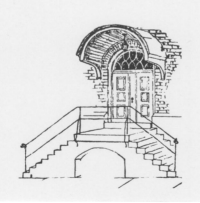

KNOWLEDGE OF HELL

ANTÓNIO LOBO ANTUNES

Translated from Portuguese by

CLIFFORD E. LANDERS

Dalkey Archive Press

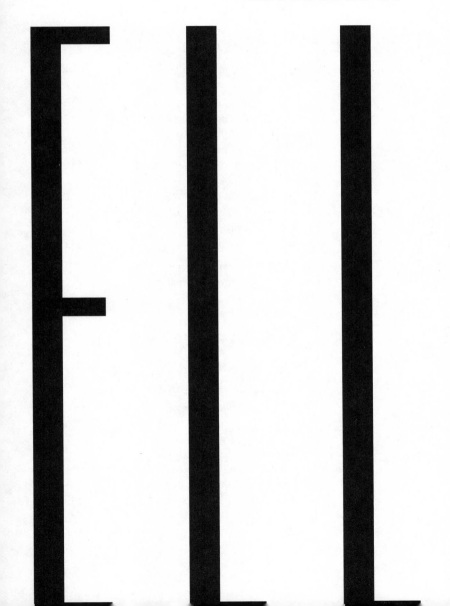

Originally published in Portuguese as
Conhecimento do inferno by Vega, 1980
Copyright © 1980 by António Lobo Antunes
English Translation © 2008 by Clifford E. Landers

First English translation, 2008
All rights reserved

Library of Congress Cataloging-in-Publication Data
Antunes, António Lobo, 1942–
[Conhecimento do inferno. English]
Knowledge of hell / Antonio Lobo Antunes ;
translation by Clifford E. Landers.
p. cm.
ISBN-13: 978-1-56478-436-0 (alk. paper)
ISBN-10: 1-56478-436-3 (alk. paper)
I. Landers, Clifford E. II. Title.
PQ9263.N77C6613 2007
869.3′42—dc22
2007039811

Partially funded by grants from the National
Endowment for the Arts, a federal agency,
the Illinois Arts Council, a state agency, and by
the University of Illinois, Urbana-Champaign

Funded by the Direcção-Geral do
Livro e das Bibliotecas/Portugal

www.dalkeyarchive.com

Design and composition by Quemadura
Printed on permanent/durable acid-free, recycled paper,
and bound in the United States of America

FOR TITA AND JOÃO DE MELO

—*Friends found at the intersection of a book*

KNOWLEDGE OF HELL

We do not believe any good end is to be effected by fictions which fill the mind
with details of imaginary vice and distress and crime, or which teach it . . . instead
of endeavoring after the fulfillment of simple and ordinary duty . . . to aim at
the assurance of superiority by creating for itself fanciful and incomprehensible
perplexities. Rather we believe that the effect of such fictions tends to render those
who fall under their influence unfit for practical exertion . . . by intruding on minds
which ought to be guarded from impurity the unnecessary knowledge of hell.

The Quarterly Review, 1860 FROM THE REVIEW OF
GEORGE ELIOT'S NOVEL The Mill on the Floss

1

The sea of the Algarve is made of cardboard like theater scenery, and the English don't realize it: they conscientiously spread their towels on the sawdust sand, protect themselves with dark glasses from the paper sun, stroll enthralled on the stage of Albufeira where public employees disguised as carnival barkers, squatting on the ground, inflict on them Moroccan necklaces secretly manufactured by the tourism board, and end the afternoon by anchoring in artificial esplanades, where they're served make-believe drinks in nonexistent glasses that leave in the mouth the flavorless taste of the whiskey furnished the actors on television dramas. After the Alentejo, evaporated in the horizontal landscape like butter on a burnt piece of toast, the chimneys that seem built from matchsticks and glue by skillful refugees and the waves that noiselessly dilute themselves on the beach in the docile crochet of foam always make him feel like one of the sugar figures on wedding cakes, the startled inhabitant of a world of sweets and croquettes on toothpicks simulating houses and streets. He had once been in Armação da Pêra with Luísa and been almost unable to leave the hotel, dismayed by that unusual hoax of backdrops that everyone seemed to take seriously, lubricating themselves with pretend creams under an orange-colored spotlight operated by an invisible electrician from a hole in the clouds: confined to the room's balcony by an absurdity that frightened him, wrapped in a bathrobe that made him look like a defeated boxer in whom the marks of punches were replaced by razor cuts, he contented himself with watching the family down there, amid a pile of sandals and slippers, like disciplined Boy Scouts around their ritual campfire. At night, a rusted fan expelled in his direction the gentle warm breath of a diabetic prompter, and a constellation of lights dangled from wires on tin boats, reduced to the plane geometry of outline. Lying in bed, embracing Luísa, he watched the curtains flutter in the phosphorescent brightness of a cellophane dawn and, intrigued, wondered whether the lovemaking was nothing more than a frenetic exercise dedicated to a nonexistent audience, for whom he articulated his moaning responses with an actor's pathetic conviction. And now, so many years later, as I was leaving Balaia for Lisbon, I hoped, almost unwillingly, to find you in the garden, in the midst of blond foreigners, tragic and motionless like Phaedra, in whose vacant eyes dwells the resigned solitude of statues and dogs. I would sit on a bench, between the affectionless varicose veins of an old German woman and the intertwined thighs of a teenage couple floating on a raft of hashish, smiling at no one in the contentment of an unknown dimension, until suddenly seeing you, on the other side of the square, with a wicker basket on your shoulder, your hair parted in the middle like a squaw, coming toward me like the girl in the Repimpa mattress commercials who recycled Greta Garbo's eyeglasses.

The uniform impersonality of the hotel produced in him an exalting sensation of freedom: no object of his marked the furniture like dogs' urine on the bark of trees. The long corridors full of numbered doors brought to mind fantasies of an expensive brothel, just as the small grocery stores of his childhood had been transformed into gigantic supermarkets similar to space stations, and trotting down the hallway from room to room, he enjoyed imagining men plunging headlong, panting over pairs of knees perfumed by essences from the Orient, before washing with Ach Brito soap in the contradictory jets of the shower. The employees at the reception area, amid books and keys, officiated with clerical dignity. Guys with pipes slept off their lunch fillets with blankets of foreign newspapers forgotten in their scrawny laps. And he felt, entering the revolving door, as unpredictable as a roulette ball, capable of the winning bet of meeting some Norwegian woman or of losing, of sitting on a beachfront esplanade, ruminating acrimony over the fizz of ginger ale.

At the end of the day I licked your skin as cows do the hollow of rocks, that whitish spider web that the sun extends on the belly in concentric designs like pitch in the sands of ebb tide and stretches to the hairs of the pubis in an unexpected shellfish taste. Little by little the cardboard sea changed color as night approached, illuminated by a purple filter that confers on the Queen Anne furniture the melancholy of seaside tercets. The last few people were deserting the beach, staggering with baskets, umbrellas, and chairs in the downcast exodus of refugees of war, pursued by lilac clouds of twilight, lustrous as contented cheeks. The streetlamps revealed plastic bushes in which windup crickets trilled the tinfoil monotony of their wings. And I slowly ceased to see you, as you dissolved into the blackness coming through the bedroom window in irresistible surges of garlic breath, forcing me to feel my way toward you as one searches for the light switch, in the hope that your smile would open a crack of light in the darkness of the pillow and your tremulous octopus gestures find mine in a timid challenge of tenderness.

He was leaving Quinta da Balaia toward Lisbon, from the walnut and egg-white villages of Balaia where plastic people spent their plastic holidays in the plastic boredom of the rich, under trees resembling tissue-paper garlands that the green pupil of the swimming pool reflected in the methylene blue of the water. He had sometimes awakened in those marzipan houses with the eye-liner sun underscoring the eyelids of the shutters and con-

ferring on the crumpled sheets the tone of the wadded brown paper of mountains in Nativity scenes, and moved about on the
floor tiles as if inside a snow globe, looking in the kitchen for
grapes as heavy as those in the canvases of Spanish painters,
whose white flesh left in his mouth the thick taste of blood. In
the sky that resembled a river of open hands, round clouds
swung gently, hanging by nylon threads from transparent
clamps of air like room keys in a hotel lobby. On the varnished
grass, an old man in bathing trunks was reading the newspaper,
suddenly without the dignity of his suit, the pomp of a tie, the
competent cough of winter, crossing his thin legs like silverware
on a plate, staring at the calligraphic birds drawn on the notebooks of two lines of branches. He had sometimes awakened
in the silence of a still house, motionless like a dead butterfly
among the bodiless shadows of the night, and gazed, sitting in
bed, at the diffuse outlines of the armoires, the clothes scattered
on chairs like weary spider webs, the rectangle of the mirror that
drank the flowers as the banks of Hell drank the distressed silhouette of the dead. He would go outside to observe the insects
around the light bulbs in the quiet of summer's secret womb,
woman's warm and secret womb in summer, feeling the sweet
putrescent odor of the East on his skin, hearing the disordered
sound of the acacias, and thought I'm on a sunflower farm in
Baixa do Cassanje between the hills of Dala Samba and Chiquita,
I'm standing on the transparent plain of the Baixa do Cassanje
turned toward the far-off sea of Luanda, the roiling sea of Luanda
the color of oil from trawlers and of the easy laughter of the
blacks, thought I'm at my grandfather's country house near the

tile benches and the idle henhouses, if I close my eyes, floating white feathers will descend on me on the inside of my skull with the lightness of snow, and he squatted on the porch, incredulous, under the glassy stars of the Algarve, glued to the ceiling of the set in some mysterious geometry. And, as always happened in the course of insomnia, the crazies of childhood, the tender, humble, indignant, arm-waving crazies of childhood began parading one by one through the darkness, in a procession, at once wretched and sumptuous, of poor clowns lit from the side by the oblique spotlight of memory, to the sound of old music from the gramophone in the attic, groaning a rheumatic waltz about wooden horses covered with the dull mire of dust:

There was Monsieur Anatole, the French engraver of whom his father had spoken, Monsieur Anatole to whom he attributed, not knowing why, the white head of hair and the lead-colored irises of Marc Chagall, painting watercolors of clocks with wings, blind violinists, and lovers embracing, Monsieur Anatole who was writing the novel *Livre Plus Que Social*, and had answered a doctor, when asked if he had children, with disgusted disdain:

Docteur, je ne fabrique pas de cadavres.

There were the crazies of Benfica, the elderly man who suddenly opened his raincoat at the schoolhouse door to exhibit the rag of his sex, the drunk Florentino sitting in the walkway in the rain, in a grandiose pose, insulting the rapid legs of passersby with the complicated vehemence of wine, the gentle crazies of Benfica faded like photographs in the confused album of childhood, the bell-ringer who played *Papagaio Loiro* during the Elevation of the noonday mass, his surplice trailing in the wind like the cape of a galloping knight, the woman who kept the host-wafers at home in a small box in hopes of one day reconstituting the entire body of God, the crazies of Benfica who would gather at night in packs like stray dogs and scream their horrible barking protests in the silent vastness of the countryside.

He passed by the office in Balaia, next to the tennis court and the beds of yellow flowers whose petals were slowly opening like thighs at the gynecologist, submissive and inert between the gloved fingers of the sun, and there came into his head the deranged man in a baby carriage reading magazines about quantum mechanics in the Monsanto woods, heedless of people's surprise and astonishment, a composed guy in a coat and glasses reading magazines about quantum mechanics in the Monsanto woods in a rusted baby carriage and how, upon noting the man's strange naturalness and the stupefaction halfway between laughter and alarm on the part of others, he had decided to become a psychiatrist to better understand (he thought) the strange ways of adults' lives, whose insecurities he sometimes suspected behind their cigarettes and their mustaches as they bent over their dinner soup with pontifical gravity. And he remembered, driving the car along the streets of Balaia, with the sea behind as if illuminated from the rear by a clear light bulb, how the gray-haired woman, with an umbrella wedged under her arm and men's shoes hidden under the stained folds of her skirt, came suddenly from a thicket, muttering words no one understood from her lipless mouth, and began pushing the guy with the magazines along the floor of leaves and pine needles with a horrible squeaking of wheels, as if conducting an inattentive child through the city, until they disappeared in the crease of a hill leaving only the groan of the wheels, like the smell of perfume in an empty bed. It was then (he thought) that he decided to become a psychiatrist in order to live among distorted men like the ones who visit us in dreams and to understand their lunar speeches and the agitated, rancorous aquariums of their brains, in which swim the moribund fishes of fear.

There were, therefore, the crazies of Benfica, the thin young man loaded down with cricket cages who chatted with the indifference of buildings inveighing against the closed windows, the guy masquerading as carnival barker directing traffic on a street corner, plethoric with energetic authority, the two old-maid sisters, as hook-nosed as cockatoos, daughters of a seaplane pilot whose picture on the wall in helmet and fur-trimmed jacket futilely threatened the cat's slumber, the sisters who on summer evenings invaded the churchyard from which departed the slow composure of the funerals, imitating with their dentures the clatter of propellers, trotting around the wagon like stumbling birds ready to rise above the trees in the faltering commotion of weary angels. He would never forget the coffins covered in black and gold cloth, whose sequins sparkled in the August sun like reflections in a pail, one of those à la minute beach pails where our face is drawn little by little on a piece of paper, or the family members who hid the lit joint behind their backs in an absurd ceremony, as if the cadaver would lift the lid to scream reproaches at them, never would he forget the silence of the doves during the funerals, nor especially the seaplane pilot's daughters who zigzagged over the acacias in awkward partridge bounds, their plastic incisors clacking in a bizarre imitation of engines.

He would never forget this, he thought when the gate at Quinta da Balaia appeared at the summit, open to the road to Albufeira, and he slowly headed toward the encounter, the private hospital on the outskirts of Lisbon that he visited with his parents at Christmas, corridor after corridor where footsteps and voices acquired the disquieting amplitude of caverns, enormous rooms full of motionless women installed in high-back chairs, gazing at him with the fixity of wax statues positioned in attitudes of waiting, and of nuns who glided soundlessly over the floor tiles, their bell-like multilayered skirts lightly swaying, who greeted them by dipping the starch of their headdresses in a murmur of prayer. Christmas for him was deformed adolescents who drooled on wooden benches opening and closing horrible toothless mouths, old women in pinafores prancing about with coquette-like gestures, the distant sound of an upright piano fumbling a waltz, plucking feathers from Chopin like a live chicken. He would never forget the creature with thin colorless hair and long fingers as white as those of the infantas on crypts, darting from the doorway to declaim for them, with the jerky movements of marionettes, the verses of William Butler Yeats

When you are grey and old and full of sleep

in an unreal timbre that conferred on each word the vertiginous depth of a well. Christmas wasn't the kiss, enveloped in the red ribbon of his uncles' aftershave, or the old servants in the kitchen huddling around the trays in insect-like agitation, it wasn't the cousins from Brazil with their tremulous amiability of cypresses, or the priests hovering over the sweets with Eucharistic appetite, it wasn't the shyness of the caretaker folding his beret in enormous hands, it wasn't the rain outside on the patio, sharply outlined against the vine on the wall, stripping away the fragile sadness of the wisteria: Christmas was the private hospital near Lisbon and its women immobilized in pathetic contortions in dusty chapel light like the weary silhouette of the cork oaks in Alentejo, among which from time to time floated the pale eyes of animals.

He groped for the throat of Paul Simon in the glove box and introduced it into the poor-box slot of the tape player, intending to hear, en route to Lisbon, the hesitant and tender appeal, delicate and wounded, of a voice so equal to the one that lay curled up in his gut that at times the odd sensation assailed him that each one of the singer's words had been yanked out of him, syllable by syllable, from the innermost part of him, and it embarrassed him that the man would display in public, shamelessly, the intimacy of the anguish that he tried in vain to transform into the lucidity without bitterness that in him, in his best moments, took the place of happiness. A grazing of violins, light as a feather duster, ascended from his legs to his chest the way the tide dons, in the river, the chestnut mud of the rampart in a powerful aspiration of water:

> Still crazy after all these years
> Still crazy after all these years

I'm like that small, ugly guy (he thought) and it surprises me not to find over my navel, when I scratch it, a stave of guitar strings, it surprises me that my saliva, my urine, and my sperm don't taste like the foam of warm beer at the bars of blacks in Harlem that slides down the throat in a blues lament, this cardboard stage setting for make-believe holidays surprises me, this overly bright Algarve that puts to flight madmen and specters with its neon sun, reducing the penumbra to a vague geometry of dark lines accumulated in the angles of the rooms. As in Lisbon, he checked an infected pimple on his neck, the only city in the world where night doesn't exist: there are mornings, afternoons, twilights, dawns, the translucent, orangey, purple clouds of sunset, which parade and stretch out like bodies in orgasm in elastic and tranquil jubilation, there is the brutal revelation of daybreak that calls forth in our faces in the mirror the contours of the aged that we will be, but night does not exist: perplexed tourists photograph identical statues and chocolate generals, get lost, map upraised, in a labyrinth of cross-streets steaming like intestines, invade small neighborhood pastry shops where bald gentlemen drink lemon tea looking at checkers problems in the newspaper and finally return, exhausted, to their hotels to try to sleep in the dazzling glare of perpetual noon.

It was in Africa, in Luchaze country, that I learned that in Lisbon night did not exist. Luchaze country is a red plateau twelve hundred meters above sea level where brick-colored dust penetrates our clothes and sticks to our skin, entangles itself in our hair, clogs our nostrils with its smell of earth, much like the acidic dry smell of the dead. Luchaze country, almost devoid of trees, is a country of lepers and darkness, a country of restive forms, of noisy ghosts, of gigantic butterflies emerging from their dark cocoons to flutter off in search of streetlights, in a desperate tenacity of rage. It's the country where the deceased sit and watch the ritual drumming, frenetic from the invisible presence of the gods, their eye sockets, as concave as school inkwells, wide with pleasure, brimming with thick tears of joy. It's a country poor in manioc and game, dimmed by fog, that the spirits abandoned on their way to the forests of the North, as touched by life as the May awakening of the apples. In that country of small narrow rivers like folds of skin, minuscule as scars or laugh lines, I found friends among the poor blacks of the PIDE, Chinóia Camanga, Machai, Miúdo Malassa, the leaders of the civilian troops that the PIDE had conscripted to combat the guerrillas, and who left for the jungle at dawn to fight the MPLA and UNITA, as silent and rapid as shadowy animals. They were courageous and proud men deceived by perverse propaganda, by cruel assurances, by the regime's lying promises, and I was in the habit of talking with them, in the evening, in their adobe houses, squatting on a tree trunk, looking at the white stain of the barracks on the hill, where the headlights of jeeps effected an indecipherable dance of signals. Skeletal dogs in the thickets barked their distressed childlike moans, hens sought shelter in the matting, Machai, brother of the teacher, brought a chair for me and said:

"Tumama tchituamo, Muata"

and stood beside me contemplating his country at war, the

parched land of the dry season, the coming of darkness with its cortege of ghosts, stood contemplating his country with the impassive expression of the Luchazes, or he was patiently teaching me his strange language with an amused gleam in his eyes. Sometimes, António Miúdo Catolo, the Muata of Muatas, the chief of chiefs, would come to talk with us in Machai's hut on the hill where the civilian hospital stood, near the *quimbo* of Sandindo and Bartolomeu, the crocodile hunters, who swore to me that upon opening an alligator you'd come across diamonds and sand in its belly, diamonds as thick as eye sockets emitting reflections of blood in the gelatin of its intestines. António Miúdo Catolo resembled Zorba the Greek with his enormous drooping mustache and the proud carriage of his body, replete with disdain and kindness, his broad shoulders, his long muscles like tensioned levers of quiet strength, his calm eucalyptus laughter in which his teeth moved about with the gentle sound of leaves. One day as we were walking along the barbed wire, near the sentry post where the militias clutched like shipwrecked sailors their outmoded and useless blunderbusses, he turned to me and stated, in his reinvented Portuguese, in an outpouring filled with the miraculous freshness of a Bernardim rondeau, that in Lisbon there was no night, amazed that I came from Portugal and wasn't aware of that obvious fact, never having perceived, in twenty-eight years, that in my city night didn't exist. Some time earlier, the government had awarded him a War Cross and a trip to Europe: they took Catolo to Luanda, put him on the plane, led him out of the airport, bought him a suit and tie on sale at a clothing store on Fanqueiros (how can a hero not be in a suit and tie?), rented a room for him in a shabby boardinghouse on Figueira Square, gave him five hundred escudos, and forgot about him. The woman who owned the boardinghouse locked him in the room so "that fool of a black wouldn't run off and get drunk and do a lot of stupid things, you know how those niggers are," and Catolo stood there, intimidated and rigid, between the armoire and the bed, leaning against the enameled wash basin, in the petrified attitude of portraits, with the War Cross in his lapel and money in his pocket, a piece of paper that crinkled like tobacco leaves if his fingers squeezed them. He was hungry, he was sleepy, he wanted to urinate but couldn't lie down, because the Luchazes only lie down at twilight and twilight didn't come: after the daytime of streetlamps came the daytime of the sun, and António Miúdo Catolo anxiously went to the window to await the night, to glimpse the blue of the first darkness on the crest of the rooftops, to divine the shadows that would allow him to lay his exhausted body on the sheets, contorted with cramps like that of weary young bulls. Automobiles continued to blow their horns in the street, voices rose constantly from the square, the neon ads licked the window ledge in the cardiac rhythm of their purple tongues, driving far away the silence of the dark and the chrysalis peace necessary for sleep. Even the pigeons remained alert around the statues, staring at him with the small accusatory marbles of their pupils, and he felt he was being watched by the panicked souls of the dead, come from the earth in the form of birds, intent on forbidding him to sleep. António Miúdo Catolo fasted for seventy-two hours, urinating in terror in his new pants, his nose pressed against the window to which was glued a never-ending noon, until the owner of the boardinghouse opened the door, tapped him on the shoulder, and without a word he slid down her body to the floor, where he lay crucified on the mat like the corpse of a cat run over on the highway.

So, years later, on the plateau of the Bundas, after having shaken the hand of some official, posed for newspaper photographs, and returned to his country of murmuring darkness, to his warring country of murmuring and troubled darkness, the Muata of Muatas, free now of the nightmare of a diurnal city, looked sidelong at me, amazed at my ignorance of Lisbon, of the stupidity that kept me from understanding that in Europe, in that aged and sad continent of cathedrals and hubbub, night doesn't exist and the people have been transformed, little by little, into pallid walking specters staggering through the streets in search of an impossible repose. We were near the militias' sentry post, facing the narrow trail that leads to Luena and where the enormous machines of Cetec were felling trees with their iron shoulders, vociferating and smoking furiously, crewed by mulattos in brightly colored T-shirts. The Chilala jungle was tinted a different green against the green of the afternoon, the air was starting to turn opaque with insects, and soon the shades of the first deceased, of the first late chiefs and the first dead children, would begin to move in the grass like the rats that feed on the rotting flesh of the lepers.

"Night in Lisbon is a fabricated night," I said, "a make-believe night. Moreover, in Portugal almost everything is make-believe, the people, the avenues, the houses, the restaurants, the stores, the friendships, the disinterest, the rage. Only the fear and the wretchedness are authentic, the fear and the wretchedness of men and dogs."

The eucalyptus trees of the deserted mission were no longer distinguishable beyond the cubical Administration building and the PIDE yard where half-naked prisoners were weeding. The lights in the barracks were like a garland from some sad fairgrounds, an abandoned provincial fairgrounds, and in the officers' mess the commandant sat down at the table with his customary sigh of a deflating inner tube, his body floating in the soft exaggeration of his uniform. A dead child brushed past without seeing us, with the appraising phosphorescent eye sockets of gazelles or wounded owls.

"I'm afraid of dead children," I said in a low voice, tightly gripping the Muata's arm. "I'm afraid of dead children, I fear the perverse evil of dead children."

António Miúdo Catolo ran his thumb over his immense mustache:

"White people are crazy," he declared. "Whites are crazier than children."

And only in 1973, when I arrived at Miguel Bombarda Hospital to begin the long transit of Hell, did I confirm that night had in fact disappeared from the city, from the squares, the streets, the gardens and the cemeteries of the city, to seek refuge in the hospital wards like bats, in the light fixtures on the ceiling and the old chipped medicine cabinets, in the electroshock machines, in the pails of dressings, in the boxes of syringes, until the patients return silently from the dining hall and occupy the unpainted iron beds, the custodian hits the light switch and it unfolds the loathsome felt of its wings, the loathsome sticky felt of its wings over the men lying there who stare at it from between the sheets with irrepressible nausea. The night that disappears from the city was in the face turned toward the shoulder of the patient who hanged himself behind the garages and whose battered slippers oscillated slowly at the height of my chin, it was in the obituaries that I checked during work hours, running the cold diaphragm of the stethoscope along chests as immobile as boats at final anchorage, it was in the astonished features of the living confined behind the walls and bars of the asylum, in the dust of the courtyards in summer, in the facades of the nearby houses. In 1973, I had come back from the war and knew about injuries, about the cries of pain on the trail, about explosions, about gunshots, about mines, about bellies blown apart by the explosion of booby traps, knew about prisoners and murdered babies, knew about spilled blood and longing, but I had been spared the knowledge of Hell.

2

He left Quinta da Balaia, the domesticated and snobbish green-
ery of Quinta da Balaia where the shade of the trees imparts a
light reddish, almost rosy, tone like that of seashells, and everything where the sound of the sea envelops and sings, and headed
for the village of Albufeira, in which the walls of houses resemble washed sheets, very white, white over the blue-white of the
sky. Workers on bicycles were pedaling on the highway in the
sun, Wise Men transporting the myrrh of their noonday meal in

lunch pails, and in his rear-view mirror he saw the grave features of the retable, chiseled in the dark stone of their bones, thinking that in the swarthy face of these men dwelled something of the lime and gypsum of the walls, something of Van Gogh's clouds above the ravens and the wheat, formed not by the absence of color but by the tempestuous accumulation of all colors, violent yellows, tragic purples, browns of clotted blood in an open wound, of the blood that never dries in an open wound. My country, he decided, is the panels of Nuno Gonçalves under the pitilessness of the light, barren and humble faces carved without symmetry in the wood of their muscles, lusterless eyes that do not take wing, like those of prisoners and the blind, melancholy eyes full of pride like those of dogs at night, phosphorescent with restlessness, anger, suspicion, pedaling on the Algarve highways going home amid signs for restaurants, for discotheques, for developments, for bars, pale Englishmen, ethereal Dutchmen, Swiss as light as angels, people without the weight of poor land in their guts like us, of shallow roots, of furious waves, of stones at seaside where the tolling of the bells prolongs itself, identical to the throbbing of a vein on the pillow.

And he remembered the Algarve in winter, on the road to Albufeira, the tenuous, monotonous, almost childish rain of the Algarve in winter, in October, December, February, in the course of months melancholy as the lilies of the dead, impregnated with a sweet odor of wax and lavender. He recalled the bright air fragile as glass that the petals of the rain stained lightly like the breath of tiny mouths at the window, Portimão drowned amid the clouds and the estuary in the minute grayness of afternoon, in which the outlines of all the facades emerge more sharply and precisely than the branches of trees at twilight, piled upon one another in febrile disorder, the lights of Portimão just like fake jewels in a shop window, we sat in the restaurant, I sought out your mouth with my smile, and we broke out in laughter, over the steak, the joy of mutual discovery, of inventing ourselves, like children, a passionate Morse of signals. He recalled Portimão and the sand at Praia da Rocha in winter, without any sign of footprints, the enormous boulders swollen like a sick woman, thighs sheltering dazed birds and insects, recalled Isabel explaining that she'd never had an orgasm, that I'm frigid, that sexual relations didn't matter to her, that during her marriage she'd slept as far as possible from her husband in order not to touch a body whose anxious inertia repelled her, and later, that night, he recalled her legs spilling over the bed and her startled-puppy cries of pleasure, the shrieks of a puppy startled by an unexpected miracle. I like your breast so much, he thought, passing a tractor with a person perched shaking on top of it, vibrating on top of it like a lifeless lead soldier, I like your bosom so much, the hard nipples of your breasts and the tender gentle hollow that separates them, the fuse-wire from your pubis that I encounter coiled up in the bathtub, and the toes good for biting, for sucking, for licking while your face contorts in the distance with ticklishness, saying no, your eyes closed in the disordered plane of the sheets. There was Isabel and there had been other women, before and afterwards, in the niter and windy winters of the Algarve, the color of pumice, of walnut and of olive, when he departed from Lisbon possessed by a mysterious anguish, by the pathetic distress of children who can't get to sleep and cry in the dark of their room from loneliness and fear, to lodge himself in silence before the fireplace, in his parents' house at Quinta da Balaia, as if seeking in the burning pinecones and trunks the pacifying of an impossible serenity, because he had always found in women, in their gentleness, in their mute gaze and in the acidity of their skin, something he did not find by himself and that constituted a kind of indecipherable complement of himself, the fraction of light, of clarity of fruit, of the jubilant taste of orange which he anxiously needed.

He came to Albufeira and began to descend into the center of town behind a busload of tourists that rocked and shook at each curve like a fat lady running in distress toward the trolley stop, and he suddenly smelled the odor of seagull viscera. He couldn't see the ocean but divined its presence beyond the roof tiles, the buildings that in a kind of estrus mounted trees as scrawny as my brother Miguel's shoulders and, like him, were shaken by almost imperceptible shivers. He divined its presence in the tone of the sky, in the change in the volume of sounds, in his own body, which leaned like the blue needle of a compass in the direction of the water, breathing rapidly like chicks. He sensed the sea in his nostrils, his ears, his insides, the ebb and flow of the waves withdrawing and advancing, cleaning with their knife of foam the dentures of the shells, guffawing to no one their porcelain contentment. I miss the sea, he thought, not this sea but the sea at

Cascais in September, next to Palm Beach, leaning against the wall and listening to music from the nightclub above, distorted by the deforming mirror of distance, leaning against the wall with the lights from the boats in my eyes, rocking in the darkness like the lanterns on the rear of receding trains. I miss the sea at my house in Estoril that I pulled over my head to be able to sleep, miss being in a damp beehive resounding with echoes, coral with submerged limbs that become calm, I miss the sea at Estoril that disorients the swallows in their laborious random flight, seeking in the nearby dwellings a gutter in which to anchor a nest, I miss turning on a tap and seeing the ocean pour into the basin, washing my face in the ocean, in pajamas, soap in hand, taking an ocean-shower, seeing the ocean descend into the toilet, by pressing a button, in a stormy miniature Niagara.

I miss the sea, he thought, not this sea but all the seas that I've known since childhood, this small, harmless, tame cardboard sea, we were children, lying on the damp sheets of the boardinghouse annex, above the pharmacy, the taurine voice of the sea called to us, we went to the window, disoriented, and on the beach, in the moonlight, they were erecting one of those wonderful and pitiful traveling circuses that appear and disappear in summer, suddenly, with its cortege of repulsive animals, sick lions, limping camels, magician's doves in silvery cages, hairless chimps coughing the resigned bronchitis of old age. Leaning on the parapet, we saw dozens of clowns, contortionists, acrobats with gleaming muscles, obese managers in tailcoats, jugglers in striped costume, dwarfs with enormous cubical heads on minuscule trunks, raising the patched tent in the moonlight, the tent that grew and stretched out in the moonlight like the enormous canvas corolla of some fantastic tulip decorated with garlands of light bulbs that sprinkled on the artists' painted faces dusty little clouds of flour, while from a trailer swelled a dramatic beating of drums. They erected the circus and the acrobats leapt in the darkness, dressed in colorful sweaters, feathers, scarlet capes, the tightrope girl was carrying a Japanese parasol between the two barking trained dogs, cards were falling from the pockets of a gentleman in a morning coat, the bearded lady was staring at the sea, hands on her hips, growling with rage like a make-believe bulldog, a plush bulldog incapable of true fury, a fury of nerves and flesh, beyond the string that moved its jaws in the mechanical imitation of a pout.

I miss the sea, he thought on his way to the sea, the sea of Carcavelos in January, when the birds leave furrows in the wet sand similar to crow's feet, delicate furrows similar to crow's feet: he ran into two elderly Americans in bathing trunks, pipes between their teeth, whose skinny legs slowly knitted their way, red from the unmoving raging Algarve sun tacked onto the blue plank of the sky, and looked for a parking space in the square among the automobiles with their noses hidden on the sidewalk like rows of young calves in stables, looking sidelong with the rounded eye sockets of headlights at the people approaching. The crafts shops displayed urine-colored wicker baskets, idiotic cloth dolls, bunches of leather coin purses hanging on strings, straw chairs as uncomfortable as scrawny laps, in which one's kidneys suffered the stiff tortures of lumbago. And the esplanades suddenly seemed to him replete with cadavers, placid cadavers awaiting some kind of resurrection, cadavers that talked and drank, leaned toward one another, moved away, told the dead lottery vendor *no* as he tried to foist the dream from table to table forgetting that the deceased do not dream, that they detest the dream, the plans, the future that has excluded them, that they hate what they do not know, what they do not command, what escapes the narrowness of their understanding, and they remain stubbornly seated in old waiting rooms, contemplating each other in silence, with cups of nothing on their knees.

When one misses the sea, he wondered, in the square in Albufeira, in August, should he walk under the arch and see the beach or go to Harry's? I've always found something of the deck of a ship in bars, something of a shipwreck, of the brightness of a submerged ship in bars, and I'm certain that minuscule transparent octopuses entangle themselves in our hair, spring from our gestures, circulate in our mouths, attracted by the coral of our gums. He pushed against the door and felt like Alice when she falls down the rabbit hole at the beginning of the story: the sudden transition from the excessive brightness, dense, palpable, almost solid, of the outside, to the cave of shadow, vertiginously hollow, into which he had the sensation of having fallen, produced in him a whirlwind of dizziness similar to that of years earlier, when he arrived at Miguel Bombarda Hospital to begin his journey through Hell.

Miguel Bombarda Hospital, former convent, former military

school, former Rilhafoles Mental Asylum, is a decrepit old building near Campo de Santana, the dark trees and plastic swans of
Campo de Santana, near the large, damp house of the morgue,
where as a student he had sliced into bellies on stone slabs with
immense disgust, holding his breath so the fat, repugnant smell
of guts wouldn't assail his nostrils with the rotting perfume
of lifeless flesh. Later he had carried out autopsies in Africa,
outdoors, in the light from jeeps and Unimoogs around which
thrashed thousands of panicked insects, autopsies of bodies de-
voured by the vigorous young appetite of the green land of Angola, whose roots are reflected in the sky in the transparent network of rivers. He arrived at Miguel Bombarda Hospital with a
paper in his pocket, his marching orders like in the troops, it was
June 1973 and he sweated from the heat under his jacket, shirt,
tie, the lay civilian uniform he was wearing. I'm in the troops, he
thought, I'm arriving in Mafra again, they're going to hand me a
rifle, cut my hair, teach me with discipline to die, and send me to
the dock at Alcântara to embark on a ship of the damned. And he
stopped to look at the vulgar facade of the convent, the military
school, the asylum, and the courtyard where men in pajamas
dragged their slippers under the sycamores, their strange faces as
empty as uninhabited carnival masks.

He paused to look at the hospital facade, which the leaves reflected from trunk to trunk and crown to crown, as on a tremulous sheet of water, and a bald little guy in a checkered shirt came
sashaying from a glass cubicle and grabbed effusively onto his
arm, his face split in two by the enormous wound of his smile:

"Well, I'll be damned if it isn't the professor's son."

And he remembered as a child accompanying his father to the laboratory filled with flasks, cubical vessels in which floated gelatinous brains, test tubes, microscopes, Bunsen burners, and perching on a swivel chair to listen to his father's conversations with that man, then younger, then larger, hairier, wearing coveralls, a cap on his head, who took up all the attention that he demanded for himself.

"How is your dad, boy?"

How is your dad, boy? he said aloud in Harry's Bar to the deserted tables, to the employee cleaning glasses behind the trench of the counter, to the lamps extinguished like empty pupils. The guy returned to the glass cubicle without releasing his arm and cupped his hand around his mouth to call out like a newsboy:

"Dona Alzira, come see who's here. Damned if it isn't the professor's son."

A woman in a black smock appeared, her varicose veins waddling, her hands on her immense chest in rapturous surprise:

"They were so tiny, so blond, so pretty. You could see right away that the professor doted on his children."

"He was never a sissy," argued the doorman, indignant, "black nuts, big ones, right where they should be. And now the little boy is big and husky, huh? Well in that case I'm going to go have a martini at Varela's."

The patients, murmured the doctor to his mug of beer in the deserted bar in Albufeira, at first I didn't even notice the patients, only the gentle filtered light of the sycamores, the dark green of the sycamores against the light green of the sky, paler where it touched the houses and the irregular row of crenels of the roofs, the way skin pressed by a finger turns white. The acrid taste of the foam stung the inside of his eyelids, a complicit, attic-like silence surrounded him, and his limbs floated slowly into the gestures of seaweed that, with neither bones nor thickness, drifts apart. It was three, four o'clock in the afternoon, and in the distance the cardboard sea in its retreat was calm like a dog stretching out on the doormat to sleep, wagging the white plume of its tail. While I accompanied the doorman to Varela's, Dona Alzira, behind me, repeated in the startled voice of a bird deadened by the morning thickness,

"Just like his mother. Just like his mother. Just like his mother."

The mug was empty. He ordered another and stared at the yellow liquid, the color of the frightened pupils of animals, which fogged the glass with its icy breath. Since the departure of Isabel, of sad memory, months before, since Isabel's departure, he had become accustomed to being alone, without assistance, clutching onto the mane of life with the stubborn strength of despair and hope and for now he felt utterly exhausted from the struggle: he just wanted to go home, lock the door to the empty apartment, sit down at the desk and finish the novel he was writing, the narrative of a chaotic and feverish war, he wanted little by little to reacquaint himself with isolation, the unanswered echo of his own footsteps down the endless tunnel of the hallway. He recalled having read that Charlie Chaplin would speak about the need, upon finishing a film, to shake the tree in such a way that the superfluous branches, the superfluous leaves, the superfluous fruits fell off so that there remained, as it were, only the essential nakedness, thought how profoundly that idea had engraved itself ever after inside him, forcing him to constantly rethink his life, the books he had written or planned to write, the projects that continually seethed in his head, contradictory and intense, the people who sought him out to travel with him in the difficult waters of analysis.

Varela's was a mongrel tavern and pastry shop with a television set on a high shelf near the ceiling, as imposing and sacred as an icon, and a group of orderlies playing dominoes in one corner, gravely examining the blocks like a general staff leaning over a battle plan. The doorman released his arm and stuck in his chest the peremptory dagger of his index finger:

"Your daddy's a fantastic guy, boy."

And to the boy busy at the counter serving packages of diet crackers to an obese lady who was telling another woman, in catastrophic tones, of the misadventures of her pregnant bitch:

"Two stiff martinis. No lemon."

A martini at eleven o'clock was all I needed, he lamented silently, lacking the courage to offend by the impoliteness of a refusal, because refusing a drink in a tavern constitutes the most serious, most unforgivable insult, the rudest and stupidest of cruelties, and the doorman was proud to offer the drink not to him but to his father through him, to the important gentleman who taught at the university and spoke to the lab workers as equals, seeing under the microscope red globules identical to distant planets bobbing in the pink gelatin outer space of plasma. It was his father who was there in Varela's through his intermediary, and he tried to represent him as best he could by swallowing heroically, in a single gulp, the purple liquid smelling of cologne with sugar, attended by the satisfied attention of his friend. The hands of a square electric clock whirled on the wall, one of the players shuffled the domino blocks on the table like the chattering of false teeth. The doorman stifled a belch of joy with his fingertips and paid for the drinks with money from a coin purse laboriously removed from the back pocket of his trousers, swollen with cards, old papers, lucky numbers, tattered photographs. A man with a briefcase and a thin Errol Flynn mustache, who was observing the domino peripeteias with erudite graveness, limped toward the counter, summoned by the bald guy who was overflowing with happiness in his threadbare coat:

"This boy here is the son of the professor. I've known him since he was this high."

And he lowered his hand to thirty centimeters from the floor, soiled with sawdust, cigarette butts, candy wrappers and lupine shells. The mustache of the man with the briefcase spread in a respectful smile:

"Since his daddy left, the hospital's not the same."

How's your daddy, boy? How's your mother, boy? he asked himself in Harry's Bar lining up the empty mugs on top of the table. Three or four in the afternoon, and he felt very alone in the Albufeira summer, with the sea out there slowly, calmly licking the fishing boats that at night populated the distant horizon with lights in the heat of August, duplicated by the tremulous mirror of the water. He leaned back in the chair and saw, through the half-open door, the movement on the beach: since his daddy left, the hospital isn't the same, proclaimed the Errol Flynn mustache from some corner of his memory, and when it's my time to leave who'll say that to me? What will Luísa or Isabel say one day, what will they think about my temperament, my acts, my deeds? The worker came to the doorway to look at the street, the houses, the people, and the sun ran along the floor to meet him, wrapping itself around his ankles like a happy dog. Everyone is fine, boy, everyone is always fine, boy, with every beer I drink people get better, Luísa is going to remarry, Isabel is going to meet some other guy, and I'll stay here leaning against the counter the way sick people from their beds watch the departure of their visitors, with a weak artificial smile dissipating from the pillow.

"Yeah," he said, while the martini spread through him like an unpleasant knot in his stomach, "I grew up faster than I should have."

In the hospital courtyard, under the transparent, almost waxy glare of the sycamores, disseminating on the ground stains as mobile and light as the tenuous shadows of sleepwalkers, a patient with biblical sideburns suddenly sank into him eyes like the buttons on spats:

"A cigarette, sir."

And an imperious, imploring throng in pajamas surrounded him, shuffling in slippers, moaning, barking, sniffing his coat, touching his body, fingering his tie, spilling into his nose a sour mixture of dirt and sweat, cawing:

"A cigarette a cigarette a cigarette"

from enormous, toothless, elastic mouths framed in bristles of hair, advancing and retreating like the frenzied coming and going of a pack of hounds: like in Elvas, he thought, just like in Elvas, in 1970, during the inspection in the barracks gym.

It was in June or July (or the end of May?) and the unbearable heat of the Alentejo, where he had arrived by train the previous evening, nodding from fatigue against the darkness of the journey, twisted the houses like birthday candles consumed by the furious flames of summer. The white sky, the stone walls softening from despondency, the circular horizon clouded in the distance by a kind of purple haze, as immaterial as breath or a sigh, singed the barracks flowers, the flowers that the commander maternally braced with rods next to the gym, inside which, galloons on my shoulders, I watched march before me the young men from Elvas that the army had drafted, called, regimented to defend in Africa the coffee plantation owners, the prostitutes, and the merchants of explosives, those who ruled in the country in the name of confused ideals of oppression. I was awaiting my own embarkation, counting the days, the hours of pleasure that remained to me, by hurriedly memorizing your body like an unfamiliar book before an exam, and, sitting at the desk, saw the young men from Elvas march before me in the closed gym, which the stench of groins, the excess of people, and the clothes abandoned on the floor contaminated like some squalid and tragic bullpen. I got up on the pretext of urinating, the sergeant in charge of testing for colorblindness went on showing his cards with colored spots, and I went out into a kind of enclosure where the second lieutenants and cadets were teaching weapons-handling to the recruits, aided by noncommissioned officers who herded the squads the way sheepdogs herd flocks. The barracks flowers were rotting in the sun in the ammoniac damp, in the damp of the pus of the dying flowers, their stalks bending toward the ground in pallid anemic spirals, and from the walls ran like resin the paint that the heat had liquefied, transforming it into thick cloudy tears like the spiritless weeping of old men. I stood there for a few moments, hands in pockets, observing the company's exercises, raising and lowering their rifles in the yellow dust of the enclosure, thinking that they had sent me to Elvas not to save people from war but to send them to the jungle, even the lame, even the hunchbacks, even the deaf because patriotic duty excludes no one, because the Sacred Overseas Lands needed everyone's sacrifice, because The Army Is The Mirror Of The Nation, because The Portuguese Soldier Is As Good As The Best, because sonofabitch motherfucking cocksucking shiteating cunt bastard assholes, I saw, leaning against a stone column as gnarled as the ancient trees, the future heroes, the future mutilated, the future cadavers, the commander, watchful, bending over his dying flowers with a watering can in his hand, I went back to the gym, sat down at the desk, raised my head and my nose found itself at the level of dozens of penises that surrounded the table waiting to be observed, to be measured, to be approved for death. They weren't faces, or necks, or shoulders, or torsos, they were dozens and dozens of enormous limp penises that had accumulated there in my absence, hanging testicles, repulsive long dark pubic hairs, dozens and dozens of penises nearly pressed against my panicked eyes, threatening me with the flaccid snouts of their skin. They weren't men, they were penises that pursued me, cornered me, oscillated before me in their blind inertia, I closed my eyelids forcefully and longed to scream from disgust and fear, scream from disgust and fear like, in childhood, in the middle of some unbearable nightmare.

"A cigarette a cigarette a cigarette"
whined imploringly the pajamas leaping about him like frenzied poodles. A patient with a minuscule head, incapable of speech, tried to kiss his hands in a furor of spittle. Another, on his knees, sniffed at his navel, introducing his damp nose into an opening in his shirt. And it could be said that new strange beings emerged constantly from the sycamores to limp toward him in a hurried cortege of gargoyles. The martini doorman, coming to his rescue, removed him from hands extended like Christmas turkeys, brandishing an imaginary cane at the end of his arm, and he thought

"What am I doing here?"
just as he had thought at the barracks gymnasium in Elvas

"What am I doing here?"
as he sometimes thought in certain bars, certain nightclubs, certain dinners, certain gatherings of opinionated intelligent people

"What am I doing here?"
listening in silence, at one corner of the sofa, to the spiraling vehemence of their arguments, just as he thought

"What am I doing here?"

at Harry's in Albufeira, letting the sour foam of his fifth beer descend into his glass and observing the sun slowly crawling along the floor to meet him. Soon he would return to the car, cross the Alentejo toward Lisbon, toward a city without night, huddled into itself as if it enclosed a treasure that no one knew among marshals of bronze and cemeteries without grandeur, a treasure like those he imagined hidden in the fists of sleeping children, eyelids descended over the simplicity of their mystery. He looked for the money in his pockets the way he had looked for cigarettes in the hospital courtyard, in the tremulous green well of the trees crossed now and then by oblique eels of sparrows, small gray eels whirling in the air in a confusion of wings, and began climbing the stairs that led to the office of the asylum director, where the new doctors gathered near a desk with a plastic flower on its surface in shy small groups of newcomers.

Here I am in the realm of plastic flowers, he verified by caressing with his thumb the proud artificial petals, among the plastic sentiments, the plastic emotions, the plastic piety, the plastic affect of doctors, because in doctors almost nothing but horror is genuine, the horror and the panic of suffering, of bitterness, of death. Almost nothing but horror bleeds in those who attend to the anguish of others with their complicated instruments, their books, their cabalistic diagnoses, like in childhood when I would bend over mollusks on the beach, turning them over with a stick to look with curiosity at the other side. On the floor below, in the immense tiled corridor of the floor below, an invisible man was screaming the distress of pigs at the moment of slaughter, of a neck pierced by thick knife blades. Maybe that's why, he calculated, they put plastic flowers in the vases, because plastic flowers are like stuffed animals: they watch with total indifference the spectacle of pain: I've never seen a plastic flower that was moved by the sight of a corpse.

He left the bar for the cardboard afternoon of the Algarve, with its background of fake waves and the warm wind like a woman's thigh clinging to the sticky sweat of his shirt, and stood on the sidewalk, the lukewarm car keys in his hand, looking at the small thin trees in the square, the benches packed with people, the crypto-Hindu creatures with hollow eye sockets, selling bracelets, earrings, necklaces, brooches, rings, squatting on Moroccan mats. Gigantic imperious women led on a leash bald guys with panama hats on their heads, for whom the long flexible legs of the English women, their buttocks as soft as embroidered pillows, banished the narrow tyranny of the office. Entire families in baseball caps circulated erratically around the garden like merry-go-round animals, jumping in time to the rhythm of the motor's growls. A cross-eyed republican guard, whistle in his mouth, moved about restlessly making protracted signals to a long line of impatient automobiles, behind whose windshields old Belgian women exhibited the crocodile skin of their naked shoulder blades. And at the doors of taverns, at the doorways, in the frames of windows as white as dogs' teeth, the people of Albufeira, the Moorish people of Albufeira, hidden in shadow, with minuscule eyes set in the hard asymmetry of their features, watched the strange fever of the summer people whom the sweetish odor of the water made dizzy, like the light young wine of Lagoa.

He stood on the sidewalk watching the wire of the trees twist in the redness of August, blown by the dry breath of Africa that at twilight rocks the fishing boats, as he had stood, years before, in the waiting room of the asylum director, running his thumb along the plastic petals, between a screened cabinet filled with books and the shy silhouettes of the new doctors, talking among themselves in monk-like murmurs. We were safe now from the patients, safe from the coarse, eager faces of the patients floating in the courtyard in cotton pajamas, safe from the screams of pigs in agony in the hospital corridor, in the dignified, cushioned atmosphere of the masters of the crazy people, of those who determine insanity according to their own horror of suffering and death.

"What am I doing here?"
he asked himself descending in a procession with the other newcomers to the room dominated by an enormous painting of Marshal Saldanha, in which had lodged the mangled bullet that had gone through the head of Miguel Bombarda leaving in the canvas a tragic finger hole, the enormous painting of Marshal Saldanha, fat, white sideburns, covered with sad majestic medals, staring down at us with the dull pupils of a defunct hippopotamus, disguised in cardboard glory.

"What am I doing here?"
he asked himself arriving from the limitless space of Angola, where the horizon retreats to the end of the sky in an infinite

blue plain of sunflowers and cotton, farms of tobacco, rice, manioc, minuscule settlements like warts on the earth's wrinkled skin.

"What am I doing here?"
he asked himself, looking at a man urinating in the sun, singing, against the asylum wall, the wall that the sycamores' reflection turned into a moiré, why don't I run out through the gate and specialize in dentistry, or pediatrics, or physiotherapy, or general practice, or otorhinolaryngology, anything concrete with concrete diseases, tranquilizing, solid, compact, real, cavities, tumors, spinal deviations, sinusitis, hernias, anginas, why the fuck do I go with the others into the dark office of the hospital director, where he awaits us, standing up, protected by an enormous desk with an enormous glass inkwell on it, cutting him in half at the waist and reflecting his inverted bust like the king of hearts, an older man with white hair who straightens his tie, coughs to give his voice a presidential tone, rests his fingertips on the rectangle of the blotter and states

"Psychiatry is the most noble of the medical specialties"
with the pomp of someone offering the world a discovery of genius. Off to the right, in the clouded lake of shadow, shone a silver brilliance as sharp as a boiling droplet, transfixing with its delicate rapier light the respectful sideburns of the interns. Budding Bombardas unthreatened by any pistol. The rescue squad was removing from the ambulance a stretcher on which writhed the bound outline of a woman whom the pajamas immediately surrounded, their arms out, barking

"A cigarette a cigarette a cigarette"
out of hairy slack mouths with sparse brown teeth planted randomly in the rotten sponge of their gums. The director's mouth, on the other hand, was as clean and clear as that of a bass, the fusiform oblique bass that pitilessly devour defenseless sea mollusks with their tender pink throats, a mouth that smelled of Emoform and American tobacco, the impeccable mouth of an executioner, the impeccable mouth, devoid of remorse, of an executioner:

"Psychiatry is the most noble of the medical specialties."

I'm in Auschwitz, he thought, I'm in Auschwitz in an SS uniform, listening to the welcoming speech of the camp commander while the Jews mill about on the other side of the wire tripping over utmost misery and utmost hunger, I'm clean-shaven, shoes shined, well fed, well dressed, ready to learn how to do my job as guard, I belong to the superior race of the jailers, the castrators, the police, the school principals, and the stepmothers of fairy tales, and instead of rebelling people accept me respectfully because Psychiatry is the most noble of the medical specialties and it's necessary for prisons to exist so we can harbor the imbecile illusion of being free, of being able to circulate in the square at Albufeira spurred by an authoritarian wife, terrified by Saturday after the dinner in which she will devour me, in bed, with the gigantic mandibles of her vagina, forcing me to sweat over her gelatinous body the calisthenics of resigned despondency.

I was on the sidewalk at the door to the bar, breathing in the sweet odor of the beach, where the waves were little by little taking on the transparent hue of young girls' bones under their skin after making love, like the first light from the shutters in the dawn of a cold, when every sound, every smell, every tint injures and offends us like some unjust anguish, and then the English women with their long greyhound thighs, the bearded men with their Moroccan knickknacks, the children in baseball caps, the cross-eyed republican guard, the guys lying prone on the esplanades for endless breaks, the country people hidden in the shadows of their window frames began coming toward me shouting

"A cigarette a cigarette a cigarette"

in a confused rush, in a tumult of limbs, in a whirlpool of eyes ever larger, more menacing, redder, while I, gripping the wall, disappeared under them like the woman on the stretcher still making with my free arm a gesture for help that no one answered.

3

The homes, the restaurants, the boardinghouses, the car rental agencies were receding in the distance, one after the other, but he didn't realize he had left Albufeira until he stopped smelling in his nostrils the sweetish odor, of candied squash, from the sea. It was a smooth and bland odor identical to the perfume of coloring agents, to the aroma of liqueur-filled bonbons, to the lavender that emanates from linen in chests, the breath of the Algarve beaches from whose waves are sometimes born, as in the Greek isles, the blind-gypsum statues of gods. Even in Tavira, even in Faro, even in Lagoa, at the airport, in train stations, in small suburban cafés where the wine bottles enclose a pure morning clarity, that feverish imbued smell of birds pursued him, watching him with insistent animal eyes. From the beginning he had been assailed by the impression that things were observing him, the chairs, the furniture, the ironic wineglasses in the sideboard, his own face in old photographs accusing him of some shortcoming of which he was unaware, that things were observing him with the severity of eyebrows from their volutes, the reproving cough of creaking wood, the chains of a pocket watch on dresser knobs, but it was the first time that he found himself being watched by a smell. For example, I was in bed in Armação de Pêra, in the hotel room so sparkling with light that objects floated, weightless, in a golden mist and I myself floated in a golden mist slowly moving the hand with the cigarette between ashtray and mouth, the blond hairs on my elbow shone like cheerful eyelashes, my burnt skin resembled that of potatoes in the oven, and the smell of the sea climbed the wall in a glycine spiral and perched, blue, on the parapet sitting on its hind legs, looking at me with the large humble pupils of its horse-eyes, wet from tears of foam. I pulled the sheet over my head to flee the curiosity from the sea, and the melancholy shyness of its restless obliqueness of a wounded man seeking me out among the pillows with anxious haste, rolled over on my stomach, clasped my hands around the back of my neck, drew up my legs, sucked in my belly and chest until I reduced my body to the dimensions of an embryo, an insect, an insignificant chrysalis lost in a fold of clothing, but the sweetish odor of the sea, smooth and bland, perforated the pillowcases to stare at me, silent as the touching plaint of a woman. Odors are normally heedless: they pass by us in a hectic rush, linger a few seconds, and disappear into the air the way smiles hover before our mouths like the shadows that envelop in a diffuse veil of mystery the houses where we were born. As a child I would distinguish aromas with a dog's quick sharpness, I could anticipate by smell the arrival of people before hearing their steps in the hallway or the vestibule, was able to guess those who were going to die by the greasy halo that surrounded them, heavy with the strange dew of cadavers. Later, when I grew up, I achieved what adults call "the practical sense of life," which deep down remains the automatism of uselessness, and lost the gift of the affectionate and startled attention of children, in which echo, as in dreams, enormous footsteps mingling joy and fear. Until in the hotel room in Armação de Pêra, whose walls sparkled with light, after many days painful, and happy, and faith-filled, and desperate, I saw the odor of the sea sitting on the parapet looking at me with the humble pupils of its horse-eyes.

The odor of the sea looked at him from the parapet, with eye sockets wet from tears of foam, and he got up and went to the balcony to examine the beach. One descended directly from the hotel to the sand and stood there in the middle of the naked people, like some modern angel, a towel around his neck, come down from above in an elevator to impart an unmistakable mechanical touch to the miracle of his presence. At the beach the smell enveloped us in the white vapor of its breath, which panted softly like that of a girl awaiting someone, her hair spilling onto the pillows of the rocks and the profile of her belly seeded with small boats, colored freckles that crept slowly along. Leaning back on the balcony he waited for the odor of the sea, following a shy and lengthy hesitation, to leap onto his shoulder, like circus monkeys, and went back inside to shave carrying on the nape of his neck a hoarse constellation of seagulls whose cries shattered in the mirror the swift geometry of his movements. At night, in contrast, the sea was a fish with a dark luminous back, an anchored fish whose eyes, behind the curtains, undulated lightly the round jelly of its irises, illuminating the room with the indecisive gray of an endless twilight, identical to that which dwells in photo album smiles, yellowed by the orange tea of time.

So that he knew he had left Albufeira when only the water's sweet odor of squash was little by little replaced by the dry dense aroma of the earth, as lean as a large porous horn, in which tree roots twist and break like the antennae of butterflies against the oil lamps of summer. They were trees both insignificant and pathetic, reduced to the rust of their branches which extended in every direction the petrified pleas of their gestures under the towering porcelain sky, devoid of birds and clouds, hollow like the useless eye of the strabismic lost in the corner of the features in a kind of contemplation. He left Albufeira, the homes, the restaurants, the boardinghouses and the car rental agencies of Albufeira, and found himself in the dusty fields of the Algarve, ugly and acid like the detritus of ebb tide, on the road to Messines. Its snout downward, a dog trotted between the shafts of a cart and he thought how sad my country is where the sea doesn't reach, nocturnal even in the sun, somber even by day where the sea doesn't reach, small cemeteries in which the dead, unkempt, swirl in the labyrinth of the crosses in search of an impossible way out, road workers repairing the highway with the sleepwalking movements of prisoners, the hermits he saw in Monsanto as a boy, working in the open under eucalyptus trees as large as the shoulders of his uncles. There dwelled in him a raging piety, an angry tenderness for his strange emaciated country that he remembered, when far away, not by way of landscapes, fragments of cities, statues, streets, people, but through a sound, one single sound, the whistling in the crown of the pines like weathervanes, secretly calling him to mysterious adventures. In London, in Madeira, in Angola, when he would lie down in unfamiliar beds in hotels where freight elevators ran continuously with their tiny whistle of comets, that multiple, injured, abstracted and moaning vibration forced him to sit up, completely awake, in the sheets, imagining himself at his parents' beach house in September, when the equinox blows from the east like the wheezing of an asthmatic child.

He left Albufeira and headed toward Messines and the color of jaundice, the cancerous color, the yellow color of the earth reminded him of the Miguel Bombarda courtyard, across from the 1st men's ward, seen from the dusty window of the doctors' office, with two wobbly desks facing each other and a mirror over the wash basin whose faucet dripped the constipated eye drops of an eternal tear. The first men's ward consisted of dozens and dozens of patients shuffling their slippers like fetters through the hallway, empty mattresses, globes of dingy glass, an old man squatted on the wooden floor, his hands in his pockets, trying to bite whoever came by, with the enraged snarling of a country villa dog, one of those that at night take offense far off, in cruel barks of insomnia. From time to time heads with uninhabited features introduced themselves into the narrow gap in the door-way to peep at him, their unshaven chins moving in a strange prayer that reached his ears like the vague rustle of feathers.

"I'm going to be a dentist," he declared to the thick convent walls painted a dirty moss-green, because he was frightened by that miserable and unreal place in which he was beginning to feel as much a prisoner as the others, those who stretched out in the sun like great repugnant lizards, their belts replaced by strips of bandages and twine, as quiet as the crocodiles at the zoo and like them acquiring little by little the mineral texture of the rocks, the trunks, the nuns' embalmed cadavers in glass coffins on church altars, whose fingers resemble those of stone octopuses.

"I'm going to be a dentist," he said, because he was beginning to fear that the assistant when he arrived would stare at him side-long, suspicious, hand a piece of paper to the orderly on duty, his clothes would be replaced by a cotton uniform, he would be in-jected in the buttocks with a battery of syringes and they would make him lie in the courtyard, dazed and dizzy among the other crocodiles who were snoring, their hands wrapped around a crumpled pack of cigarette butts.

He examined himself in the mirror, making sure of his tie, his jacket, the part in his hair, and thought

"I'm a doctor"

just as children repeat

"I'm grown up"

as they walk through unlit corridors, shivering with doubt and fear. I'm a doctor I'm a doctor I'm a doctor, I'm thirty years old, have a daughter, came back from the war, I bought a cheap car two months ago, I write poems and novels that I never publish, I have an aching upper wisdom tooth and I'm going to be a psychiatrist, understand people, identify their despair and their anguish, calm them with my competent smile of a lay priest dispensing the host-pills in chemical Eucharists, I'm finally going to be a respectable person leaning over a prescription pad in hasty abstracted nobility, take it after meals, take it before meals, take it in the middle of meals, when you get up, when you go to bed, with a hot drink, at breakfast, at lunch, in the afternoon, no wine, brandy, vermouth, liqueur, come back in two weeks, come back in a month, call and tell me how it went, I'm normal you're sick I'm normal you're sick I'm normal you're sick I know semiology, psychopathology, therapy, I can spot depression a mile away, paranoia, unhealthy excessive joy, epileptic seizures, organic equivalents, the character-based ones, request an EEG through the Health Service, pay the secretary, don't forget to pay the secretary, be sure you pay the secretary, behave yourself, or I'll put you on sleep therapy using morello Serenif Largactil Niamid Nozinan Bialminal, good afternoon, he tightened the knot in his tie guiding himself by the left-handed image in the mirror, scrutinized himself fullface, at three-quarters, in profile, I'm a doctor, I'm a doctor, I'm an intern in psychiatry, the old man in the hall bayed incessantly, he returned to his desk, sat down imperially in the chair, and through the window glass had the dizzying impression of seeing a man flying, an ordinary man neither young nor old, flapping the sleeves of his jacket in the blue of July and flying. He thought

"I'm fucked"

and when he raised his head he saw the assistant by the door, staring at him in great surprise.

"The first time you come here, it impresses you," he said apologetically, looking sidelong at the window: the flying man had yielded to the decrepit ward across the way, near whose entrance on a worn bench sat a Last Supper of pajamas, their gestures suspended from nothing like those of waterfowl he imagined always in the middle of an unpredictable journey suddenly interrupted. The assistant looked around for something, opened a drawer, took out a plastic rose in an aluminum vase, deposited it on a round mat on the other desk, and drew back a step, his head inclined, to observe the effect:

"Nothing like a flower to raise morale."

He resembled the oval portraits of eighteenth century French poets, in which the eyelids, heavy as drapes, cast a dense velvet shadow over soft cheeks. I felt like asking why he didn't wear a La Fontaine wig and, instead, heard my own voice replying, independent of me like a wind-up toy:

"If you put a Benfica team poster on the wall the room would be complete."

And he recalled Cavém, number 11, making his way downfield along the left sideline, until passing to the center, next to the penalty area, toward José Augusto of Águas, of Santana, in the stadium jammed with flag-waving enthusiasm. He could smoke at will in the stands because his father never attended football games: he stayed at home listening on the radio, sitting on the sofa, impatiently and nervously gnawing his pipe.

"That's an idea," said the assistant, considering, "why shouldn't we put the Benfica team on the wall?"

He began rummaging through the desk, shuffling papers, and I thought He's going to put a dozen plastic roses on top because the guy is the Holy Queen of the atomic age, with a Dacron lap full of fake petals. Leaves are going to come out of his fly, his lapel, his belt, the openings in his shirt, he himself is going to turn into a gigantic monstrous flower, installed in the vase of the swivel chair like the palm trees in hotel lobbies, brushing past us the frayed bristles of their branches. I want to become a dentist before that happens, he decided, I want to become a dentist as fast as possible before the old man baying in the hall comes crawling into the office and bites my shins, hangs onto the seat of my pants like postmen in cartoons, before the plastic roses soak up all the oxygen from the air and leave me writhing on the floor like a drowning shark, thrashing the desperate fins of my jacket. Someone in the ward began to shout: it was a hoarse moan, persistent, monotonous, similar to that of the sea in the cracks in grottoes or the

wind at the sharp crests of cliffs, bevel edges of granite raised toward the lips of the clouds, and his body stretched out, tense, in
the direction of the sound, like a bowstring plucked by the finger
of the moan. He listened to that nocturnal sound in the hospital
morning, laden with mysterious resonances and impalpable
echoes of darkness, that kernel of shadow in the dusty, excessive
light of morning, with the same dolorous expectation, the same
unspeakable fear he once felt at the approaching thunder in
Africa, heavy with unbearable anguish. The administrator's cook
passed around the room a tray of fruity drinks, the glasses
clinked lightly against one another in a tinkling of crystal and
the large trees outside bent under the menacing rain, come in
great thick sheets from the north in a whirlwind of lightning. He
always imagined

"I'm going to die"

when the thunderclaps arrived and tenuous sparks rose from his
hair into the saturated humidity of the room, to swirl freely from
person to person like strange magnesium eels. He always imagined

"I'm going to die"

just as he imagined, on the road to Messines, through the yellow
pumice-stone landscape of the interior of the Algarve, rendered
hard and acid by the absence of rivers, a restless and humiliated
landscape, that he would never reach Lisbon and that he would
remain, for years and years, inside the car, drifting along highways that he barely knew, listening to the voice of Paul Simon or
Gal Costa on the cassette player

My love
everything around me is a void
everything okay
everything okay
like two and two are five

gripping the steering wheel as a sleeping baby does a useless doll. He crossed one or two villages with strange names, a lonely chapel on a hillock, sparse sterile cultivated fields, and he remembered the house without water or electricity near Lagoa, Bia Grade's house, with the well bucket constantly attacked by the soft buzzing of bees, where last summer he had spent three weeks with Isabel to finish *Elephant's Memory*, which he had dragged out for months in annoyed discontent, building chapter by chapter with his usual slowness, awaiting the arrival of the words like a martyr of improbable Revelations. Gripping the wheel, he remembered Bia Grade's house distant from the sea, among the almond trees and the vineyard reflecting the sun on the dull ochre of its leaves, the light of the kerosene lamps that transformed shapes on the walls into towering herds of shadows approaching and retreating like monstrous amoebas, making love on the floor so as not to awaken Dona Deolinda and Mr. Manuel sleeping in the next room, and once, at the time of the afternoon nap, having gone to urinate in the bathroom and seeing, lying on the basin like some smiling animal, a set of dentures baring its canines to a piece of blue soap. I wrote the entire day, outside, next to the wash-tub, behind the house, pushing my chair back and forth according to the position of the sun, the paper rolling up and crackling under the pen as if aflame, and when I raised my head from time to time I saw the poor land, without grandeur, the ugly land of the Algarve bowing in humiliation under the sumptuous gleaming of the sky, whose transparent skin shone like a limitless sequin.

"What are you ruminating about?" asked the assistant, looking in the glass cabinet for some clinical process or other. The old man who barked fell silent: an orderly must have placed a bowl of leftovers before his knees, pieces of meat, bits of rice, a rotten bone, and the man surely must have lowered his wrinkled bald scalp to the plate, showing the long parallel tendons of his neck like a drinking giraffe.

"About why he didn't become a dentist," he replied, with Bia Grade's house, surrounded by the cry of crickets, still in his mind, and the dust of the hospital whirling in the courtyard in desolate spirals, dashing against the asylum's melancholy walls or the tiled cloister in back, as delicate and transparent as the shell of an eyelid. He should have been a dentist, he added, all of us should have been dentists, repairing molars with a jeweler's attention to detail, calmly tending to incisors and canines, saying Rinse and feeling at peace, he realizes, free of inquietude and remorse, making molds of gums for elderly ladies, while from the window a mustached statue points its bronze finger at us, to general derision.

The first houses of Messines appear in the distance, surrounded by the ochre gouache of the fields above which summer weighed its open limbs like a sleeping body with an enormous hot mouth slowly breathing over the surface of the land: summer is a very fat man, I thought, summer is a very fat man who snores, a gentleman as fat as the one we're used to seeing at the restaurant where I take my daughters to eat, a working-class tavern of mechanics, truck drivers, lottery vendors and soldiers, silent and slow people with the eyes of a dead mare, swallowing their soup with noisy harvesting lips. The fat gentleman would arrive in shirtsleeves, suspenders, rolled-up illustrated newspapers under his arm, and he would say to himself Humpty Dumpty has invaded Benfica, he lives in Poço do Chão, works in a nearby office, smokes nauseating cigarillos and eats seed germ when he diets, and the three of us stare, stupefied, at the mattresses of his buttocks, spilling over the chair in soft pleats of straw, his belly, his shoulders, the absence of neck, stare at his bulging toad eyes, his resigned gestures, the successive, overlapping double chins, and if we stuck a pin in his leg the guy would deflate and zigzag around the tables like a balloon until nothing was left but a useless little tatter hanging from the neck of a bottle of Bucelas, with his features visible in miniature on the leftover piece of rubber.

"No, don't say it," he told the assistant who was about to push the button on the wall to call the orderly, "he didn't go into dentistry because psychiatry is the most noble of the medical specialties."

"Psychiatry is a hoax," his father declared. "It has no scientific basis, the diagnosis doesn't matter, and the treatment is always the same."

"Have you ever noticed," his friend asked, "that psychiatrists are humorless lunatics?"

They both worked at the time at Santa Maria and the psychiatrists startled us daily inside and out, their way of speaking, of walking, of dressing, the dime-store profundity of their concepts, the little games whispered in the corridors, the perverse alliances that were made and unmade, the enmities, the hatreds. People greeted one another with a smile and stabbed each other in the back distilling the dark, repugnant, filthy cruelty of cadavers, entangled in Freud's beard in cloying admiration. He would see the psychiatrists, thinking those who consulted them healthier than they themselves, and it distressed him that through ignorance the living embraced the dead, in hope of impossible relief.

"This stinks like the carcasses of dead mules," he thought whenever he entered the doctors' office, where they sat pompously in a circle for discussions that had nothing to do with real life, real happiness, real suffering. "This stinks like the carcasses of dead mules, talking among themselves about their own putrefaction." And whenever one of them lifted his cigarette to his mouth he saw the smoke disappear into the decomposing gums, into the swollen tongues dirty with clots and scabs, into the lips purple from the lividity of nitrogen. In the hospital meetings, during the day, he was assailed by the odd impression that it was the patients who treated the psychiatrists, with the delicacy that the apprenticeship of pain brings, that the patients feigned being sick in order to help the psychiatrists, to disguise a bit their sad condition of ignored cadavers, of the dead who suppose themselves alive and circle slowly through the corridors with the measured graveness of ghosts, not authentic ghosts, the ones who from the porches of abandoned houses watch the movement in the street hidden behind the lace of curtains, but false ghosts with oakum sideburns and cardboard noses, ridiculous ghosts bloated with useless wisdom. From Santa Maria he could see whether the river in the distance was in April or May and the sky panted like an enormous mute lung, a lung as blue as if the Tagus poured over the houses and the clouds its stream of sparkling shadows refracting the city upside down in the mirror of the birds. The trees, the churches, the buildings, sharply outlined and colorful, shone with pleasure in the brightness of morning, and in the hospital meeting room the psychiatrists, sluggish, dun-colored and flaccid, argued interminably their dialogues of dead mules, analyzing Freud's beard hair by hair with the cheap reagents of their imagination. In the bar they would meet in a separate group like nuns or the lead cows in a bullfight, whispering Oedipuses in a drone of conspiracy. Schizophrenia, a viscous schizophrenia, hovered over them and enveloped them in gestures and behavior identical to a repulsive spider web: Psychiatrists are insipid lunatics, he thought, rich clowns tyrannizing the poor clowns their patients with slapstick psychotherapies and pills, rich clowns in the whiteface foolish pride of police, the ungenerous ignoble pride of police, of the owners of other people's heads, of the labelers of other people's feelings: he's obsessive, phobic, phallic, immature, psychopathic: they classify, stamp, pry, rummage, they don't understand, they get nervous because they don't understand and issue from their decomposing gums, from their swollen tongues dirty with clots and scabs, from their lips purple from the lividity of nitrogen, authoritative and ridiculous pronouncements. Hell, he thought, is psychiatric treatises, hell is the invention of insanity by doctors, hell is this stupidity of pills, this inability to love, this absence of hope, this Japanese bracelet for exorcizing rheumatism of the soul with a pill at night, a vial to be taken at breakfast, and lack of understanding from outside of bitterness and delirium, and if I don't go into dentistry right away I'll become as crazy and sordid and humorless as they.

Messines emerged before him, around a curve, unfocused because of the heavy mist of the cellophane heat, and he remembered the first time he had arrived in the Algarve, the day after his wedding, and the flower of blood on the hotel sheet, a small open poppy that glistened, red against the smooth, foam-embroidered blue of the sea. Sitting on the room's balcony at night they could smell on their necks, their hair, on each other's shoulders the salt of the muscles, the algae of the pubes, the fishlike texture of the thighs, making love with a wedding ring on my finger and feeling your ring on your open hand against my kidneys, I've forgotten what the priest said but remember very well your smile, the innocent Latin, the angelic language of orgasm against a wheat-colored devastated body. He arrived in Messines, that August of 1970, in the large slow-moving car lent him by his grandmother, which rattled along the highway like a rocking cradle. The bushes by the road traversed the profile of his wife at his side as if the purity of her face had turned into transparent glass, crystal features lightly tinged by the tanned skin where the sun focused the intimacy it bestows on fruit. The bushes turned the back of her neck green, the damp line of her lashes, the long interminable question mark of her neck, and her phrases were green, her vulva was surely green, green and soft as the moss of grottoes. They reached Messines and I said We're in the Algarve because this is Gildásio's land, because for them the Algarve was Gildásio, Gildásio's light-colored eyes, Gildásio's roaring laughter, Gildásio's uncloying friendship in the mess hall at Tomar full of doddering old colonels and generals, of reservists dripping stress medications into their water at lunch, of elderly well-mannered gentlemen talking in hushed tones about chronic ailments and fainting spells, having forgotten the warrior glories that never were. The fields of the Algarve, the trees, the poles, the houses traversed the glass of your face, darkening it with edges and shadows, your curls fluttered like the narrow leaves of a lemon-tree, on the wall of your brow the brightness of morning expanded and grew, and I said We're in the Algarve because we came to the town of Gildásio and of João de Deus of the reading primer *Cartilha*, and in some square or other we may run into that poet's stone beard among the illiterate indifference of the acacias and the pigeons. But there were only garages, buildings, cafés, the quiet stir of the province composed of an incomprehensible eternity, and your transparent profile, lightly tinged with the bronze tone of your flesh, on which the sun slowly ripened like the skin of pomegranates.

"Do you have any experience with this?" asked the assistant, his finger on the button in the wall to call the orderly on duty, and he felt like answering that he was familiar with the psychiatrists' stench of mule carcass, the psychiatrists' obscene stench of mule carcass, felt like talking about the petty angers and the cabalistic speeches, like telling how when he had first entered Júlio de Matos Hospital, still a student, he had rebelled against the dreadful misery of the patients, against the neglect of the garden, against the filth of the dormitories, rebelled against the resignation of the ill, pushed behind bars by an absurdity that exceeded them, by irrationality they couldn't understand, by the grinder of a medical profession that persecutes fantasy and dreams, a moralistic, castrating, authoritarian profession, the profession of the lords, of the owners, which detests deviation, hates difference, can't stand the capacity for invention, the dead profession of a dead society, whose greasy viscous odor had repulsed him at Júlio de Matos when he smelled it floating among the wards in the midst of the trees, breathing into the throat of the grass like the nocturnal wind.

The assistant looked at him from head to toe, waiting for a reply, and he thought, I'm an SS with doubts, I'm a seminarian suffering a crisis of conscience, Hitler is great, God is good, and Psychiatry is the most noble of etc., etc., he thought You can't be a merciful executioner, he thought You can't be a tender-hearted tyrant, so I pulled a chair up to the desk, plopped down into the seat like a crown prince on his throne, no one was flying outside the windows, at the entrance to the 5th ward my subjects lay motionless in the sun like victims on the tracks after a railway catastrophe, I checked the knot of my tie with my fingers, buttoned my coat, and received the paperwork for the first patient, just as earlier I had accepted a rifle in Mafra, on the firing range, to learn how to kill efficiently.

The light of the Algarve, around four in the afternoon, starts to mellow, forlorn, as twilight approaches, and the houses begin to open slowly like nocturnal corollas, to the rhythm of the wall clocks to which the great slow hearts beat, unhurriedly, like those of sleeping cattle. The static convex vitreous sky reflects and deforms them, the fields disdained by the sea, the land that the sea rejects like a useless horn, the land as dry and hard as a horn, a crust of pus, a worthless remnant. The sunset is a butter stain, the hint of a butter stain similar to a translucent blot of clouds, or not even clouds and only a light accentuation of color, a diluted tear watercoloring the air, an undefined something ready to crystallize and grow. He had felt that in Lagos, in Albufeira, in Armação de Pêra, in Tavira, with a strange throbbing in the chest, an inchoate nameless anguish in his body bowed in wait, he had felt his veins dilate with blood in the darkness of broad daylight, heard them groan in his temples like the wood of old houses under the weight of the ghosts of his childhood, felt the seed of darkness in the interior of his body like Beira's black mica stones, and thought It gets dark so early in me, thought When they open my belly on the operating table, looking for my liver, or my gall bladder, or my stomach, they'll find instead of viscera the silence of deserted farmhouses and the distant barking of dogs, the restiveness of startled dogs summoning the dawn. The light of the Algarve, the light of Messines, stuck to his thumbs like butterfly dust, if I touch a house, or a street, or a river, the mark of my hand imprints itself on things like on the wet clay in school, the hollow of the palm, phalanges, nails, I can steal a piece from this afternoon, carry it to Lisbon in my pocket, take it out and stare for a long time at the fields disdained by the waves, the downcast dogs that trot among the vineyards with the oblique pace of foxes, the timid penumbra of the porches, the land that the sea rejects like a useless bone, a bone as hollow as those of birds, killed in flight. The orderly stuck his head through the opening of the door in the glare of Messines, brushed aside a cloud that clung to his brow, that adhered to the sweat of his forehead propelled by the east wind, and said

"Good morning doctor"

The assistant answered

"Good morning Gouveia"

one seated and the other standing, like me in front of my superiors in the troops

"With your permission, colonel?"

and the colonel's porcine eyes measured me behind the desk, next to a map of Angola full of white and red dots, unable to shout If you only knew how I hate you, you bastard, but the orderly smiled, the assistant smiled, I smiled too, the colonel's porcine eyes disappeared into the outer room, and the white and red dots floated before me until they vanished like the flakes in a snow globe.

"I wanted to talk to Nobre"

said the assistant to the cheerful head that was waiting and then evaporated into the brightness of Messines. He didn't leave through the door: he evaporated like smoke evaporates on the roof, like the features we loved evaporate into memory, like my body evaporates into yours in a gentle salt of sweat and moans.

"You're going to take care of Nobre"
the assistant informed me, you're going to take care of Nobre, a simple case, a delirious puff of smoke, I quickly looked for delirious puffs of smoke in my mental notes and found nothing beyond the usual poor treasures, my grandfather, Luísa at the beach, the little girls' first steps, the brownish crayon color of the lemon tree in the backyard, the dental braces, the displeasure of never having broken an arm, thick missals with the images of dead people, with every answer I gave on the Psychiatry examination the professor bent over in his chair laughing like a compliant audience in the presence of humor that escaped me, I'm one hell of a comedian, I thought, rummaging in my head for definitions and treatments, a simple case, a delirious puff of smoke, in Messines the absence of the sea is so total that the wind hawks the phlegm of bronchitis in the throats of the streets, a wind as sad as the cough of a librarian or a widow. Good morning doctor sir, Good morning Gouveia, corridors in half-shadow just like those at the Vasco da Gama Aquarium where from time to time emerges the unexpected mushroom of a mouth, the coral of an arm, the medusa of hair, the patients are the silent algae of these floating pajamas, the pumice stones of these opaque features, the palpitating gills of these phrases, the door opened and closed with a bang and Nobre entered.

"Hello, Nobre," said the assistant in that special tone reserved for children, the dying, and boutique employees, carefully storing the glass ashtray in a drawer, the signboard pointing to Lisbon was missing the L and I thought That clown Gildásio's been fooling around here, what else can you do in this desert to keep from falling into using drugs, at the mess in Tomar we would grab the elastic of the servants' bowties which would snap back with a pop, and through the windows the trees of Mouchão were a heap of dark whispering heads. When I'm asked to list the finest moments of my life Tomar is there, he decided, it was the year of the Tabuleiros feast and the fishing competition, he courted the teachers from the school over the weak lemon tea of melancholy abstainers, I fixed the dislocation of a paratrooper's shoulder by a foot in the guy's armpit until the bone gave a pop, crack, every night a suspicious old man would spy on me, following me from window frame to window frame making faces like a stuffed crocodile, our profiles merging in shoe stores, in clothing shops, in travel agencies, the teachers' breasts flattened obediently under my palms, their lips rose to mine, blindly, like famished colts butting one another, the ill outside the city awaited me in dark concave houses, stretched out in the dirty disorder of the sheets.

"In the name of the Father, the Son, and the Holy Spirit" bellowed Nobre on his knees and his hands joined, from the other side of the desk. He was a small fat man with a mustache, his pajama lapels covered with sports emblems, medals, various badges, prizes from Christmas cakes, and pieces of paper attached with pins, imitating decorations and insignias. The assistant removed the stapler, a potential hammer, and suggested in the inviting whisper of a priest at the start of confession:

"Would you like to sit down, Nobre?"

"In the name of the Father, the Son, and the Holy Spirit," Nobre repeated indignantly. "Parlez-vous français? Speak English? Habla español? Speak German? Turkish? Russian? Armenian? I only talk to polyglot doctors. Blessed be our Lord Jesus Christ and his Holy Mother Mary. Hurray for Sporting."

"I see a chair right there at your feet," advised the assistant, chest inflated, cooing persuasively. His eyebrows fluttered restlessly.

Nobre grabbed the chair and smashed it against the wall with all his might. One leg skidded along the floor and was lost from sight under the glass armoire.

"When you're in the presence of God," he explained, bellowing, "anyone who lacks respect goes directly to Hell. You know what Hell is? Speak English?"

A delirious puff of smoke, he thought, what the hell is that? Nobre's arms moved back and forth in the rhythm of a seagull's desperate flapping, his pale lips sipping the air beneath the sieve of his mustache, like the jutting-jawed fishes in drugstores that gulp without appetite the water cloudy with moss. He calculated that the other man must be about his own age and imagined himself on his knees yelling at two men strategically entrenched behind an enormous desk, listening to his distress with scientific detachment.

"We have to go back to the needles," sighed the assistant as if reluctantly assigning a penance of eight hundred Hail Marys.

Nobre leapt up, whirling in outrage. His pupils did in fact resemble those of gulls perched on the walls of the Marginal roadway on rainy afternoons, small glassy spheres simultaneously in-expressive and hallucinated. The waves crashed onto the rocks in acidic fans of foam, near the Mónaco restaurant and the doorman dressed as a wily aviator, the sky was composed of successive lay-ers of overlapping gray, the river shuddered with fever all the way to the sea, and the rain furiously burrowed hundreds of crystal braids into the highway. The windshield wipers moved their shaky automaton elbows, shaving away the persistent acne of the raindrops. Perhaps the Spanish pianist Shegundo Galarza would be playing a fado in dance tempo to the empty tables.

"Needles my ass," roared Nobre, turning toward the assistant, breath to breath, like a pair of elephant bookends without books to hold. "Speak English? Speak German? I work in tourism, I know all the languages, I want out of here."

He moved in leaps between the window and the door like an obese squirrel, medals and emblems jingling on his chest with the sound of tin cans like the long tail of pots and pans dragged behind the cars of newlyweds. His sparse tufts of hair rippled chaotically over his reddish ears, his belly oscillated and vibrated like a timpani struck by invisible drumsticks. In the courtyard, crates of sparkling water were being unloaded from a rusty white truck. Spirals of dust rose occasionally from the ground and spun from tree to tree driven by the sudden wind of June, that kind of flame without smoke that arises from the pores of the earth with implacable vehemence, under the cloudless sky like a marble plaque streaked with fine luminous veins. The assistant surrep-titiously pressed the button on the wall and I thought If deliri-ous puff of smoke means thunderous agitation I might have one of those every week but I blow off steam silently, on the road to Montijo, gnawed by the thousand acids of anguish. The glass of the armoire reflected the face that he had become accustomed to seeing in mirrors and that didn't resemble the features he presumed to be his, the glorious nose, the happy mouth, the jaw of Julius Caesar arriving in Rome: there they were, he and his assistant, installed in their regal chairs, there Nobre was, appearing and disappearing like a frantic insect, shouting his angry tirade at an uncomprehending world. I'm still young, he thought, there's time to get out of here, to go home, to become a dentist, to enroll in economics, agronomy, mathematics, he thought. It's time to run away from here looking at the reflection in the glass of the armoire, the way he saw himself, minuscule, in women's pupils when he moved closer to touch them, minuscule and convex, reflected in women's pupils as in a silver skin, the cheeks, the forehead, the eyebrows, the little squares of their teeth, Nobre knelt at the window, extending his arms toward the trees in the courtyard, the sycamores and acacias in the courtyard, gilded by the electric light of the sun, and at that moment a redheaded youth in undershorts, his orangish pubic hair sticking out from the loose elastic, came staggering in, braced himself against the desk, and began saying

"Doctor sir doctor sir doctor sir doctor sir doctor sir"
through crusted freckled lips without saliva, the lips of a gluttonous child, a distressed little boy talking in his sleep, the lips of my brother Nuno at three years of age, sick with peritonitis, repeating I'm going to die and I want my daddy in a voice I'll never forget, the terrible accusatory voice of the very young in agony,

I've seen children die of leukemia, wrapped in sheets, carried them to the hospital refrigeration unit, children who cried for the vial of morphine, raising their ecchymosis-swollen elbows to the interns in panic.

Gouveia's head appeared at the door, like a bald rosemary suddenly springing up in the chipped wood of the doorframe, an obedient and ugly flower with a mustache. The cloud floated now into the flaccid shell of his ear:

"Did you call?"

How real this guy is, how soothingly real, he thought, even to his breath thick with booze, even to the obsequious vulgarity of his features: a concrete, actual, solid man anchored in the logical world of taxes, parking tickets, cutlets with sausage, and petty marital hatreds. A man like the men and women at the Trindade Tavern, I verified, the frustrated sour women and men at the Trindade Tavern the night I met the writer Luiz Pacheco. I was leaning against the counter with Zé Manel, listening to him talk about sadness, loneliness, the perplexity of his life, in that enormous tiled pool populated with voices, the clinking of glasses, the rustle of fabric, it was March and the people were plunging their noses into the foam of their beer like horses at the beach, a cloud of smoke hovered over the waxy, overly white necks of the people, the stearin features and sweaty hair of the people, and who should arrive but the writer Luiz Pacheco, carrying two plastic bags filled with newspapers, a Lenin-style beret on his head, his protuberant eyes of a skinny turtle behind the glasses that kept them from tumbling to the floor with the tinkling sound of china. He was dead drunk and the frustrated sour women and men at the Trindade Tavern, the untalented women and men at the Trindade Tavern mocked him, rummaged in his bags, took off his beret, tugged on the ends of his grubby raincoat, laughed behind his back with the spoiled-milk sourness of envy or shook his hand as one shakes the hand of circus stars, with a strange mixture of condescension and disdain.

"Shit," I said to Zé Manel, "for God's sake get the old man out of the claws of those sons of bitches. They're the grandchildren of the bastards who used to throw rocks at Gomes Leal in the Rato district, they're the limp-dicks who complain that everybody in this country does a shitty job and when somebody shows up who doesn't do a shitty job they start snarling in fury and envy at the other guy's hard-on because they feel the withered piece of meat in their underwear, because they're incapable, because they're definitively not capable of screwing life."

"This is António Lobo Antunes," said Zé Manel in an affection-ate and gentle voice that transformed the words into soft stuffed animals. He brought Le Monde with him the way guys in the nine-teenth century carried their silver-handled canes, and I thought, Le Monde is his tie as I looked at the clothes thrown carelessly onto his small body, the leather bracelet, the hair spilling over the col-lar of his shirt.

The writer Luiz Pacheco swayed lightly on unsteady legs: his poignant pride, his unbearable irony, reduced the penises of the impotent to soft little shriveled things for pissing, curled up in their pants like shameful worms. A discolored wisp of hair waved like a feather against the wall tiles. He put aside his raincoat, laid down the bags and slapped me in the face with both palms in amused jubilation:

"Ah, boy!"

And the three of us were the only living guys in that cemetery of lupine.

"We need to change Nobre's therapy," the assistant told the orderly. "And the redhead isn't mine. I don't know him from Adam."

"Adam? Did you say Adam?" Nobre interrupted. "I am Portuguese. Habla español? Do you speak English? Speak German? Deutsch?"

The patient in the corridor began barking again. Something metallic (a plate, a mug, silverware) fell to the floor making an enormous report, amplified by the silence that clothed in anxiety the patients' actions, the unbearable silence growing in the intervals between screams, like the storm clouds in Baixa do Cassanje, separated by the turbid waters of the Cambo. Gouveia expelled Nobre and the redhead from the office like someone brushing away shadows of an uncomfortable nightmare:

"Go, go, go," he repeated in the slow patient tone of a shepherd, and the sounds seemed to come from his throat like the gushing of a river depositing stones. A distant telephone started to ring. The assistant leaned back in his chair, relieved:

"Wasn't it you who said that Psychiatry is the most noble of the medical specialties?" he asked. "Shit, if I'd known what I know today I'd have been a dentist."

I discovered that loneliness, he said aloud to himself in the empty car, en route to the mountains, is a child's gun in a plastic bag in the hand of a frightened woman. The afternoon now had the cloudy yellow color of the deceased, the melancholy yellow of the iodine in old portraits, the dirty yellow of the coffin against a tree trunk or a wall, the rusty yellow of limping dogs on the beach, running in packs beside the sea in the September twilight, under the immense silent sky where in the distance can be divined the equinox migrations of ducks. Gaunt tragic plants rose to the fat, convex, almost violaceous cheeks of the clouds, multiple frenetic maestro's hands immobilized in the midst of a whirling waltz, and from time to time, on the edge of the road, tools and highway equipment dissolved in the sparse grass into the soft odor of the dead. Everything in the Algarve is feeble and gentle, he thought, even the waves that fold onto themselves like successive eyelids rendered transparent by anemia, even the soapstone faces of the peasants in whose veins runs a secret, mysterious wind, even the quickly aging mornings that immediately turn heavy, hanging like fruit from the branches of the sky, by thick incandescent peduncles of sunlight. No birds were to be seen because there are no birds in the mountains: only the tools abandoned on the banks by highway workers and the ochre soil that seems to croak, breathing slowly like an enormous frog. Neither birds nor people were to be seen: the highway resembled a scar, a fold, a wrinkle in the skin, and on both sides the horizon, too near, fogged the windows of the car, the square mirror, our very eyes, with its dense animal breath: no landscape seemed so menacing beneath its harmless appearance of theatrical scenery, and he imagined that if they hoisted the cardboard hills with pulleys, behind the boxwoods, the hillocks, the sluggish calming palpitation of the earth, he would find restive and agitated darkness, such as dwells in the round pupils of the eyes of children, hidden in the false complicity of a smile. Everything in the Algarve, he thought, reminds me of moonscapes, the entrapped algae, the quietness of naps in the summer, when only the apples on the sideboard remain awake and alive in their porcelain bowls, roused by the red shadow of the light, and it's not impossible for a school of fishes to suddenly cross the asphalt, wiggling the lilac eyelashes of their tails in tiny spasms, or for the thousand arms of an octopus to drift among the bushes, uncoiled in a woman's languid goodbye. Like in the emergency room of Miguel Bombarda Hospital, where the faces wrinkle and the silhouettes float by, staggering, leaning against the faded green walls, old alcoholics with trembling fingers like compass needles, drugged men with convulsed eyes like the heavens during a storm, old ladies in whom a discreet and incommensurate sadness concentrates in the circumflex angles of the mouth, dragging under their nightgown painful menopauses. At dinnertime, a long line of beggars approaches the frosted-glass door of the emergency room, feigning imaginary insanities, weird illnesses, made-up suicides, in the hope of a bed or a plate of food to escape from the forced fast of the poor. They are the bums who circulate in the vicinity of the river near the warehouses at the docks and on the steps of the Alfama district, the neck of a bottle sticking out of their pockets so they can light up the night with the wick of booze, concave unshaven icons, dreaming of vegetable soup in the garbage cans. They head for Miguel Bombarda Hospital through the dark trees of Campo de Santana, through the little narrow sidewalks that form a kind of wig of lanes around the bald walls of the asylum, through Rua Luciano Cordeiro that my adolescence still associates with heavy thighs spread on threadbare velvet, and pour into the emergency room the supplicant sad gaze of dogs, barking at the doormat their humble hunger. But loneliness, he said aloud to himself in the empty car, en route to the mountains, is a child's gun in a plastic bag in the hand of a frightened woman, standing before me at the other end of the table, escorted by an exhausted fireman.

I slept in a bedroom as impersonal as a mess hall, whose sheets exuded the acrid odor of a grave, with a water bottle just like those in provincial boardinghouses, and a telephone that from time to time weeps a baby's distressed moans. Close to a thousand people were snoring in unison around me in a slow tidal movement, and I felt as if I were floating on the surface of the sound, stretched out in the sheets like the corpses of seamen that slide into the water enveloped in a canvas shroud and slowly sink beneath the waves like strange rigid cylinders of lead. When they called me to the emergency room I would enter an unreal grotto in which steps multiply and voices echo, shattered, reduced to meaningless fragments without vowels under the neon of bulbs that conferred upon the white of the smocks a glaucous tone, almost incandescent, of whitewashed surfaces, moving about slowly, noiselessly, just as the houses in the Algarve move away behind us, staring at us with the square blind eyes of their windows. Policemen, firemen, the Republican Guard, families, wait on worn benches fearfully whispering church monosyllables. A dense night of crepe, the predawn night, compact, opaque, almost solid, the night of insomnia or influenza which neither breathes nor lives and yet shivers from indecipherable frights, the way floors quiver in silence or flowers grow gigantic, impatiently, in the darkness, extending toward us the carnivorous digits of their leaves, pushes against the porch its soft weary breath. I sit at the desk, sticky from sleep, with the baby's cries of the telephone in the distance vibrating in my ears like some faraway but still present pain numbed by a pill, and grope for the ashtray, awkwardly, with the fingers with which I look for the water bottle if I awaken, in order to find in my hand the hard smooth contact of glass and through it the calming presence of familiar objects, and meet the gaze of the woman standing before me, clutching to her chest the plastic bag like someone slowly rocking a sick child: and I understood that loneliness, he said in the empty car on its way to Lisbon, isn't the trace of lipstick revealed on a glass in the empty office lit by blinds, or coming out of a bar where we perhaps left hanging on a chair the snakeskin of fake happiness intended to disguise anxiety and fear: loneliness is the people standing before me and their gestures of wounded birds, their damp gentle gestures that seem to drag themselves, like dying animals, in search of impossible help.

When I tried to show you the hospital, Joanna, you refused, with the stubborn, rocklike, unmovable firmness of children, to pass through the gate: the sycamores glistened in the sun, the asylum offered the serene image of a neutral and friendly large house, free of ghosts, the August brightness lightly shaded the tulle face of the dust of summer, which rounds off corners and reduces angles, turning them diffuse like observers behind the curtain in a house, reducing them to the vague contours of cheekbones. From nearby streets came a happy smell, a sound of life, the jubilant blue reverberation of tiles, and I thought to my-self, I'll show you the dressing room, the interiors of the dressing room, the enormous marble bathtub lying like a dead rhinoceros, I'll visit the vegetable garden with you and we'll walk hand in hand through the sea of greens, becoming smaller and smaller and happier and happier like the end of films until we dissolve gloriously into the horizon of houses on Gomes Freire, I'll intro-duce you to my friends the orderlies, My daughter, and hear the laughter of your shyness that wraps around my legs in distressed embarrassment. You refused to go into the hospital, your eyes full of tears and your arms clutching my waist like some fragile tenacious animal, your hair a skein of light-colored curls against my belly, and I suddenly remembered the well-kempt and servile little man who sold tin plates, tin vases, tin basins in the lobby of the asylum, and who always greeted me with the respectful bows of a muzhik, bending at the waist like a folding rule. He was a bald guy, in glasses, dignified and serious, an old patient whose lenses sparkled with the acid reflections of a teacher, who asked me one day in the slow, cautious, vaguely ironic voice of a school-master, an explainer, a disillusioned lecturer, if I hadn't noticed that in the asylum there were neither children nor animals, and that children and animals avoided the asylum the way they avoid death, impelled by some mysterious dread, the denial of agony, of putrefaction, of the morbid and funereal feelings of those in-habiting it. I listened to the little man speak as he circulated in his pointed patent leather shoes amid his vulgar tinware, amid his pretentious, ornate, useless, vulgar tinware, and I added that not even birds perched in the trees in the courtyard, as devoid of wings as the eyelids of albinos with their lashes ruffled by the hollow summer wind.

"Not even sparrows," the guy said, "want anything to do with the asylum, you can see that. Not sparrows, or pigeons, or blackbirds. None of the kind."

Then, confidentially, nudging:

"We're under the ground, you know? This here is the purgatory of the living, full of burning people."

"When there aren't any birds," I said, "it's as if there wasn't enough air, as if we're suffocating in air, belly up, like pink-mouthed fishes in the green foam of aquariums."

The little man bent down to adjust the horrible tin tray with the national seal at its center, which an elderly lady was contemplating absorbed, and poked me in the chest with a finger as hard and stiff as a piece of fishing pole. A strange smile twisted his mouth into swirls of saliva:

"Maybe one of us will learn to fly, doctor. Maybe one of us will perch in the sycamores in the courtyard."

And he set out running, limping, over the tiles in the lobby, shaking the tin sleeves of his jacket and crying

"Cheep cheep cheep"

in sharp batlike caws.

However, the girl standing before me didn't fly. I was sitting at my desk, surrounded by papers, my pen suspended over the file card (white for men, blue for women, different colors like baby clothes), looking at her and the fireman pallid from fatigue who accompanied her, dark translucent circles under the eyes from lack of sleep, under the high lunar lamp on the ceiling that emitted a melancholy phosphorescence, and with difficulty I freed myself from my own darkness, from my own ghosts, to listen to them. They came from Serpa, from Serpa to Faro, and from Faro to Lisbon, driven away from hospital to hospital by the impatience of doctors.

"We don't have beds"

"We don't have specialists"

"We don't have resources"

melting in the heat of an old ambulance whose engine coughed like a faltering kitchen appliance constantly on the verge of irreversible coma, steaming through the nostrils of the hood the sluggish vapor of its final breaths. The girl lived by herself on a deserted hillside, two or three haylofts in ruin that smelled of goat dejecta and rotten bones in the rain, and one day she suddenly appeared in the village and squatted in front of the Guard post, on a kind of wall in front of the Guard post, talking to angels. Little by little, the corporal of the squadron, the parish administrator, the priest, a group of stupefied peasants, the blind man with menacing opaque glasses like slate disks that no chalk illuminated, the poor circus acrobats who set up their tent in the square, gathered around her, amazed and apprehensive, to listen to her question the archangel Gabriel with intriguing familiarity that sprouted in the prior the mushrooms of envy. The veterinarian, quickly summoned, interrupted the difficult birth of a mare, groaning softly in her resigned suffering, to alert the lunatics' doctor from Faro, who should be able to understand the celestial hosts and invisible creatures. But the doctor from Faro, impatient with angels, sent the girl with the plastic bag to Lisbon along with a letter authenticated by a rubber stamp and an indistinct signature. During the journey the woman, installed beside the fireman driving the ancient ambulance, shaking like tractor operators perched on their iron seats, answered the seraphim's questions in the half-Latin, half-Russian language that surely must be used in the frozen spaces of the stars. And now there she was, standing in front of me, looking at the walls with strange quartz eyes, waving silently to the floating gaseous creatures whom we couldn't see in the office's glare of spectral insomnia. The fireman had plopped his aching body down on the sofa and was looking through his pockets for the oxygen of a cigarette. At the other end of the corridor, an alcoholic tied to his bed howled ceaselessly like a lighthouse in the fog, confused roars that distance blurred and muffled. In the intervals between his bellows I seemed to hear, very close to my ears, the rustling murmur of feathers. The nurse pushed aside an inopportune quill (outside, the trees at night were beginning to coo like doves, as if each leaf were a dove calling to us) and in an irritated tone, bothered by the odor of the thickening incense, sulfurous and sweet, in the emergency room, asked me:

"Why not give her an injection against angels? You must have learned to kill angels at the university: the autopsy cadavers are deceased angels, angels who allow themselves to be cut apart without a word of protest."

"Maybe call a bishop?" suggested the custodian, checking the file cabinet drawers so no seraphim could hide among the papers. "Bishops know all about angels and devils, as long as they dress in red like souls in Hell."

The girl, immobile, standing very straight, clutching to her chest the plastic bag, allowed the angels to alight on her shoulders, in her hair, on her arms, like birds on statues in parks, perched on bronze heroes like clothes on hangers. If I didn't act quickly the asylum would be transformed into a celestial aviary, replete with the rustle of tunics and sidereal droning, and dozens of winged men would invade the emergency room, breathing light laughter on the backs of our necks like the bubbles from gills that dissolve in green bursts of moss.

"Why not give her an injection against angels?" insisted the orderly. "There's got to be an injection against angels like there's rat poison, roach powder, or treatment for phylloxera. Angels are easier to kill than phylloxera."

And for an instant he imagined, as he wrote some prescription or other on the file card, angels in agony on the floor, sweaty and pale, calling out to him with the smoked-glass pupils of the moribund, which little by little shed expression and color until they resemble hollow crystals without reflections, identical to the hard plastic eyes of stuffed animals. He imagined the city's garbage trucks loaded at night with biblical astronauts with porous eagle bones and divers' fins, piled on one another in the attitude of castaways, he imagined a young cherub hanging from a gutter, lilac ankles rubbing against the porch's parapets, imagined his own guardian angel lying at his feet like a shadow, arms spread, a bloody remnant of the Milky Way evaporating from the corner of his lips. The fireman, who had remained with him in the office (from the injection room could be heard, like commotion in a henhouse, panicked cackles, breaking eggs, the custodian's voice railing against the archangels), had meanwhile fallen asleep on the sofa like a child in the backseat of a car, and the flickering light of the bulb in the ceiling conferred on their silhouettes, motionless till then, the mobility of gravel silently colliding with itself, pebbles hurling themselves at one another, crumbling, propelled perhaps by the thrashing of the angels' agony. The night rested against the windowpanes a tree branch that fluttered like an aspergillum, and the patients' sleep hummed the way empty houses hum if we but listen to them, merging with the throbbing of our temples, the throbbing of the veins in our hands, our bellies, our temples, when, lying down, we feel our bodies shrink into the sheets until they assume the size of useless, anguished dust. I felt the urge to stretch out on the floor like a dog and rest my face against the boards, as cool as a clean pillowcase, until the dead cherubim were swept from the hospital, the drunk who went on screaming from somewhere now unlocatable to me (to the left? to the right? the floor upstairs? in the exact center of my stomach?), the laughter of the unkempt horrible women from the first ward, advancing in a halting duck-like march. I wished I could be far away from the profound interior misery of people, from their fragility and their fear, wished I could sleep like the fireman a sleep without childish remorse and brush my teeth in the morning in a pink plastic cup with Mickey Mouse printed on it, without the promise of Hell awaiting me. I dragged my arms along the desk and rested my chin on the rectangular blotter like an old terrier on a doormat, a sick terrier with sad, red, timid eyes: I was falling asleep, I was surely falling asleep in the office, where the light vibrated like a trapped wing, milky and smooth, burning under our skin in a kind of slow combustion, I would add my sleep to the hundreds of poor sleeps accumulating in the decrepit building, approaching and retreating in a grave tidal purring. It was three A.M. and I was starting to gently absent myself from myself as gas slowly escapes from a balloon, as water flees between the fingers that hold it. The nurse's footsteps approached in the corridor outside, rapid and hard, as if nails of pain were being driven into my weariness, stabbing nails of pain into my weariness, they penetrated into the office, angrily percussing my forehead, stopped next to my chair with the whisper of starched uniforms, identical to the gust of wind in July, through the lemon tree in the yard:

"Want to see what she was carrying in the bag?"

And with the easy grace of an illusionist she took out a Bakelite pistol and a rusty hammer.

The imbecile of a custodian appeared in the doorframe, as unexpected as a street fair marionette popping out of his canvas hole:

"When you live alone up in the hills, a woman has to defend herself, doesn't she? Defend herself from bums and dogs, defend herself from the ghosts, full of gold teeth, from the rich?"

"Bang bang bang," said the nurse, pointing the toy gun at the light fixture in the ceiling.

"Bang bang bang," echoed the custodian, gripping his esophagus with both hands as if in a gangster film, staggering on the linoleum, writhing in pain, his guts riddled with imaginary lead slugs.

In the empty car en route to Santana, the sides of the mountain range, carved almost upright, seemed to him like cloudy mirrors into which the afternoon pressed its fat yellowish face, surrounded by motionless ringlets of bushes. A hare dashed across the asphalt and disappeared into the bright shadow of a thicket. The landscape was beginning to take on the texture of the kraft paper in church Nativity scenes, lit by the large bluish dripping candle of the sun. A torn bullfight poster flapped like an arm from a piece of wall that the heat was dissolving, and I thought Loneliness is the bitterness of dignity, thought Women's loneliness is the most melancholy form of nobility, thought about the final years of my grandmothers' lives, sitting in the living room among portraits of dead military men, waiting for death like Eskimos on ice floes, thought about the agony of the pigeon in Tomar, alone on the roof facing the mess hall, which every afternoon, as I sat at the table in the bedroom to write the long novel that I would never publish, that I will never publish and on which all my books feed, I seemed thinner, more wrinkled, more exhausted, chilled by the breath of June and by fever, I thought I called the head servant, showed him the pigeon, and asked

"Do something about that animal"

and that the man leaned out the window, examined the bird, turned to me and said

"It's dead. If you want, I can sweep it down with the broom."

I thought about the man's indifference and the indifference of the other pigeons that went on flying in a flock around the station, above the willows and the mulberry trees in the square, now white now dark like the two faces of playing cards, thought Soon at night the ghost of the pigeon will keep me from sleeping by sinking its anguished claws into my neck, thought about the loneliness of people and pigeons and about the hammers that frighten no one, thought about the woman from Serpa, filled with gentleness and hunger and fear, threatening with her Bakelite pistol the derision of the bums, I thought about the young girl from Serpa surrounded by the inaudible sighs of dead angels, benumbed in a hospital bed amid the drunkard's horrible cries and the patients who meandered in the dark like dazed automatons. The nurse handed the gun back to me and said

"Bang bang bang"

and I fell into a soft mound of feathers, dragging with me a pile of file cards that danced in the air until they covered my body the way leaves in the park in autumn cover the carcasses of dogs.

It's going to start getting dark, I thought, it's going to start getting dark in an hour or two, the afternoon is going to turn as delicate and fine as tissue paper, the smell of jasmine will rise from the earth, insistent and sickening like the flowers of the dead. The darkness grows from the pores of the ground, first lilac, then reddish, deep blue afterward, populated by insects, murmurs, exclamations, small tears, the trees shake without changing position like brooding hens, while the branches take on the extraordinary sharpness of twilight, engraved on the soft waxen plaque of the sky. Nothing yet heralds the night, but a light veil, a tenuous web of shadow separates us from things, establishes between us and them the mysterious distance of darkness, where clocks tick to the panting rhythm of the blood. Night, he thought, is the cardiac anguish of alarm clocks, the unfindable switch of the lamp that the hand gropes for blindly and never locates, the glass of water on the nightstand that seems to contain a slice of the moon and all the rivers of the dark, those that are born in the thighs of women to flow, through the sheet, toward our arched bodies, tense with the slow rage of desire. It's going to start getting dark, he thought, and as it always does when night falls an undefined melancholy, a diffuse restiveness, a vague tremor in the bones causes to vibrate in me, before the orange, the gray, the faded ochre of sunset, a wind with neither origin nor destination, prolonged like a moan or sigh that precedes the oblique flight of owls hidden in tree trunks like gaunt, cruel specters. To the right of the highway, in a hollow of packed dirt where the road workers' enormous kettles of asphalt, strips of wood, traffic signs on tripods, rollers and shovels were stored, a few vans were parked in front of one of those types of restaurants sometimes found in deserted areas of the provinces, displaying wicker or painted metal tables under a thatch roof. Half a dozen tiny speckled chickens trotted austerely in the dust with the jerky motions of husbands. A goat tied by a piece of rope bobbed sadly its withered beard of an unpublished poet, apathetically grazing in a corner of the café on mimeographed grass from magazines. He stopped the car next to a tall tractor, similar to the throne of a tennis referee, smelling the manure and the oil, and got out to have a beer in the lonely mountain restaurant, against whose counter leaned the soft sweaty shoulders of the truck drivers, hanging from their necks like padded jackets on a nail. The horizon was pleated with clouds like a folded accordion. A flock of hoopoes glided diagonally on the other side of the roof, in the direction of a yellow-gray thicket, waddling the farewell of their wings in a quick tinkling of glasses. My muscles, tight from the journey, reluctantly uncoiled with the slowness of worms, observed by the antiquarian eyes of the goat which was masticating the chewing gum of an unfinished alexandrine, and he seated himself near the window, chin in hand, looking at but not seeing the sooty shoulders of the highway. Behind him a monotonous whisper of voices rose and fell in a dolorous sound, the sound of the foam from waves in the siphon of the rocks, similar to that of the female patients in the Marias Club, in the fifth women's ward of Miguel Bombarda Hospital, before the doctors' arrival.

The fifth ward, on the top floor of the asylum, accessed by way of an enormous elevator, sobbing from floor to floor its sharp shrieks of panic, was, when established, a sad purgatory that the psychiatrists made a futile effort to enliven by covering the walls with mirrors that multiplied and reflected the dusky shapes of the patients, their miserable condition as prisoners (they were forbidden to go out alone, forbidden to take a walk, forbidden any contact with men because "we don't want the responsibility, we don't want any confusion, we don't want problems, we don't want protests from families"), so the only amusements allowed consisted of taking their medication, of doing vague useless sewing, and in attending, piled in the dining room in chairs as precarious as baby teeth, the Club meetings, one morning a week, run by technicians imbued with the unctuous good will of Christian jailers.

The doctors would arrive at eleven, clinically look at the river's tongue through the locked porches, a river also imprisoned by the frame, blue and flat like long vacations, commune their ritual coffee in their lay confessionals separated by narrow wooden dividers, increase or decrease dosages according to the patients' frenzy, and finally go in a group to the dining room, dispensing to all sides the smiles of healers. Each smile shouted, I'm sane and you're crazy but if you behave maybe I can do something for you, make you as normal as us, as normal normal as us, as normal normal normal as us, three pills at breakfast, three pills at lunch, three pills at dinner, the sick women calmed down silently, the interns disseminated strategically among the public. Make believe for a while that we're all equals, the assistant installed himself facing the audience with the kindly indulgence of a minister at a provincial soirée, crossed his legs, and between his cuff and sock shone a piece of hairy flesh identical to the gelatin of octopuses, to the gelatin of the thick marine flora of Sesimbra, and always at that moment, at the exact instant when the session began,

I felt like barking and leaping up to bite that round chunk of shin, the shin of power that with patient, pendulum-like serenity, swung the patent leather shoe.

"The minutes," requested the leg, with the inflection of a canon.

A nightshirt rose in the rear and in the style of an elementary-school version of *Ballad of the Snow*, read slowly and poorly from a book with a waterproof cover like the ones housewives use to keep accounts. Fragments of meaningless sentences fluttered randomly into the saturated air, seeking in vain some kind of escape. There was no escape: the nurse, her arms crossed, stood guard at the door, and he thought as he looked at his colleagues The dream of guys like these is to be psychiatrists by divine prerogative, to be right by papal infallibility, to impose their pomposity and melancholy order on the disorder of others, to themselves determine, with marks on a chalkboard, the volatile limits of suffering and joy. If I bite the presiding shin, barking out my raging indignation on all fours, the canon will limit himself to laying a friendly hand on my shoulder and suggesting You're not well: why don't you go into analysis? with the amicable comprehension of hangmen. The cotton nightshirt suddenly fell silent (in mid-syllable?) and the leg asked

"Does anyone wish to comment on the minutes?" scratching his other ankle with the polished shoe.

Angola, he thought in the mountain restaurant over a warm beer, feeling the almost imperceptible presence of darkness in the still-intact daylight, darkness that could be discerned in the shadowy speckles of the day like a face in the mirror, I almost miss the war because at least in war things are simple: you're trying not to die, trying to endure, and we find ourselves so occupied with that enormous, desperate, tragic task that we have no time for perversity and dirty tricks. I would go into the company's storeroom (the eucalyptuses were sobbing softly outside, far above our heads, in the dull fog of the drizzle), observe the biers in their wooden crates and say aloud, I don't want to go there I don't want to go there I don't want to go there, tripping over the sacks of supplies in my enormous rubber boots, crushing potatoes, onions, soft things, a dog who moved aside protesting quietly. The supply corporal jumped up from his hammock beside the coffins, sat up rubbing his eczema-encrusted eyelids and recounted in the barracks that a ghost that looked like the doctor was wandering among the vegetables and the caskets, the soda bottles and the packs of cigarettes, murmuring the absurd speeches of ghosts. Angola, he thought in the mountain restaurant over a warm beer that tasted like snail slime and bath foam, perhaps the war goes on, in a different form, inside us, perhaps I am still occupied with the enormous, desperate, tragic task of enduring, of enduring without protest, without rebellion, of enduring timidly like the patients of the fifth ward at Miguel Bombarda Hospital, looking at the psychiatrists in a strange mixture of hope and terror: those who behave, my dears, have the right to weekends at home, those who don't behave get a quick punishment of injections, eh, and sleep chemical sleeps surrounded by absolute darkness, a blackness as total as that of the nights of the blind, whose eyes resemble dead birds lying in the cages of their lashes.

"If no one wishes to comment on the minutes," declared the leg, "we'll move on to the information phase."

A doctor with a beard out of *Colóquio Letras e Artes*, who possessed the composure of the stupid, that species of imbecilic restraint that masquerades as good sense, raised his nicotine-stained index finger and announced the important purchase, thanks to the Club dues (the sweeping gesture of a bullfighter), of a new coffee machine for the members' use: as the psychiatrists were almost the only ones with money, its general utility was obvious, and he thought of the announcement by the officer responsible for the delivery of mail The bottles of whisky are intended exclusively for officers, the soldiers drink orangeade, wine on Sunday and that's all, he thought When I was living at home with my parents coffee was something for adults, you earned the right to coffee when you got your degree. After you graduate you drink coffee and smoke, the river panted next to the windows like a winded horse, its mane floated against the tiles of the houses in the manner of the oakum beards of the prophets, and a hollow neutral silence, the silence of death, the silence of empty bedrooms and of corridors in the darkness of death, surrounded the psychiatrists, suffocated the psychiatrists the way the gardener's fingers strangled sparrows in the yard, and I saw the pink beaks open and close in asthmatic distress. The La Fontaine profile of the occupational therapist, straight from the oval portraits of the Pleiades, announced in the tone of a fable the Marias' next visit to the zoo, to the napless animals of the zoo sorrowfully mooing behind the wire nets, staring at people with gentle expressions full of loneliness and shame, which the sycamores concealed like wrinkles.

"Any further information?" asked the leg, still swinging.

And he imagined the patients in a closed circle, shepherded by the nurses, trotting from cage to cage with total indifference. Only the old women who couldn't get out of bed remained in the asylum, poking their gray noses toward the ceiling, sunk in the round cheeks of the pillowcases. Only the old women, who gave up the mattresses for the funeral homes, on bumpy stretchers, wrapped in the yellowish stains of the sheets. At Santa Maria, he recalled, in Surgery and Medicine there were individual rooms for the terminal cases so that the anguish and sighing of the moribund wouldn't disquiet the other patients, inflict upon them the horrid spectacle of agony. When a bed was wheeled into the corridor, the patients would spy in panic to see which neighbor was leaving, scrutinizing his thin face, almost of plaster, the deep, soft, repugnant wrinkles of death. And the dying person moaned and protested greatly, crying, imploring them to let him stay in the ward because staying in the ward meant, despite everything, a delay of sentence, the certainty of a few more hours of life. The bed would disappear, squeaking down the corridor, a new patient would fill the vacant spot, and the intruder would be looked at askance as if he were to blame, as if he were truly to blame, as if it had been he who wheeled away the bed down the corridor, en route to the final bedroom. I had finished the course weeks earlier, knew nothing of the suffering of men, of the miserable, poignant, unjust suffering of mankind, and stood in the middle of the room, rolling the rubber tube of the stethoscope in my hands, angry at my useless young science, my impotence, and my fright, stood in the middle of the room with its large windows beyond which Lisbon spun in the light in the uneven slowness of a carousel, causing its ugly, complicated monuments to turn like wooden giraffes. The patients at Miguel Bombarda Hospital, he thought, looking around at the multitude of nightshirts sitting wordlessly in their Formica chairs, didn't sob, didn't protest, didn't cry: they are gray cadavers, poor castrated cadavers that breathe lightly, doped with tranquilizers, bloated from pills and capsules, moving with the sluggish motion of algae from compartment to compartment, dragging their slippers on the boards, concave from wear, of the floor. As a result of the lack of water, the flushing mechanisms don't work, the dejecta accumulate in the toilets, the urine putrefies, foaming, in the urinals, and an unbearable stench from the latrine, a faceless stench, unpleasant and foul, wafts through the offices without alighting on anything, identical to a bird without compass, meek and desperate. The patients of the Club must smell the odor, be bothered by the odor the way mules are bothered by the smell of blood, agitated on the inside by disgust but with nothing showing in their immobile features, absolutely still, as unmoving as those of landscapes, of photographs, of summer sunsets, nothing showing in their ever-horizontal features, decomposing silently in the Formica chairs.

"No information?" the leg repeated with beatific insistence.

The smell came and went in the room, but the psychiatrists bore courageously, without blinking, without change of expression, the smell of others, the insanity of others, the despair, the anxiety, the agony and fear of others.

"I wish to inform you that you're crazy," I feel like shouting. "I wish to inform that all this, this meeting, this asylum, this scientific shit is the final proof of your stupidity, your uselessness, your insanity, I wish to inform you that I'm going crazy along with you and I want you to take me away from here before I turn into one more cotton nightshirt full of pills wandering around the cages at the zoo on Sunday mornings."

At that moment, before I could open my mouth, a patient stood up, pointed to the leg, and exclaimed ecstatically:

"You, doctor, are the Holy Father."

The doctor smiled at her with tenebrous gentleness:

"The Holy Father?"

"You, doctor, are the Holy Father," repeated the patient, "and the other doctors civilian governors."

The doctor's mouth opened in immense satisfaction:

"This case is an excellent teaching tool. An excellent teaching tool. Don't change her therapy and keep her for my class."

Once a week the students would enter the asylum as if in a lepers' hospice, keeping as far as possible from us as if by touching us they ran the risk of catching some abominable disease, of losing their minds, of winding up in the jacket with the ridiculous tin medals. They were afraid the doors would be locked on them, that they would be put into regulation pajamas and never again be allowed outside, to go to the apparently free, pale-colored city, to the city that seemed to convalesce in the dull glass of morning, in which the Tagus and the sky merged like two faces staring at each other at close range. They were young men and women with skin still marked by the acne scars of adolescence, those pinkish bubbles that come to the surface of smiles and burst in the air like fragile little spheres of happiness, young men and women whom for now disenchantment and cynicism had not had time to metamorphose into wise, composed, acrimonious and incredulous beings, had not had time to metamorphose into executioners. Because we're executioners, he thought in the mountain restaurant watching the afternoon gradually fade into the spare narrow landscape of the Algarve interior, where the sea doesn't penetrate and an aridness of cartilage inhabits the people and the land, we are in fact executioners, executioners of cadavers, executioners of these inert soft cadavers, of these silent cadavers, abstract, defenseless, motionless in their rooms with the lightness of statues.

We're executioners, he wanted to shout to the Club, ignorant and perverse executioners, mired in the rotten odor of stagnant piss and shit, talking about coffeemakers, trips to the zoo, and other similarly shitty entertainments, we're executioners and when we go home we exhale in the vestibule, between the coat hanger and the console, annihilated odors of Marias, because when we hang up our raincoats it's a bit of ourselves we hang, our bodies withered like the partridges in still lifes, pointing the beaks of our lips toward the floorboards.

"As there is no further information to convey," decreed the leg, "we'll move along to the order of the day. If my colleague would be so kind..."

A female psychiatrist of the Norman mare type, with a large trunk, large limbs, a large, heavy, ridiculous horse-like chin chewing at a bubble-gum mouthpiece, dissertated at length, consulting memorandums and notes, about the mirrors that lined the living room and in which, whatever our position, we were malignantly confronted with multiple images of ourselves, like at the tailor's when he marks us with chalk, pads our shoulders, the rough sketch of the wings we don't possess. That stubborn persecution of oneself, of one's eyes endlessly, anxiously, searching for approval or a smile, that constant presence of the profile that he inhabited and poorly understood, poorly commanded, whose reactions, tastes, impulses he poorly perceived, produced in him a kind of torture, of vertigo, of nausea, as if the floor were oscillating from side to side, the hesitant rocking of a boat, forcing upon him a difficult balance among the restless furniture. The doctors had decided that the mirrors returned the patients to a much-needed contact with external reality, so they surrounded them with an abracadabra gallery of reflections, of sparkles, of vertical metallic brilliance, on whose surface gestures acquired the odd textures of ballet, of some strange immaterial dance, of serpentine farewells, of spirals of smoke that dissolved and thickened in the rhythmless rhythm of a doleful breeze. The Norman mare was laying into a prolix report on the therapeutic effects of the singular invention, swearing that if they flooded the asylum, the city, the country, the entire universe with hundreds of thousands of millions of mirrors, mental illness would soon be as much a thing of the past as collar stretchers, and people, free of homosexuality, fetishes, schizophrenia, Oedipus complexes and depression, would live for two hundred years in a dazed paradisiacal happiness like mongoloids and hospital administrators. The patients listened to the long discourse in silence, coughing from time to time the stifled maladies of mummies. River and sky came together now mutually in the manner of closing lips, and the shadow of the clouds glided lightly over the boats like a bunch of fingers through the scales on a piano.

"Would my colleague please make a clean copy of that as soon as possible," the leg decided solemnly, "to be presented to the proper authorities."

"To the Ministry of Social Affairs," suggested a psychiatrist wearing sneakers like some lucid beggar, who bobbed in his chair with enthusiasm at the marvelous prospect of a reflecting planet.

"To Public Works," timidly added La Fontaine, in the inviting tone with which the fox must have addressed the crow with the cheese. "If we started with the facade of the hospital maybe it wouldn't even be necessary to admit the sick people: they would come to their senses at the entrance to the gate and automatically be cured."

The Norman mare raised her fist in agitation:

"Caution is called for. An American study was published a short time ago about the dangers of an excess of mirrors. There are even those who try to commit suicide by spreading their arms and throwing themselves onto their image."

"Sandford and his coauthors," observed the *Colóquio*, irritated at the mare's success, "describe the case of an insurance agent who slashed his wrists with a piece of the glass that reflected his face: it was as if one part of him were cruelly assassinating the other half."

"In the twentieth century," commented an ugly female psychologist covered by some Mexican singer's poncho (Luís Alberto del Paraná, he laughed inwardly), beneath which must crawl multiple arachnid appendages with gnawed nails, "in the twentieth century, narcissists find themselves uncomfortable in prosaic professions."

"Down with the company gas," bellowed a voice from somewhere in the back of the room.

"It's important," opined the leg, "to study the percentage of surface that will remain uncovered."

"Twenty-four point three percent, according to Rabindorff, Hages, and Metch," clarified the mare.

"The French," countered the lucid beggar, fanning himself with Reich's *Sexual Revolution*, "argue twenty-three point four."

"The Swiss school of Professor Heinemann replaced the mirrors with coated yellow plastic," explained an undefined creature who, for six years in Geneva, revealed in French the sorrows of early childhood to a silent and impenetrable psychoanalyst who probably already felt dead after the fifth or sixth session, and who smelled mildly bad in his wing chair.

"Which is cheaper?" asked a nurse whose practical sense of life and the rise in the price of grouper kept her close to immediate realities.

"That type of decision is beyond our scope," replied the leg in a proud transport of scientific humility. "Our task is limited to composing a memorandum to the proper authorities."

A respectful silence fell, and at that moment the door opened and an old, fat maid wearing a wig and an apron around her hips came in, carrying a tray of coffee cups, which clinked on the saucers like the crystal drops of chandeliers. The black liquid gave off oily sparkles of tar, the white convex china of the cups had the glaucous and morbid sheen of eyes with cataracts. The elderly maid, her wig rigidly atop her head like a helmet of hair, placed before the leg a cracked plastic sugar bowl, and smiling to right and left with papal urbanity, he spooned the sugar into the doctors' cups with the stately gestures with which priests cast incense from censers, murmuring exorcisms in Latin from the corners of their mouths. The head nurse shooed the patients toward the mirror room as if she had an invisible rod in her hands, and the nightshirts staggered like geese down the corridor, puffing their cotton belly feathers in a pandemonium of quacking that grew in volume, deformed, divided, pulverized into the glass surfaces in a raucous tempest of sound. If one face in the mirror becomes strange and different, menacing, left-handed, disturbing, the echo of a sound, of several sounds, of many sounds, acquires the aspect of an unbearable sight, a deafening nightmare, a landscape of grotesque moans that envelops us until it submerges us in its dance of clamorous shadows. The occupational therapist began distributing pieces of wrapping paper to make grocery bags, and the members of the Club, sitting in a circle, folded the grayish light cardboard in slow inattentive creases, looking at themselves in the mirrors with ineffable terror: they were forty or fifty women whom psychiatric treatments had reduced to indifferent animals with hollow mouths, hollow eyes, hollow chests, vegetating in that extended summer morning of flashes of blue lightning. Smoke from the Other Shore resembled bloodied rags clinging to the wrinkled plaster wall of the sky, raised vertically before us to prevent the flight of the gulls: it imprisoned us in its white bell jar, spotted with clouds, cleft by fissures, by that mysterious complex of tiny pleats that rests like a web on the mysterious alarming features of old pictures. The sky imprisoned us the way the mirrors imprisoned the patients and transformed us as well into mournful, sad creatures, talking to one another over cups of coffee, in smooth and imbecilic horse whinnies. We smelled like stuffed animals, Joanna, we smelled like doctors, with the unmistakable aroma of doctors, which took me back to the PIDE jailers in Angola, repellent and filthy, furiously smoking cigarettes in the carbonized glare of morning. The leg asked me amiably, taking his cigarette holder from its case:

"How are your daughters?"

and I understood, staring at his tumescent porcine face, his fat fingers, the rubber smile unfolding on his cheeks like an accordion, a smile that squealed, off-key, the asthma of a harmonium, staring at the doctors who, brandishing their coffee spoons, were discussing bitter dialogues of Landrus, that we should attempt, like seagulls, to break through the sky of plaster that walled us in, smash the mirrors, reject the paper bags and get out of there before they medicated us, measured our IQ, our powers of reasoning, our memory, will, emotions, and catalogued us and finally labeled us and tossed us into the dark drawer of a ward, awaiting in terror the immense bat of night.

The leg lit his cigarette with the silver lighter, blew the smoke through the napkin ring of his lips, and I remembered, mired in his dense courtesy, in his dangerous congeniality, how, when I wanted to show you the hospital, Joanna, you refused to go past the gate, with the stubborn, rocklike, unmovable firmness of children. I remembered the sycamores that sparkled in the sun, and the asylum that presented the serene image of a harmless old house, free of ghosts, I remembered the faces that the August brightness underlined with the tulle dust of summer, turning them diffuse and vague like observers behind the curtain in a house, reducing them to the out-of-focus contours of cheekbones. The bags were piled in the mirror room, which the occupational therapist crossed in large strides, as ostentatiously resolute as a lion tamer, a tamer of unhappy somnambulant beasts that from time to time emit the insignificant catarrhal roar of a poodle.

"I don't want to go into the hospital," my daughter said, the frightened curls of her hair crushed against my belly, "I don't want to go into the hospital because I'm afraid of the sick people."

Through the open door I saw gliding along the corridor the aluminum lunch pails, rocking on a kind of wheeled cart that a one-eyed custodian, as bent as a bow, was pushing like a recalcitrant plow. The aroma of the food, hot and humid, penetrated my nostrils with its weary sweetness. A rattling of silverware vibrated in the distance. An absurd familiar atmosphere, an agreeable torpor, a sleepy fatigue was beginning to invade me, to insinuate itself into my body in repose, when the guffaw of the Norman mare suddenly burst out behind me, in a carnivorous, almost brutal explosion of jubilation.

"I'm a lot more afraid of the psychiatrists," I answered.

5

The Alentejo, he thought, extending his hearing beyond the motor, feeling the flight of the black butterflies of afternoon born of the holm oak like tremulous leaves of shadow, of the yellow fields of summer and the eternally mysterious olive trees, forever nocturnal, silver and lilac in the hot air of afternoon, the Alentejo begins by being this different color of silence, this white texture of silence that distant dogs rip asunder from time to time with red barking like a clown's clarinet. It's a dead landscape, a horizontal body with its limbs splayed, from which rises a light exhalation of herbs indistinguishable from that of the wax flowers of the deceased, animated still by a tenuous breath of wind. A green body like that of the bridegroom who showed up at the hospital one day, disguised as a vocalist with a band, in a profusion of lace, his nails polished, his hair lacquered and a suitcase in his hand, smiling wanly amid distressed apologetic laughter. He remembered the groom, in the automobile surrounded by the large menacing butterflies of afternoon, by the color of the smell of the Alentejo which is like the odorless smell of metal or light, and as always when he recalled him, he shifted in his seat and smiled. He was a young man, very thin, very tall, stooped from anxiety and fear, whose mustache, hanging from his nose, shook like a wet towel on a clothesline, and who, coming toward him in a cloud of cologne, put his hand on his shoulder, and declared

"I need to be admitted because I'm crazy"

staring at him in an entreaty both touching and ridiculous.

It was just after lunch and my blood had the slow, lulling thickness of sleep. I felt like stretching out in a beach chair and going to sleep without talking to anyone, without listening to anyone, hearing the rustle of the trees outside and the footsteps of the orderlies in the offices as if through a muffled veil of water, drawing around me a muted ballet of sounds. I had the urge to take a nap like a python to digest the hamburger-and-egg from the nearby café buried under potatoes like a casualty among rubble. I had the urge to close my eyes and feel the sun wrap around my knees like a blanket, to pull the sun to my neck and breathe in its smell of wool while my body drifted weightlessly like an astronaut in a landscape of pleasant phantasms. But something insistent, repetitious, sharp, kept creeping into my sleep, preventing me from dozing off, just as the sound of footsteps disturbs silence, or a curious nose against the back of the neck keeps you from reading the newspaper in peace. Little by little, chewing on the sticky saliva of dreams, I began returning to the overly defined, geometric universe of the emergency room, to the glass ashtray on the table that suddenly struck me as enormous, shining dolorously like sarcasm or remorse, to the faces stuck atop their white smocks like pineapples on a shelf, huge pineapples without eyes, without noses, without mouths, who were waiting for me to get settled at my desk, open the list of patients, and ask

"What's troubling you?"

in the competent, abstracted tone of doctors on duty.

"I want to be admitted because I'm crazy," repeated the man in lace and green suit, with cologne running down his temples in a panicked sweat.

His arm drew me from my siesta the way a midwife's forceps extract a child from its mother's uterus, and my mouth, upon waking, emitted the unhappy howls of protest of the newborn, shaking their limbs in futile spasms. Just like in the morning with the alarm clock, when I struggled to return to the concave womb of sleep, where the shades of childhood float on the screen of the eyelids. But the pallid green man covered in absurd lace clung to his sweater, begging

"Admit me immediately admit me immediately admit me immediately"

enveloping him in a cloud of cheap cologne and desperation.

He finally rose, staggered toward the desk, ran his fingers randomly over the papers like a guitar player mechanically exploring a scale for the sound of the strings. The ashtray began to diminish in size, the walls stopped weaving, from the street came the protracted sigh of an ambulance's siren. When he took the pen the orderly extended to him he did so with the assurance of a bullfighter accepting the sword: I'm the psychiatrist, with injections I'm going to kill the sixth patient the sixth of the afternoon, and receive winks, the tail, and be carried from the hospital on shoulders to the next contest before an arena filled with doctors.

"So, what's wrong?" he asked, beginning with an elegant fluttering of the cape.

The banderilleros of the custodians withdrew to the background of the barrier, where their denim suits of light merged into the neutral anonymity of the walls. Only I and the green man, face to face in the linoleum arena of the office, until the final sword-plunge of the syringe. Whatever happens, you always end up losing, he mentally told the other. When anyone enters here, he always ends up losing.

"I need to be admitted," informed the guy, constantly casting sidelong glances of fear at the door (Normal suspicion, thinks the doctor). The nail of his pinkie scratched the varnish of the desk, identical to a first-quarter moon in a clouded Formica sky, a first-quarter dimmed by earwax.

"Admitted?" he murmured, leading the sick man by *chicuelina* cape movements toward the center of the arena: try not to ask any questions, he had taught his assistant when still an apprentice matador. Take advantage of the words they say to you to get what you want. Remember that interrogations scare people: give them the impression that you understand them, esteem them, and you'll have them in the center of the ring in no time.

The fellow's eyes possessed the damp stupidity of anguish, the fear of bulls amid the palms and the music, spurred by the cries of the trumpet:

"I should be getting married right now."

"Married?" (You're moving toward the banderilleros and will charge the way I like.)

The ambulance siren evaporated into the air, like a mere echo, but something prolonged itself, inaudible, in the room, similar to the reverberation of a seashell held to the ear. The patient who imagined himself to be a plane soared, arms open, above the roof tiles, the landing gear of his shoes waving from his belly. Cologne ran down the man's neck in thick transparent drops:

"I can't get married because I'm already married."

A current of ants descended from the window along the frame and disappeared into a hole in the baseboard. Here, as in the Algarve, night was beginning to fall: a rustle disturbed the uppermost branches of the sycamores, in the tiled cloister the marble tubs thickened into a water of shadows. Red window frames emphasized the contour of the buildings: soon the custodian would turn on the light, like the still-pale headlights of cars before the slow coming of night, when everything seems to tilt, floating, into the weightless landscape of twilight. One of the orderlies leaned forward, intrigued.

"If the bride's brothers catch me they'll make mincemeat out of me."

And shaking the lace of his wrists in a pathetic plea:

"The only way out is to be admitted to the hospital as a crazy person."

The patient who thought he was an airplane buzzed the porch: upon landing in the courtyard, under the sycamores, he rose as usual from the ground in a cloud of yellow dust. Down here, another sick person, promoted to the control tower, guided the maneuver by making his arms into large windmills. A third spun around and around, imitating radar. The man who thought he was a plane never flew at night: he remained seated in bed, elbows raised, his large phosphorescent eyes shining in the dark. From time to time he coughed the bronchitis of propellers.

"A kind of political asylum," suggested the orderly. His square glasses shone with irony.

"I have to get out of this," explained the guy, like someone making a case. "If you send me away I'm going straight to São José Hospital. A guy I play pool with works there, maybe he can come up with some kind of disease for me."

"We're full," I said, forgetting my bullfighter's cape. "Full of alcoholics, epileptics, schizophrenics, paranoids, people without beds to sleep in, other than my own, beside the water bottle and the telephone. Take your pick: either I scoot over or we sleep in each other's arms."

And I imagine myself up against the groom's green suit like a moss-covered trunk, with my naked legs wrapped in the absurd cloth of his pants, breathing the liquefied resin of his aftershave lotion, from which was dissipating the acrid sea odor of Alcântara barbers, in whose metal undulates invisible river water, and gulls spin about the sheared heads like small clouds, scant and angry. When the brush touched the back of my neck a strange shiver ran down my spine as if an animal were crawling from my knees toward my genitals, and icily flowing back, inside my testicles in a stinging exhalation of acid. The man who fancied himself a plane whirled in the air in a sudden handspring like some rudderless bird lost in the chaotic sea of trees.

"Ask for political asylum at São José," the orderly advised. "Have them put your leg in a cast and say you broke it in three places."

"They're all at São Jorge castle waiting for me," howled the guy, in anguish. "They've come from Torres Novas for the wedding. If her brothers catch me they'll murder me like it was nothing!"

And to the custodian who was observing him, leaning against the filing cabinet like an old woman with lorgnette against the parapet of a loge:

"Hey man, I'm begging you, get me out of this!"

A tame bull, he thought, what the hell can you do with a tame bull like this? He got up from the desk like a matador giving up on a useless bull, a lame bull in the arena, a sad, scared, motionless bull under the pitiless sun, and went back to his siesta chair near the window, curling around the lunchtime hamburger the way a woman would her pregnant womb. The pale man went on pleading

"I'm begging you, get me out of this"

to the indifferent group: open the corral and let an animal appear, lots of firemen, lots of police, lots of equipment, lots of shouting, lots of banderilla ampoules to calm the beast. I closed my eyes, laced my fingers over my fly and could almost feel the scrambled egg yolk under the folds of my skin, the French fries that my intestines were grinding up in rubbery wormlike undulations. The orderly went to open the door for the guy with the suitcase, clapping him on the shoulder like a manager:

"You got to understand, man. You only get political asylum at embassies."

In the courtyard, a guy in a smock was summoning with broad gestures the airplane-man for evening medication. Several sick people who were learning to fly were awkwardly wielding dust rags from tree to tree, twittering the purple croaks of owls. In the mirror room, millions of faces stared at one another, intrigued. My body slowly sank into the silent waters of sleep. Independent of me, one arm had already dissolved, far away, formless and dark like a cloud at night. I vaguely heard the key turn in the lock, the muffled sound of voices, the great cold muteness of the stone corridor. And I immediately began to dream of the sea and the docile murmur of the waves of September, began to dream of the wondrous freedom of the sea, the fingerprints of tar on the beach, the foam hardening and popping in thick white bubbles of saliva. I dreamed of the sea, the sound of the sea, the groaning of the rocks covered with mollusks, with mussels, with shells, when the tide goes out. A cool wind young as the breath of my daughters mussed my clothes and hair, a sail rose to my chest and swelled, and then there was a knock at the door, the custodian went to open it, came back to the office and announced

"The entire wedding party's here"

with his mouth rounded in an expression of astonishment.

They were all there: the little boy in hound's tooth and bow-tie holding the beribboned saucer with the wedding rings, his golden crossed eyes shining in the silver-plated metal, clutching the plastic leopard-skin jacket of the mandrill-mother, who was panting inside like a turtle in its shell; obese gentlemen in morning coats and matchsticks between their teeth; a maid of honor plumed like some Incan dignitary, struggling to keep her balance on her cork heels; the group of pool-playing buddies nudging one another in embarrassment; an extremely old woman with a cane leaning on a young Catholic Action never-masturbated type with the look of an intransigent convert; and the photographer, a camera around his neck, who tried by brute force to line up the guests for a clichéd church-steps portrait Now smile everybody a little bit over that way please.

"The bride's missing," I said without thinking, flabbergasted at the intrusion of so many ties and necklaces, so much perfume as violent as a punch, so much face powder and so much shaving cream, in a world of sad gray morning coats.

"She stayed in the car," muttered one of the morning coats hatefully, holding in his fist a pair of traffic cop's gloves, just like those in the story of the three little pigs: the house made of straw, the house made of wood, the house made of brick, I'm going to huff and puff.

"Are you going to tell us where the son of a bitch is?" asked a bald sergeant, one of those concentrated and obtuse types who play fife in the Army Band: Mozart's *Turkish March* and an adaptation for brass and woodwinds of the *Ninth Symphony* in bolero rhythm.

The patients emerged one by one from their rooms like Lazarus to observe the wedding ceremony or to touch, fascinated, the amulets hanging from the bridesmaids' necks: tiger claws, magnetic jewels, silver talismans to ward off the evil eye, enameled hearts with photographs, gold zodiac symbols, coral poodles whose eyes looked like bulging sapphires of goiter. These two apparently incompatible universes, the one of morning coats and the one of pajamas, the combed and the unkempt, the back-stick and the openly dirty, mingled in the asylum in the slanting sweetish brightness of afternoon. The banquet was getting cold, skewered on toothpicks, somewhere at a pastry shop.

"I asked where that son of a bitch is," repeated the fife, addressing me in a tone of authoritarian disdain usually reserved for a washroom attendant.

A limping creature, with the gigantic sole of one shoe the thickness of a sidewalk curb, came forward rocking like a metronome, pushed aside the musical warrior with an elbow to the belly, pointed at me with an index finger where the polish was flaking off, and shouted

"I want to speak to the doctor"

in a bearish asthmatic rage. The patients who were learning to fly gathered flapping their arms, against the windows, in search of an opening in the frames that would allow them to buzz into the hospital like the flies in the half-shadow of a bedroom, laying their sticky enormous insect hands on the beds, the settees, the glass armoires. From where I stood I saw their vapid faces, their hollow eyes, their expressionless mouths, the clothes that flashed in the worn light of afternoon, standing out among the sycamores whose shadows were lengthening, crucified, in the dust of the courtyard. It was my patients who were flying, the sick people from the second men's ward, Durand, Baleizão, Luís, Sequeira, blind Lino tripping in the air as if over unexpected stairs, the sick people I sometimes attended to in the corridor, always hurriedly, always sleepily, the ones who asked for my help in agitated supplication, in submissive supplication, and from whom I would disengage myself with a quick clap on the back. We'll talk tomorrow, I would tell them every day, Tomorrow we'll go to the office and talk, but I never sat at the desk to listen to them, to let them share with me their suffering and their anguish. We'll talk tomorrow, I would say, shaking their hands and leaving, thinking Nothing can be done for anyone, to justify to myself my lack of interest and my haste, I would disengage myself from them with a clap on the back and disappear down the corridor, Baleizão stood contemplating the greens in the vegetable garden and silently losing weight, the kale, black at night, in the vegetable garden, which shone in the darkness, and now my patients were flying in the courtyard against the windows, flying flapping their cotton wings like unsteady wheels against the glass, flying toward me perhaps hoping for a word, a gesture, a simple, cheap, facile wave of complicit sympathy, and I felt the remorse of my indifference weigh in my stomach like a kind of pain, a panic in my insides, an intestinal indisposition that writhes in my belly like slugs, they came flying toward me and I heard the hollow sound of their foreheads against the window frames, the scraping of their hair, their fingers, their chins against the window frames, while the patients disappeared, dissolved into the wedding crowd, into the furs, the feathers, the tiepins, the wedding necklaces, the thick clouds of perfume that flowed back and forth, into the conversations in muted tones, I felt like flying off into the afternoon toward the trees, gaining altitude, touching the tops of the cedars in Campo de Santana that night was impregnating with its mysterious acidity, but perhaps even there they would phone me to provide a cause of death, attend a dying man, medicate a fever, perhaps the asylum would pursue me even among the hidden branches of the cedars forcing me to return to its thick unhappy convent walls, the boy carrying the rings began to rise vertically from the floor, to oscillate in the rarefied atmosphere, to open and close his cartilaginous mouth like a beak, his patent leather shoes hid the fragile tendrils of his paws, the lame woman pushed me into the treatment room, closed the door and bellowed

"This is a disgrace"
with her gigantic sole at the end of her leg shaking in furious indignation.

"This is a disgrace, doctor. We've been waiting at São Jorge castle since eleven o'clock, the bride's family came all the way from

Torres Novas for it, you know, even a major, even a judge are there, people of position, people of influence, and him calling every half hour from one place and another, Don't worry, I'm on my way, I've been looking for the best man, the best man forgot his ID at home, the man at the Registry has diarrhea, he stopped for a beer and I'm here waiting, it'll just be a minute, and us believing it in good faith, don't you worry I'm on my way, and us in our innocence swallowing it all, some photographs were taken with the peacocks, you could see the river, people chatted, I almost lost my youngest in the complication of the battlements, and anyway, so much old stone is overdoing it, they could cut it by half and it'd be the same thing, give the same effect, the same view, when he didn't get there by two o'clock we started to suspect, there's something going on here said my cousin Armindo, the bride's brothers went looking for him, one of them was even going to be a priest and owns an appliance store and he went too in spite of his ulcer, he's very sensitive and can't get upset, any little thing and he starts spewing blood, they searched his room, found out he was married and living with a trollop and three children behind the slaughterhouse, an old building with kitchen access, the poor bride fainted, if she doesn't go off her rocker from grief it'll be a miracle 'cause I've seen it happen over less, one of my aunts went batty because her canary died, and a canary is a canary, she died at Júlio de Matos Hospital feeding birdseed to the doctors, any doctor that approached she would give him birdseed and try to put him in a cage, at home she made her husband read the newspaper on a perch and sing Peep peep peep, he would sing so as to avoid a scene, from time to time he would look up from his crossword and say a Peep peep peep that was enough to make your heart ache, if you want to see the bride she's outside waiting in the limousine, sitting on a satin cushion, she still believes, poor thing, she keeps saying Cabé wouldn't do that to me Cabé wouldn't do that to me, she had already picked names for the children, a boy and a girl, Claudia Cristina and Roberto Alexandre, don't you like them? her brothers tried to point out the truth to her but couldn't, Give up, Suzette, Cabé is a louse, they said, the bride's father who owns two cafés and a small hotel grabbed onto the photographer trembling, Turn the car around to Torres Novas I can't take the nervousness and I want to leave now, it was a large silver Opel, prettier than a chandelier, he crashed into the edge of the gate and knocked off a headlight, the turn signal started blinking on its own, he got out yelling I'll kill that son of a bitch I'll kill that son of a bitch I'll kill that son of a bitch, my husband who's a sergeant promised to get the army after Cabé, Mr. Oscar is going to see that we find him in no time and he's going to pay for the headlight right here in front of me, the problem is the three months of pregnancy the bride's already been through, the orange blossom is already wilted tangerine, I don't know if you understand what I'm getting at, they found out about it, they saw the girl's belly, a slap here and a slap there, a couple of smacks never hurt anybody and she coughed up the bird's name in a second, it's Carlos Alberto da Ascensão Domingos, they took Cabé by the collar and Either you marry her or say goodbye to your family jewels, the seminarian threatened him from a distance with the cheese knife, the guy turned pale and said

Okay, whatever they wanted as long as they left his balls alone, he was a traveling salesman and stayed at the hotel now and then, covering the North for a manufacturer of compresses, I'll marry her, but let go of my fly, he would make eyes at Suzette who worked as a receptionist and gave the guests their keys, received the keys from the guests, the two of them would talk at night over the registration book, since he didn't wear a ring the family didn't mind too much, just the one with the appliance store, the priest, he warned Watch your step 'cause you never know and you just might find yourself gone to the dogs, but she was already thirty-seven and had a small mustache, the young men would run away howling from so much hair, she wears glasses because she's cross-eyed, and she's missing a tooth in front, my son envies her like crazy because he thinks that because of the lack of a tooth if she wanted to she could win every spitting contest, the ones for distance, the ones for height and the ones for accuracy from the balcony aimed at bald men at the trolley stop, maybe that's what attracted Cabé, going out with the pentathlon spitting champion, what's for sure is that she started visiting him in his room, with the lights out you can't see the mustache and as for moans in the night there's so many people who snore, a little blood on the sheets and there you are, a maid who's worked there for twenty years showed the stain to her father, Hey Mr. Oscar look at this it's from your daughter, as the traveling salesman was taking off his undershorts for more exercise the future father-in-law kicked him into his office, took out of the drawer his pistol from his time in the Legion, Either you marry her or I'll put a hole in you the size of the

113

one you made in that girl, Cabé turned green answered that he'd marry her, Don't blow away my bellybutton Mr. Oscar I'll marry her, Suzette ordered thirty-seven masses of thanksgiving in the church, the same number of years she waited for the miracle, the father just to be on the safe side kicked her in the shin so as to maintain his authority, had her mustache shaved off at a beauty parlor in Leiria, put a tooth in her gums, did a complete makeover for the occasion, if she tries to spit now it won't go very far, my son who used to secretly file his teeth to compete with her gave it up, these days he spits knowing he doesn't have any more rivals, Mr. Oscar arranged the wedding in a hurry before she started showing too badly, told her to get into a corset as a precaution and asked a nephew who's a driver for the court system to keep an eye on Cabé, but the nephew liked to play billiards and joined the United Eleven of the Carom Academic Recreational Association in which the salesman was an officer and he got him out of a jam by telling them to spot him ten points out of fifty, he would put chalk on his cue and not give a damn, he came in sixth in the Spring Tournament of the Philharmonic Society in Penha de França, to make a long story short the date was set, São Jorge castle was Suzette's choice, she has a thing for largeness, she's been crazy about Dom Alfonso Henriques since the fifth grade, she wanted at any cost to become a bride on the battlements like queens, to be the Grace Kelly of Torres Novas, to have her picture in the Crónica, her father went along with it to impress his friends, especially the owner of the Hotel Independente which has rooms with baths and toilets that work, the kind with a button that works really well, storms of water in the bowl, tornadoes, torrents, whirlwinds, the owner of the Hotel Independente was fit to be tied in his Mercedes, his daughter had gotten married in Leiria, he only perked up when the bride's brothers said that Cabé was already married and that he'd run away with a suitcase here to the hospital pretending he was crazy, it was his own wife who explained it, a woman who works at the stocking factory and received Mr. Oscar's sons with a slipper in her hand, she told them they could shove Cabé up their ass for all she cared 'cause she didn't want him back even for shoelaces, she was going off to live with the manager of the factory and the salesman could go to hell, if necessary she'd offer them Cabé for free and even throw in some money, she'd had it up to here with the treasurer of the United Eleven of the Carom Academic Recreational Association and cue stick for cue stick she preferred the manager, who was better at three-ball billiards, the guys were leaving down the stairs when she said If they didn't find him here it's 'cause he must be at São José and they should check carefully at the hospitals and they found him pissing from fright hiding under a stretcher, she asked them to break two vertebrae at her expense and said she was sick of putting up with loafers, even the food at home tasted like blue chalk, so we're going to run over to São José 'cause it's not every day a wedding like this happens, the guy from the Hotel Independente is drooling from delight out there, the only thing I feel bad about is the banquet getting cold back at the pastry shop, the cups of soup, the fillets, the cod in the oven, I brought two plastic bags in my purse to take something home to my Amílcar who couldn't come, those little round silvery things from the bride's cake, you know how it is, he's in bed with the gout groaning like a dog, I left the radio on by his bed, I even called to request a song to entertain him, a paso doble which is what he liked to dance at the firemen's balls when he was single, until I finally went lame like this from a stomping he gave me in the dance contest the first Sunday of Lent, when he yelled Olé and came down with his heel right on my bunion, and I was on intravenous for three months at Capuchos, it crushed my bones so bad that my leg shriveled, the nerve dried up, the doctor explained to me Your nerve's dried up and consider yourself lucky that the rest of you didn't too, getting stomped during a paso doble is dangerous and then some, every year during first week of Lent there's a dozen such cases, why doesn't someone found a League of Paso Doble Victims and organize trips to Seville, or start an Olympics for Castanet Cripples, pole vaulting with a cane, racing shells using crutches, we're going now to São José, Desterro, Estefânia, Alfredo da Costa, the appliance priest made out the entire list, because he might disguise himself as a baby or put on a fake belly and a wig and start moaning and imitating a childbirth, the sergeant brought his sword and you never know, I've seen people stick somebody for a lot less, a silly little stab and the guts come out like slugs, if I missed it Amílcar would never forgive me, his eyes will glow on the pillowcase, poor thing, when I tell him what happened, he'll forget the suppositories for pain, sitting up in the sheets, his mouth open as wide as a saucer."

Meanwhile, a kind of wind had arisen: next to the wash basin the towel flapped, the settee sheet wrinkled like a startled fore-

head, the water in the mirror curled into small waves, deforming the bony hard asymmetrical lines of my face. The pages of
the calendar, weighed down with heavy days, with heavy, gray,
gloomy days, stirred against one another in the strange rustling
of the months to come. It was an unusual wind, an unlocatable
and peculiar wind, born everywhere, with no set course, without
definite direction, moving slightly at random in the asylum like
a blind man in a room with which he's unfamiliar, probing nothingness, arms extended, in search of walls that don't exist because
the walls draw back, flee, dissolve into the air if we look for them,
escaping from our fingers with mocking cruelty. He pushed open
the door and spied outside: someone had opened the office window and the patients who had been flying in the courtyard were
now floating haphazardly in the asylum corridor, pedaling their
thin bunions in the light filtered through the afternoon sycamores. And not only the sick people: my ghosts too, the terrifying ghosts of schizophrenics, full of gums and fingernails and
grimaces and hair, shouting insults, threats, supplications, en-
treaties, curses, the viscous hairy animals of alcoholics' hallucinations dragging themselves across the floor with disgusting
challenges, the conspiratorial rustles and the invisible guffaws
that torment the paranoid, the dazzling colored visions of drug
addicts, disks, circles, pyramids, volumes that appear and vanish,
concentrate, diminish, explode: everything was floating in the
corridor of the asylum, in the attenuated brightness of afternoon, to which the fluorescent lights in the ceiling conferred the
paleness of old portraits, those faded threadbare nuances, those

raffia tones, those yellows of fat and blood. Leaning against the door to the treatment room, I saw my patients glide headfirst through the air, Durand, Baleizão, Luís, Sequeira, Lino, asking aloud Who's there? with the alarmed curiosity of the blind, the patients who were lying in the sun in the courtyard like large cold-blooded animals, or gathered in front of my desk waiting for answers that never came. And not only the patients: the orderlies rose in turn from the floor, one after the other, shaking their smocks with the slow majesty of storks, and looked at one another from a distance with the pharmacist's eyes that seabirds possess, the innocent sage eyes of marine crows, the eyes of stuffed birds in museums that watch us with accusing disquieting fixity. The crippled lady made a short crooked dash over the tiles, the dash of a crane, waving her gloved hands up and down, and then the bridesmaids, the photographer, the hotel owner, the billiards friends, the fur coats, the feathers, the tiepins, started to twirl weightlessly in the air, emitting from time to time the hoarse caws of crows. My own bones took on the consistency of foam, my flesh became fibrous and light like the wood of boats. Something chitinous, cartilaginous, vibrating, tingled on my back. A bubble of gas escaped from my anus. I no longer felt the floor under my shoes. My body bent back little by little until it was horizontal, and I began rowing in the light, chirping desperately toward the others.

I feel I had never flown, he thought in the silence of the Alentejo on the road to Aljustrel. Ourique could be seen in the distance, at the end of the highway, its mass of houses refracted by the heat, and he thought In my life I only flew the day the bride-groom showed up at the hospital with a suitcase, smothered in lace, he thought If I never fly again before I die I'll be a palmipede, a grasslands duck, a dispirited ostrich, I'll be a turkey-psychiatrist dragging its feathers along the carpet sobbing gobble-gobble at the patients, I'll be a turkey-technocrat, turkey-paterfamilias, turkey-writer, turkey-simpleton, an insipid turkey-lunatic, a turkey-doctor in the middle of turkey-friends, turkey-colleagues, turkey-relatives, all of us sobbing gobble-gobble in the discourse of boring dinners as melancholy as wakes. Sitting in the uncom-fortable car seat, amid pedals and buttons and levers, alone in the silence of the Alentejo, in the silence of the afternoon that seems to unfold and unfold like an endless beckoning, a nursemaid beckoning at night in the bedroom, which grows and deepens as we drift off, grows as objects grow in nights of insomnia, sharply defined, hostile, replete with sudden edges, unexpected angles, painful irregularities. Sitting in the uncomfortable car seat, with Ourique in the distance, the mass of houses in Ourique refracted by the heat, I remembered that we psychiatrists all resemble the bridegroom, as ridiculous and terrified as he, dragging around a suitcase stuffed with pills, syringes, concepts and interpreta-tions, the trousseau of a useless science under our arm. I remem-bered our ridiculousness, our terror, the poverty of our pomp, and started laughing. I laughed a laugh both poor and happy, the poor and happy laugh of executioners. I laughed at those who operated the electroshock equipment at the clinics in the outskirts of Lis-bon reserved for the rich, where the nightgowns smelled better and there was no dust on the desks, the clinics surrounded by sad gardens in the outskirts of Lisbon, where the bedrooms look like graves inhabited by sleepwalking cadavers, where the psychiatrists install the false hope of pills. Laughed at the well-dressed, well-fed, solemn, temperate, competent, majestic doctors, laughed at their false reassurance, their false interest, their false kindness, and the laughter sounded disfigured and humble to my ears, sounded like a complaint of sick cattle when they come to kill them, the cattle that raise their soft eyes to the hand that murders them, in unbearable gentleness. Laughed with Ourique distant in the calm of afternoon, in the peace of the Alentejo afternoon filled with wild turtledoves and silence, laughed at the psychiatrists who own the truth, playing chess in people's heads with their mother's breast and their father's penis, and their father's breast and their mother's penis, and the breast of the penis and the mother of the father, and the preast of one and the benis of the other, laughed at those who cure homosexuals with slides of naked young men and electric shocks, at those who treat fear of spiders with spiders made of wire that look like carnival insects, at those who gather in circles to dissertate about angst and whose hands tremble like redbud leaves brandished by the anger of the wind. I laughed to think we were the modern ones, the sophisticated police of today, and also something of priests, the confessors, today's Holy Office, laughed to think of the oily obese psychiatrists who imposed musical sessions on their patients in the name of obscure techniques, of the paunchy, dishonest, asexual, obese psychiatrists, of the repellent Buddhas followed by a court of ugly ecstatic disciples with goatees and dirty hair, whispering inane certainties in their ear.

After the April 25 revolution, for example, we all became democrats. We didn't become democrats because of believing in democracy, because of hating the colonial war, the political police, censorship, the simple prohibition on reasoning: we became democrats from fear, fear of the sick, of the lower personnel, the orderlies, fear of our statute of executioners, and until the end of the Revolution, until '76, we were steadfast democrats, we were socialists, we reduced the waiting time for consultations, arrived on time, spoke attentively with the families, concerned ourselves with the patients, protested against the food, the bedbugs, the dampness, the toilets, the lack of hygiene. We were democrats, Joanna, out of cowardice, he thought, seeing a flock of turtle-doves land in an olive grove, stirring the tranquility of the grove with the commotion of their flight, we were in a panic that we would be accused like the PIDE secret police, be arrested, be thrown into the street, have our names in the newspaper. And it took us a while to understand that in '74, in '75, in '76, people went on respecting us as they did abbots in the villages, went on seeing in us the only possible help against loneliness. And we calmed down. And we began carrying a right-wing newspaper under our arms. And smiled sarcastically when we heard the word socialism, the word democracy, the word people. We smiled sarcastically, Joanna, because we had abolished the guillotine.

Sitting in the uncomfortable car seat (when I have money I'll buy an automobile as comfortable as a wing chair), he laughed as he remembered the doctors' meetings in the conference room of the hospital, in the old chapel that was now the hospital's conference room, lined with blue tiles as transparent as the eyes of dolls, delicate as an embroidery of veins. It was enthusiastically proposed that a patient be made part of the asylum's board, a patient, as well as a family member of a patient, as well as a representative of the population, so the patients could discuss with the doctors' elected agent the running of the asylum. Every hand went up in approval of this democratic, this revolutionary proposal, and at that moment, behind our backs, behind our enthusiastically democratic backs, our revolutionary backs, we heard a slow dragging of slippers, a sobbing cough, ailments, the itching that a stubborn, insistent, unexpected, strange gaze triggers in the spine when it seeks us out, stares at us, touches us once, then again and again, like a child's finger. We turned around (Ourique, smaller and smaller, was evaporating in the rearview mirror, a minuscule white blot of walls that shrank and disappeared) and there at the entrance to the chapel, at the entrance to the hospital's conference room and the heavy red drapes, there where the light slanted down from the window in burning dust, a man in pajamas, small, nearly bald, wearing round dark glasses, stood motionless in the doorway looking at us. At first I thought he was blind because of the overly attentive tilt of his head, the rigidity of his body, the hands that moved slightly like the fingers of octopuses, palpating the elastic texture of the air. We turned, he removed his glasses (a wisp of hair from his forehead fell over his ear), his hollow, sleepwalking eyes settled on us in a slow, sideways, lizard-like fashion, he took one or two steps forward, tripping in his miserable espadrilles (what could he have been before coming here? a clerk? an auto mechanic? a carpenter?), his mouth was dry from medication, sticky with hardened saliva, his shoulders slack, his thighs flaccid, his trunk flabby, and immediately we, the democratic psychiatrists, the socialist psychiatrists, the revolutionary psychiatrists (and this made me laugh, Joanna, on the road to Aljustrel, as night rolled up the edges of the horizon like the corners of a leaf and the sun resembled the pale tangerine of a still life sitting on the crown of a hat), we began yelling at him Go away go away go away, accompanying our shouts with the large circular imperative gestures with which one shoos the dogs that from a distance watch us, eagerly, in dispirited timidity.

"Go away," we shouted, "go away go away," at the man who swayed among the drapes, his glasses in his hand, his sweat-glistened jowls shaking with indecision. "Go away," we repeated, "go away go away," until an orderly appeared from the corridor and grabbed the patient by his greasy jacket and dragged him away from us with a scraping of rubber soles on the waxed floor. Murmurs of outrage were still sweeping through the assembly (how dare a patient interrupt the doctors' meeting) when the socialist democratic revolutionary who was presiding, attended by two socialist democratic revolutionary doctors who were taking copious notes, advised that by unanimous vote active participation by patients in the running of the hospital had been approved, and the psychiatrists rose, full of enthusiasm, to greet this socialist democratic revolutionary measure with a storm of applause.

I laughed when I thought about the absurd arguments with which they attempted to reconcile Marxism and psychiatry, that is, freedom and their position as jailers, laughed at the inventions they came up with to placate their bad consciences, Social Psychiatry, Sectorization, Democratic Psychiatry, Antipsychiatry, laughed at their justifications and their subterfuges, laughed at the Alentejo twilight descending in great blue sheets over the crowns of the trees, causing the branches to flutter with ebb tide quivering, a sea with birds, Joanna, singing the way octopuses must sing in their colorful voices of silence, in which an algae wind throbs like an artery in the forehead.

We're like the bridegroom, I thought, caught between impossible commitments, indecisive, pallid, distressed, solemnly discussing what we refer to as clinical cases, depressed women, men who see goblins, adolescents armored in terrifying silence. What do you think about this patient? What's your opinion? Don't you want to weigh in? Haven't you triangulated? Pregenital personality? Primary narcissism? Schizophrenia incipiens? Conrad's trema phase? And he laughed heartily, thinking What resemblance does that have to life, to what's real, actual, authentic in this idiotic test tube, in this imbecilic jargon, in these explanations that explain nothing, in this pretentious *Reader's Digest*? Psychiatrists talked and pointed their fingers like batons, spoke about others, spoke in falsely affectionate tones about others, the suffering of others, the anguish of others, the perplexity of others, without realizing they were dead, Joanna, definitively dead, dissertating about the living with the envy that animates the limp phosphorescent gestures of the deceased, their hollow eye sockets, their enormous toothless mouths.

What can my colleague tell me about my case? he thought, laughing in amusement and sadness, a laugh both bitter and pure that shook his shoulder blades, raised the hairs on the back of his neck, jolted his entire being with violent sarcastic joy. The night besieged Aljustrel with its thousand murmurs, its thousand sharp eyes, with opal-colored stars adrift in the green overlays of the sky, caught in the drawn-out hair of the clouds. The towns of the Alentejo resembled in his mind clown faces in large boxes, with cheeks of painted whitewash walls. The night besieged the Aljustrel with buzzing insects and funereal veils, a blot of black ink, identical to a bloodstain, grew in the cemetery, from the earth-filled lips of the dead, crumbling into the air in dark petals of dust as thick as scales, like fingernails, like the cartilaginous eyelids of lizards, the streets coiled translucently in the manner of the spirals of seashells, drooling a pallid residue of sun through the cracks in the walls. A wisteria branch hung from the posts of a trellis like a tie from a rusted neck. The moon moved from branch to branch like a drifting balloon, a swollen round breast, a bubble of gas. The first houses of the town were disappearing into the darkness, the dogs, restless and immobile, were awaiting the moment to begin to howl. I stopped in front of a lit garage and got out of the car. I like garages. I like the smell of burnt oil and rubber, I like the cement where footsteps or a dropped tool echo endlessly, I like the calendars dirty from exhaust fumes, the benches overflowing with sparkplugs, screws, pieces of sheet metal, damaged battery terminals, burned-out headlights. I like the sound of metal on metal, the gentle angry churning of the engines. I got out of the car (my legs, numb, refused to support the rigidity of my body), ran my hand along the warm side of the hood, and the man in overalls who came to meet me, cleaning his fingers on a rag while two others were finishing washing a small station wagon with Spanish plates, seemed to me, in the precarious fluorescent light of the high ceiling, to be the guy in the beret, elderly by now, who labored in a small workshop indistinguishable from a junkyard, littered with bidets, spring mattresses, buckets, bedsteads, a thousand rusted, twisted, useless things. He was a thin guy, short, extremely polite, who had hacked to death his entire family, his wife, his sister-in-law, his mother-in-law, his children. He enjoyed chatting with him in his cubicle, hearing him talk about his life, observing his intensely blue eyes, the color of letterhead stationery, which time had not yet succeeded in fading. When something went wrong with the car, we would both stretch out in the direction of the fan, or the generator, or the points, coming together in affectionate attention on a complicated inextricable bunch of wires, united by a respectful common astonishment. And it was Mr. Carlos who came to greet me at the Aljustrel garage, his shoes tapping the cement with the lightness of an insect, calling me Sir, lifting his hand to his beret in the respectful gesture of a page. In the workshop, under a kind of arbor, insects buzzed like the stamens blown from daffodils, striking the silvery threads of a cobweb hanging from nothingness like a smile without a face. A mental defective with enormous lips, sitting on a wooden bench, followed us from the darkness of the bidets with the tense alarmed stupidity of dogs, the rather sad, whining, sticky stupidity of dogs. Hammering the metal of a dented fender with the attention to detail, the skill, the impassioned solicitude of a watchmaker, Mr. Carlos turned his enamel-blue eyes to me and spoke:

"They said on the radio that the Americans were going to blow up the world," and both of us began silently dreaming of a temple of Diana the size of the earth, from which rose traces of radioactive fire.

"Rest easy, sir, the hospital will be safe. Just yesterday I sent a check for five hundred million dollars to their president for him to postpone it. I'm making special helmets for us."

And pointing disdainfully at the mental defective who was moaning quietly in his corner:

"And for that wretched creature too."

Another blow to the fender:

"What do you think this is, sir?"

"Our helmets, Mr. Carlos."

"Later. This one is for General Nixon, doctor. A secret order. They delegated a Cape Verdean worker to alert me. Green and yellow sweater, see?"

"Uhn uhn," grunted the mental defective, rocking. He had his dick out and was caressing it the way one caresses an injured bird.

The mechanic came up to me. Like the garage, he smelled of burnt oil and rubber, and also of the Alentejo countryside, hot and sweaty in the twilight, reverberating with a myriad of sounds. The first barking of vagrant dogs slithered along the ground in a sharp spoor of magnesium.

"Good evening, Mr. Carlos," I said.

The man, who was large and dark, with broad bony shoulders under his overalls, began to shrink, to diminish in size, to curve his trunk in a polite bow. The cloth on which he wiped his fingers progressively took on the form of a twisted, useless fender, riddled with haphazard pounding from a hammer. A beret shiny from use appeared on his dark hair, forming on his brow a shadowy crease that obscured his suddenly blue eyes. Around us, the asylum (or Aljustrel?) was a chaotic jumble of ruins, broken columns, fragmented capitals, ancient dust drifting in the immense silence. The people from the station wagon stared at me in silence, sitting on a bench with the tense alarmed stupidity of dogs, murmuring, Uhn uhn, through lips as thick as cuts of meat. The mechanic removed the hose from the pump and plunged it into the gas tank: gasoline flowed slowly like blood from an open artery:

"Good evening, doctor," he replied.

6

I've never left the hospital, he thought as he received his change from the gasoline, observing the guy from whom the face, the gestures, the voice of Mr. Carlos were slowly disappearing, the same way a smile dissipates in an old picture at the beach, or the acacias dissolve in the pale fog of October, as colorless and mute as the animals in dreams. Mr. Carlos was slowly disappearing, the employees were cleaning the windows of the station wagon in circular movements using a kind of sponge, the mechanic was wiping his fingers on his rag, looking at me with the strange fixity of those Christs with exposed hearts in my grandmother's prayer niche who pursue us with the attentive and severe persistence of an urchin's gaze. On a wall blackened by exhaust fumes was written in red paint NO SMOKING above an ad for Michelin tires torn by disinterest and time, and the letters were slowly fading, slowly overlapping one another, as if the plaster were wrinkling like worn creases of skin. Inside a glass-walled cubicle, on a desk covered with scattered papers, a pile of invoices was impaled on a rusty nail. An oil stain on the floor reflected the bulbs in the ceiling, shattering the light into a kaleidoscope of colored layers. In the street, a moped with a convulsive cough shook from its ills: in the sharp, beveled mirror of the sky the first trees of night imprinted the purple blood of their branches, heavy from the suddenly opaque eyelids of leaves, thick with a motionless murmur of children or birds. Aljustrel seemed less and less like a concrete, almost geometric town inhabited by people, by voices, by the restless pictures of the dead, and more like a labyrinth of shadows, an apparition suspended between the black earth and the green sky, adrift, like an enormous boat in a silvery lake of olive groves.

I've never left the hospital, he thought in the cement lair of the garage, in which the most insignificant sound took on the immense vastness of the formless bellow of a shipwrecked man. At twilight, the other side of things takes us unawares, frightens us as if from our distressed serious faces were suddenly born the unforeseen corolla of a smile. The appearance of objects changes, clocks accelerate with anguish in the dark, the body beside us that moves beneath the sheets threatens us with its viscous rage. I entered the hospital, he thought, for a voyage as endless as this one, like the sea of olive groves advancing and retreating, twinkling in the blackness, stirred by rustling corteges of phantoms. I have never left the hospital, I thought, and despite this I have never understood the patients; I say Good morning or Good evening, I sign diagnoses, order therapy, but I don't in fact understand what's going on behind the patients' vociferous or opaque expressions, the vacant eyes, the mouths without saliva. A guy in pajamas declares, for example, "I like having relations with a six-year-old boy," the books explain why, but it's not that, it can't be just that, there's something else, other things that happen so deep down that I don't understand them, I can make out their imprecise shapes but don't understand them, so I prescribe tranquilizers, the way a person shuts up a ringing phone by burying it under a pile of pillows.

I've never left the hospital, he thought in the labyrinth of Aljustrel's narrow streets, where the houses look like the folded napkins, stiff with starch, of ceremonial dinners. The television sets in the cafés diffuse tarnished pyramids of blue glare, as spectral as dark alcoholic circles under the eyes in the morning, crinkled from insomnia, and this constellation of halos lit the town, applying makeup to the hollowed eyes of the porches or revealing the yellow silhouettes of the animals, their pupils as sharp as hard-edged fragments of slate. The bushes in the square brought to mind the square in Malanje, facing the esplanade, one without swans or pigeons, upon which only night conferred the weight of mystery, composed of the absence of cries and shapes. The fishes slept open-eyed in the lake, and he would sometimes sit in the chairs on the empty esplanade, the captive of his capricious, fury-laden, disdainful melancholy. And now he was returning to Lisbon without ever having left the hospital, because when someone enters the asylum they lock the massive gate behind us, they relieve us of our billfolds, our ID cards, our suits, our watches, our rings, they inject into our buttocks five or six cubic centimeters of painful forgetting, and the next morning our body is a jigsaw puzzle scattered on the sheet, impossible to reassemble because of the uncertain weakness of our hands.

I've never left the hospital, he thought, I'll never leave the hospital: the ones who were discharged would descend the street toward Campo de Santana, look at the houses, the pigeons, the people, the cars, and come dashing back to the asylum terrified by a city to which they had become unaccustomed, because of the traffic, the ineluctable confusion of the streets, the river at the bottom that was like an abyss over which had been laid a sheet of blue paper imitating the docile tranquility of the waters, an abyss that could swallow them up at any street corner, because at each corner the river is spying on us, waiting for us, suggesting beneath our feet a treacherous tablecloth of mud. They return to the hospital and hide trembling in the corridors, hanging onto our coats with hands sweaty from fear. Last year a patient arrived at Martyrs of the Homeland, went down into the basement urinals, locked himself in a stall, doused himself with gasoline, lit a match and transformed himself from the neck up into one horrible crackling, scorched statue, a weightless piece of wood in which shone the silver crown of a tooth. On another occasion, on one of his days on duty, a man jumped from the window in the seventh ward, smashing himself down below, his arms spread like a toad: Delirium, explained the doctors. An epileptic impulse, explained the doctors, and signed the death warrant with tranquil assurance: no one was to blame. And yet there would swell in me a kind of shame, or distress, or remorse, whenever I signed an admission form and locked into the asylum the startled and timid eyes that stared at me. No one is to blame and I have to eat, I have this State job, I went through exams, competitions, public testing, I pay rent on the house, electricity, gas, telephone, gasoline, and I justify the money I earn by imprisoning people in the asylum, listening inattentively to their misgivings and their complaints, getting to the dispensary late for rushed consultations (What does it matter if the patients wait for me from nine in the morning till noon, what does it matter if in five minutes I hear and get rid of them, what does it matter if I'm more concerned about the intern crossing her legs than about the anguish of those who come to me?), entering and leaving the asylum with the swiftness of a cuckoo clock. Guys kill themselves because they kill themselves, because of delirium, because of epilepsy, because of psychosis, they tell me, I don't know what to do about my life and I think And what do I do about mine, what do I do about my life in the flat, immense night of the Alentejo, which seems to declare to me constantly, in the buzzing of the insects and in the

September of the trees, the secret of some indecipherable message?

Slowly, gradually, the car seat transformed into the low, leprous, destroyed wall, perched on which, in the summer, I would spend long hours observing the pajamas in the courtyard, circulating in the delicate, almost transparent shade of the trees, identical to the way certain marine flowerings might project their silhouettes against the asylum walls. The dust of August and the pollen of the sycamores resembled the face powder from old boxes, floating in the air without adhering to the wrinkles in the clouds or the overly smooth cheeks of the sky, with the warm, closed odor of a drawer. The psychiatrists' automobiles seemed to be duplicated in the ground, in the excessive brightness of the ground, like batrachians on a mirror, with the bulging eyes of their headlights looking at me with the type of neutral malice of things, with that type of neutral malice of things with which things mockingly spy on us. I used to sit on the wall to feel the sun on the back of my neck, my shoulders, my entire body, and I felt like lying down on the ground or on the stone floor of the first ward, or there behind the building, where the grass was higher and a kind of wind tousled the bushes, lie down on the ground like some strange animal, my pockets full of cigarette butts and pieces of newspaper, waiting to be called to lunch. I was swinging my legs on the wall and was about to look for a cigarette in my jacket when a custodian touched my shoulder with an index finger as wooden as a sharpened stick:

"Hey, blondie, the doctor wants to talk to you."

He was a cross-eyed asymmetrical man with the enormous hands of a peasant, fisherman, factory worker, clean and thick like the roots of the blood, who was in the habit of greeting me in the halls, moving backwards, bending his gigantic body in an unending ceremony:

"Doctor sir doctor sir doctor sir doctor sir doctor sir."

I thought he hadn't recognized me, hadn't noted my position of boss, master, jailer, owner of the crazies who roamed in the courtyard, shuffling their slippers, brushing against the visitors their vacant mendicant expressions. A thin young man, his nose leaning against the trunk of a tree, was gesturing his anger to an invisible specter. Mr. Moisés, blind by now, came by, his cane cautiously groping its way toward the mortuary: his mustache, alarmed, trembled ahead of his mouth like the lashes of insects.

"The doctor wants to talk to you."

I would be going on vacation soon. My body ached from fatigue, a slow torpor of weariness, of indifference, was climbing from my ankles to my abdomen and spreading its soft wings in my belly. I was beginning to lose interest in Lisbon, in the hospital, in work, my daughters were smiling in the pine forest at the beach house, in the west the sun, orange-colored, glided over the water, my mother was placing the dinner dishes on the leaf-patterned plastic tablecloth. I would be going on vacation soon and for a month not give a shit about the misery, the decrepitude, the sickening hypocrisy of the asylum, sprawled in a canvas chair by the garage door, watching the sun turn as white as a dead man's brow. I didn't care about Durand, Baleizão, Agapito, Luís: if they weren't kind enough to die I would find them a month later, imploring and humble, stubbornly asking for the discharge they didn't want, or that I, in fact, didn't want them to want. The employees came and went from the dining hall like a stream of ants, heads lowered: I'm going to the beach, I thought as I watched them, I'm going to get away from this shit for a while, get away from this benign concentration camp, this pathetic inferno, from my monotonous job of distributing pills. Get away before Baleizão's testicles reach his knees because of his hernia, or blind Lino hangs himself from a beam, with his rotten shoes of old age level with my startled chin.

"The doctor wants to talk to you," repeated the cross-eyed custodian, imperturbable.

His enormous hands of a peasant, fisherman, factory worker, clean and thick like the roots of the blood, harpooned me under the armpit the way the chrome hooks in butcher shops do the carcasses of pigs, spreading about a greasy stench of mud. I wasn't used to being spoken to that way, to being grabbed by the armpit, to being pushed bodily in the direction of the office, among the flock of automobiles under the trees, grazing on their own shadows in herbivorous serenity. The eyelids of the headlights followed me silently, indifferently. This guy isn't right in the head, I thought, contact with the crazies sent him out of his mind for good: the man spent eight straight hours on a ward, washing the floor, serving lunches, delivering messages, scratching his sweaty back against the walls: in reality he was as much a prisoner as the others, those who stumbled from bed to bed in long underwear, trying to light newspaper cigarettes with extinguished matches, and his strabismic pupils were sometimes striped with the strange, disturbing yellow goosebumps found on the skin of dogs when they howl their piercing fear in the darkness of the streets. This guy isn't right in the head, I thought, it's from the crazies or from the summer heat, maybe cross-eyed people are different from us and sense things in a weird way, twisted or elongated like the objects magicians pull out of their star-lined tubes, which little by little lengthen and swell, inflated from inside by an invisible mouth.

"The doctor's been asking about you nonstop and you here lolling on the wall doing nothing."

He slowed as he passed a wagon with a red lantern swinging between its shafts, and he listened to the earth of the Alentejo breathing through the open window, warm and broad like a great sleeping breast. The silhouettes of the bushes fled, very straight, like figures in a carnival shooting gallery, the stars grouped overhead in indecipherable constellations. He had the impression that dozens of frightened animals were observing him from the grass, moving back and forth their snouts wet with terror. The custodian pushed him along a kind of small garden bordered by stone benches and beds of kale gnawed by the snails, where half a dozen cataleptics, chins in hands, were smoking in opaque silence, or scratching their shins in the resigned despair of caged marmosets. Under a tin-roofed shed, one outcast was unbuttoning another's fly, and both were cooing through the beak of their lips a confused soup of phrases. The custodian separated them with a slap, one of the guys started to moan, and he decided As soon as I get to the treatment area I'll have them stick you in the ass with a needle so you'll learn, not because of hitting a patient but because of what he felt was an intolerable lack of respect for his psychiatric code: like all embarrassed conservatives he accepted familiarity by subordinates as long as it came from a concession on his part, parsimoniously distributed. Still, anything indefinite troubled him: an orderly running into him without a greeting, a patient, Rainho, not offering, as was customary, to work together to overthrow the government. The wind in the leaves of the trees possessed a tonality different from the habitual, deeper and more grave, like the whisper of cellos. A repulsive sweet smell of barracks rippled through the corridor, identical to a myopic animal floundering aimlessly on the tiles. The cross-eyed custodian shooed him inside an office and bowed from the waist with the ceremony of a muzhik:

"Here's the bird, doctor sir."

It was one of the usual consultation rooms, painted green and white, an ugly green and a sad white, uncomfortable and dusty, with the small lavatory in the corner, the glass-front cabinet of historical clinics, a rusty heater broken since time immemorial, and an enormous wooden desk behind which was installed, in an armchair, the assistant, surrounded by three or four apprentices who looked at me with intriguing curiosity. I smiled at my colleague as I felt my aching armpit, and I indicated with the point of my chin the door, which was closed with respectful care:

"That cross-eyed guy there has got a screw loose. The asylum's gone to his head."

The apprentices immediately stirred like parrots on a perch, looking at one another sidelong with a complicity that irritated me. The dust in the courtyard scratched itself against the dirty glass of the window:

"Have a seat," said the psychiatrist, examining a file.

The only chair free was the crazies' chair, on the other side of the desk: as soon as they start to get agitated, tip the desk over on them, a specialist at Santa Maria recommended to his interns, the way to handle them is to tip the desk against their body and immediately call the orderly, crush them like bugs, understand? This seems like some kind of bad joke, he thought, it gives the impression that I'm the bug.

"So then?" asked the psychiatrist, with an unctuous smile. The apprentices, thirsting for knowledge, leaned forward so as not to miss a shred of the conversation. A horrible necktie with a gold- and chestnut-colored leaf-and-flower design glittered beneath the smile. The clinician's cuff links were two huge yellow gallstones. If you want to screw around with my head, good luck.

"So then, what?"

The psychiatrist unwrapped a throat lozenge, continuing to observe him. One of the apprentices lit a pipe: the first match broke and the guy stored it carefully in the box. A pleasant aroma of eucalyptus permeated his nostrils with hints of the sea, and he remembered the extraordinary limpid and sad blue of summer afternoons. He recalled the poles of the cabana erected on the deserted beach, pointing toward the clouds of twilight. Recalled the ebb tide wind skimming across the rocks and the tiny crabs, dark red, hidden in the strands of algae.

"What are you feeling?" one of the apprentices said suddenly. He had an unpleasant voice like a knife scraping a plate, and his nose rose and fell like an anxious rabbit's.

"Remembering September," he answered without thinking. "Remembering the month I was born and the equinox the month I was born, the waves breaking their teeth in a thousand tiny fragments of bone against the seawall, light and salty on my skin. Remembering the white-tailed birds that leap from rock to rock shaking their damp wings, very dignified, on the edge of the rocks."

But suddenly it occurred to him that he was a psychiatrist, that he belonged to the same professional category as the assistant, and that the other one was just a psychologist who perhaps had finished his studies a year earlier, a mere apprentice jailer without the right to a reply.

"Bullshit," he told the rabbit, who unperturbedly hastened to scratch a reply on his pad of letterhead paper.

"Bullshit," a second apprentice repeated pensively, as if taking the measure of a new word, as if his tongue were the pan of one of those high school scales in which one deposits ridiculously small bits of minerals, under the geological watch of the teacher. Tenths of a gram were extracted with tweezers from a small wooden case. It was that year, he confirmed, that I went to the brothel for the first time, with Ismael, who already shaved, and carried a picture of his girlfriend in his wallet. When we got undressed in the locker room for physical education, Ismael explained to me how to stick my hand between a girl's thighs: You do it like this, with the little finger, get it? and his fingernail went back and forth before my stupefied coffee cup. I never did use my pinky that way: good advice always ends up getting lost.

The psychiatrist cast a sidelong look of comprehension at his troops and straightened his tie with the complacent urbanity one uses with misbehaving children:

"The doctor asked you what you were feeling."

The syllables came from his round lips, light, with no corners, and crackled above, on the surface, disintegrating the way the teeth of the ocean disintegrate against the rugged back of the seawall. For some moments I felt the urge to stretch out along his speech like a naked body on the methylene of swimming pools. Stretch out and think of September and the large docile waves of the equinox, almost lilac under the extraordinarily limpid and sad blue of summer afternoons. I wanted to go to sleep in the eucalyptus aroma of the throat lozenge, which still hovered in the office the way childhood skips from room to room through old houses, identical to a lit fuse. An orderly opened the door suddenly, saw me, and exclaimed

"Ah, they caught the bird"

and turned and closed it with an eyebrow raised to the psychiatrist. It's absolutely necessary not to get them excited, blathered the specialist at Santa Maria, so they don't force us to extreme measures: for example, to throw the desk on them like bugs; or apply electroshock; or put them in a straitjacket. Despite everything, they're human beings, he added. Disturbed, but human. Different from us. A large piece of plaster from the ceiling seemed ready to fall and formed a kind of prominent scar next to the light fixture, an irregular scar like the drawing of a continent on a map; the humidity must get into the interior of the building like a canker, corroding the cement and wood. One of these days all of us will end up under dusty beams, doctors, orderlies, patients, ampoules and pills; maybe a syrup bottle and a leaf-pattern necktie will survive, ludicrous signs of a bygone era, with the man who thinks he's an airplane soaring up above, gliding like a vulture over the devastated asylum.

The rabbit insisted in his rustproof little voice:

"I asked you what you were feeling."

There's something idiotic about this, he thought, something childishly stupid that everyone, from the cross-eyed guy to these cretins, decides to take seriously.

"What's so funny?" he said to the colleague who seemed to be awaiting his answer, pen in hand, with intense interest.

"What day is it today?" another one suddenly tossed out at him. And to those beside him, didactically:

"The first thing to do is to ascertain temporal orientation."

The third apprentice hastily covered up his appointment book showing the date, putting on top of it a fifth-rate Brazilian translation of Freud, its pages replete with marks in various colors. An unpleasant psychoanalytical vapor came from its spine, like an overly greasy sauce: there was probably a photo of the author in there somewhere, gazing with his wounded-antelope eyes at the photographer's Oedipus complex. If someday they mummify me like that I'll die again, he decided. And he imagined himself, very rigid, posing in a frock coat in a studio full of dusty reflectors, in front of a myopic guy with a goatee.

"The day for you to show how smart you are, you priestling," he told the psychiatrist. Radiant, the apprentices wrote feverishly. One of them turned the page with the scholastic sound of a good student.

"Where did you dig up these bookkeepers?"

Leaf-and-flower tie leaned back with digestive satisfaction:

"Paranoid psychosis," the guy intoned, as if shouting Fire! to a firing squad. "Aggressiveness, delusions of grandeur, hallucinations. A common case: he thinks he's a psychiatrist."

And he saw that the apprentices were writing Paranoid psychosis on their pads, the same way dancers in the casino synchronize their kicks. This is going too far, he decided. He looked for cigarettes in his pockets to give himself time to think, but there were no pockets: his fingers blindly encountered the resistance of cotton. He looked down in surprise: his clothes had been replaced by a hospital uniform, long and stiff like the garments of the Jews. The letters MBH were printed in red on the gray of his pants: I look like a rabbi in a ghetto, a rabbi summoned by the SS to render account of himself and the others, those who were walking past outside, close to the walls, wearing the uninhabited faces of prisoners.

"Give me a cigarette," he asked the psychiatrist. And he noticed that his voice had taken on the supplicant humble tone of the patients, whom he had so often shaken off like bothersome flies. He had extended his hands over the desk toward the leaf-and-flower tie and implored a cigarette, the alms of a consoling curl of smoke down his throat. The lit tips of cigarettes were the only stars known in the hospital.

"Characteristic alternation of aggressiveness and submission," observed the psychologist with the pipe, his cheeks sunken like pans of watercolor as he sucked on the extinguished bowl.

"Serious problems of identification with the father figure," suggested the rabbit.

The psychiatrist swept aside his disciples' ideas with the back of his hand and smiled: two small streams of saliva appeared, foaming, at the corners of his mouth:

"António, don't you want to tell us what you're feeling?"

The canvas slippers pinched my feet, my testicles itched. Someone had stolen my clothes, my shoelaces, my belt. The stitching of the pajamas hurt my kidneys.

"I'm a doctor," I informed in a murmur. "I'm a doctor here. We were working together, we participated together in group meetings, I inherited patients of yours."

"Delirious activity delirious activity delirious activity," quacked the pipe in unbearable jubilation.

The admirer of Freud brought his fingertips together and lowered his eyelids with withdrawn unction.

"Introjection because of inability to compete. This man has an oral personality."

"Oral or not, we're going to double his dosage," decided the psychiatrist, pressing the button.

"I'm a doctor, I'm a member of the Order, I pay my dues," he argued, his hand outstretched toward the tie's pack of cigarettes. Mentholated Kayak brand: it keeps you from getting a hard-on. In any case, if they double my dosage I'll lose it on the spot: the medicines in the hospital are enough to castrate a whole army, they transform people into pitiful, patient steers in the corral, mooing their tame grief. Maybe they'd like to yelp, howl, bark, strangle the orderlies, break the glass in the windows. Maybe they'd like to die but the medicines in the hospital castrate even the simple, angry, natural, almost pleasant will to die, stop the blood in the arteries, suspend movements, wither smiles, reduce steps to the hesitant teetering of a child: asylums are nothing more than gardens of human cabbages, of miserable, grotesque, repugnant human beings watered with the fertilizer of injections. He lowered himself from the chair until he was on his knees on the linoleum:

"I don't want to be a steer, I don't want to be a vegetable, I don't want to lie out there in the sun like the bodies in a disaster lined up along the tracks. I don't want the Sunday visits, the trips to the zoo, the Christmas program on television. I don't want to play checkers with the deceased."

"Schizophrenia?" the pipe asked his assistant, raising a sage eyebrow. During the course he had surely studied all the notes, memorized dozens of symptoms, and now he was making an effort, unsuccessfully, to articulate a coherent mosaic.

"Strange and absurd language, no contact with reality," said the Freud. "He speaks of vegetables and cattle."

The streams of spittle from his smile increased in a repellent unfolding, like that of plants that feed on the gelatinous juices of coffins:

"Double his dosage and let's see. And take away his clothes so he won't try to escape."

I remembered Sequeira: I ordered them to leave Sequeira in his underwear, locked in, so he wouldn't run away. Sequeira and his skinny legs, his confused way of talking, his grandiose plans, the old anarchist with a white mustache showing everyone his union card: Libertarian communism, doctor, will be the world's salvation. Sequeira, in his underwear, stared at me from behind the glass like a caged animal, he had a plastic charm hanging on a silver chain, his mouth opened and closed with words I couldn't hear. He would escape to his mother's house and immediately initiate impossible frenetic dealings, passing bad checks, contacting stores to sell hundreds of pieces of sports equipment that he didn't have, proposing marriage to willing women in the street. I remembered Sequeira, naked, sitting on the bed, trembling, looking at me from behind the glass like a caged animal, a poor, defenseless, caged animal. And I began to cry silently before the psychiatrist, feeling the tears running down my cheeks like drips of dampness that seek a path on wall tiles, leaving in their wake the viscous spoor of snails.

"Emotional lability," the pipe verified disdainfully, as if observing me under a magnifying glass. "He manifests emotional lability."

"The mentally ill often have unpredictable reactions," explained the doctor. "It's never advisable to speak to them alone.

It's one thing to feel for them, but you can't take chances with aggressiveness. Why, just the other day I was punched in the corridor."

Sequeira died a few months later, suddenly, in the street, on one of those small side streets near the asylum, full of itinerant peddlers, children, octogenarians, rusty three-wheeled carts transporting bottles of gas along the sidewalk: syphilis. A few injections of penicillin would have been enough to cure him, but I was concerned only with taking away his clothes and locking him in the deserted ward. In the next bed an enormous black man roared all day long, demanding to be released, brandishing a crutch:

"I'll knock the shit out of anybody who comes near me."

Sequeira rested his cigarette on a dented aluminum plate and raised to me, his owner, the submissive eyes of a dog: I can do whatever I feel like to these guys without anyone lifting a finger to protest: I can lobotomize them, rob them of their potency, forbid them to eat, forget about them. I can stay away from the hospital for weeks at a time. I can interrogate them about a man's most intimate matters, their secrets, their shameful miseries, I can inflict on them my plastic certainties, my twisted view of the world, the grandiose hollow pomp of my discourse. Push the desk over on them like bugs. The knifelike voice suddenly scraped against the terrine of my ears:

"How did you get along with your parents when you were a child?"

In summer the wind from time to time raises small vortexes of dust and leaves that spin furiously in the courtyard, collide against the windows, the corners of buildings, the trunks of the sycamores, then fade in the green sun of July, soft and swollen like a furuncle of light. We could see them rise obliquely near the fifth and seventh, send a shudder through the grass, increase in size on the embankments, swallow up the patients lying in the shade sucking on their cigarettes made of newspaper. A runaway beret danced in the air. The aluminum sky reflects our faces, deforming them, streaked with veins, as if the clouds palpitated with blood. The Freud rapped on the desk to get my attention:

"The doctor asked how you got along with your parents when you were a child."

When I was a child with my parents I was too little to remember. There was Lagos, and I don't remember Lagos, the sea, my mother as a young woman. Atemporal people pass vaguely through my memory, the fig tree above the well still shakes its unfocused branches, the abbot's maid, her hands folded over her apron, smiles. No, wait, my brother fell into the pond one day, he floundered around in the algae, among the fishes. I began to shout. They dressed us alike, before the long and painful saga of inheriting our uncles' clothes. The seamstress who came to the house would eat at the machine, on a board, her back bent over . the plate. Sometimes I would sit on the stone steps in the yard, near the window that looked out on the street, and feel like crying. No reason: just crying. I was six, seven, eight years old, I can't say for sure. If you don't mind, let me have a cigarette. Just today I had an itch in my throat, that craving, my body suddenly tense, hard, heavy with inexplicable anguish. Sunday nights, for example, when everything becomes absurd, ridiculous, and sad, and I look like a mummy squatting on the kitchen floor, waiting, there comes into my head that small boy on the steps in the yard, filled with soft and cruel melancholy. And yet (you will never understand this) I think that in a way I was happy: I wasn't going to die, my family loved me, I watched the caretaker arrange the plants with his thick but inexplicably delicate fingers, arrange a plant like a living statue, of flesh. Petals, sepals, stamens, the straight fragile trunk of a woman. When our grandfather died, Pedro came running into the house: he had by then almost the voice of a man and his eyes looked like twin drops of varnish. They're buying the coffin for one of us. In fact, despite my fear of the dark, my savage loneliness, and the lack of money, I was happy: as John Updike's Pop Kramer would say, we lived under the eye of God.

"We won't get much more out of him today," the psychiatrist told the intern-jailers, who were assiduously writing suggestions and questions in their notebooks. One of them was underlining certain words with the pencil he clutched horizontally between his teeth like a bit. "Once the drops start to take effect we'll repeat the interview. You'll see how differently all this will come out."

They want to change my childhood, he thought, make it aseptic, deserted, uninhabitable. They want to rob me of the knick-knacks of the past, the solemn communion ceremony, the first masturbation, the clandestine cigarettes on long holidays, transform my life into an ugly, impersonal hotel room, with artificial flowers on the night table and the lifeless spiral of the radiator in one corner: pull back the curtain and Filipe Folque street down below gazes at us with the hollow withered eyes of statues. The heads of people seen from above, the bald spots, the gray roots of their hair. The white birdshit on the tops of cars, on roofs. The weary, livid trees of morning. They want to rob me of anxiety, fear, joy, offer me on weekends a pack of little cigarettes, El Ropos, that enter your lungs like a poisonous rain of razor blades. The psychiatrist rang the bell behind him to summon the orderly, the apprentices closed their notebooks like students at the end of class, and we fell silent, immobile, waiting, hearing the feminine puff of wind against the window frames, or the sound of tiny glass bells made by the sycamore leaves, which collided in the concave air of the morning, the color of river pebbles. The guy with questions about childhood tapped his extinguished pipe against the sole of his shoe. The psychiatrist smiled. How does his wife put up with that eternal smile, I thought, that infinite comprehension, that limitless indulgence? And he imagined the smile serenely chewing his dinner, or lounging in front of the television, or making love, with the lights out, glowing in the dark, bristling from a double row of gigantic teeth. The smile took up the entire office, dispensing around it a cool breath of throat lozenge, a whiff of eucalyptus, a spearmint breeze, and he instinctively drew back his chair to escape a bit the aroma that pursued him, thick and heavy like the nauseating smell of the dead.

"I've never seen a crazy person," he said aloud, "but if there are such people, you smile and talk to them." Sometimes, you know how it is, at Campo Grande, at a traffic light, a group of patients from Júlio de Matos will show up, armed with filthy rags, to clean the windshields of the stopped cars. They wave the rag with one hand and ask for money with the other, they have empty deserted faces like stone plaques, but if by chance you smiled at them they would smile back at you the twisted evil smile of the dead. They must take away his clothes and lock him up in underwear like Sequeira, Sequeira with his hairy and pendulous breasts, sitting on the edge of the bed, with his warm tearful dog-eyes.

The psychiatrist loosed his smile again without replying: Unfortunately putting up with aggressiveness is part of our profession, until it becomes necessary to push the desk over onto their chest, the specialist at Santa Maria told his interns; he was a fat guy with bristly hair and an eternal hectic, stupid expression on his puffy cheeks. The bad taste of his tie pained me like an aberrant shout, the sound of blunt chalk on a blackboard, a long fingernail on the wall: a pompous bedbug surrounded by pompous bedbugs, pompously sucking our blood. One of the insects stood up to wash his hands in the office basin, under the mirror, oblique and slightly turbid like an unreal sea, and the water spurted from the faucets in successive brown discharges of rage, accompanied by borborymi that recalled a sputtering engine. Leaf-tie unwrapped another lozenge with a great rustling of paper identical to the crackling of dry pine needles, and the odor of eucalyptus returned, stronger than ever, and with it the subtle attenuated smell of the September equinox, as delicate as a Japanese ink drawing. The September equinox brings to my mind the dogs on the beach, russet from autumn, running along the deserted shore in downcast packs, licking the algae, the pieces of wood, the waste that the waves return and reject, fragments of cloth, animals, shells. The dogs lick the algae and the waste, rub their scrawny scab-encrusted flanks against one another, the attendants collect the last unused beach umbrellas, the water has the pinkish hue of a child's back, fearfully beating against the slime on the seawall. A bearded orderly half-opened the door with the respectful care with which priests at the altar turn the shutters of the sanctuary:

"Did you call, doctor sir?"

The tie handed him the papers with complicitous urbanity:

"Increase this fellow's medication. And keep his street clothes: if he's naked we can be more certain he won't fly the coop."

The orderly gave a brief chuckle in his throat at that subtle witticism:

"Alcoholic?"

"No, paranoid. Three days from now he'll be as tame as a paraplegic."

And I remembered Joaquim Carlos, Lourenço, Valdemiro, Manuel, wandering about the corridors of the asylum with pupils like burned out bulbs, obedient and submissive. Their grandiose visions, their fantastic plans, the constellation of their dreams were reduced to a meager present of walls stained with damp and mold, of the viscous gray fungi of mold, devouring the wooden window frames with their soft dun-colored jaws. Valdemiro presided over the movement of the stars, standing at attention in the courtyard, whistling at a flock of stars. All the radio stations talked about him ("A Portuguese commands the firmament"), all the newspapers wrote about him, the people who saw him in the street stared at him in superstitious terror, murmuring behind his back in cafés, on the esplanades, in bus lines, at traffic lights. They had brought him to the hospital, left his buttocks lumpy from injections, and a week later the people, the radio, the newspapers went back to worrying about a cure for cancer, pole-vaulting, and the Polish mathematician who after eighteen years of study had demonstrated that one and one are seven. The stars floated at random in the uncontrolled sky, and Valdemiro, clothed like some kind of beggar, asked visitors for cigarettes in the hospital atrium.

One afternoon, in Montijo, I heard someone call my name. It was a happy, full, jolly voice, the warm tender voice of a friend. I was with Jorge beside the river (we were going to return to Lisbon once the consultation was over) looking at the muddy banks strewn with large rotting boats into which water was slowly penetrating in dark spirals of algae, starving gulls were desperately skimming the grass, the city distant on the other bank as if reflected, shakily, in a tin plate, like a faded smile. The dirty smoke of Barreiro advanced menacingly toward us, creasing the eyebrows of the clouds, dense with the distress of a cough. We were at the edge of the river, breathing the waves' putrescent odor of a long-dead corpse, the gelatinous sweetish odor of the waves, and behind us a labyrinth of narrow streets, passageways, alleys, one-story houses, depositories, small forgotten stores, folded and refolded upon itself like a closed fist, clutching in its fingers a nonexistent treasure. We had just finished listening to a cortege of lengthy complaints at the medical post and were going back to

Lisbon along a highway packed with bicycles and trucks, talking about cycling greats like Fausto Coppi, Gino Bartali, Charlie Gaul, the Angel of the Mountains, Federico Bahamontes, the Eagle of Toledo, the Swiss Hugo Koblet, who carefully combed his hair before the beginning of each stage, Freddy Kubler, about the mythic heroes of the Tour de France of our youth, talking about Carl "Bobo" Olsen and his tattoo that said Mama on his left arm, Sugar Ray Robinson, Rocky Marciano, about boxers and gangsters, and that was when a happy, full, jolly voice, the warm tender voice of a friend called my name amid the cries of the seagulls and the monotonous sound of the dead body of the water, a voice that expelled the dirty smoke of Barreiro and echoed from alley to alley with an amused smile:

"I'm working with the stars again, doctor."

Valdemiro had long hair, was unshaven and wore a greasy jacket with one shoulder torn, the tattered slippers from the asylum, and he was smiling. He smiled beside the polluted river of Montijo, beside the hulled boats sunk into the mud, and the gulls moved restlessly about his round head lit by the afternoon sun, like the doves around the saints in church retables, the saints that seem to rise in the air to merge with a mystical nothing, possessed by incomprehensible and unshakable jubilation. Jorge spoke of Ma Barker, Baby Face Nelson, Machine Gun Kelly, the great John Dillinger treacherously killed by the police at the entrance to a movie theater, spoke of Carl "Bobo" Olsen and his famous Mama tattoo, spoke of Louison Bobet, Geminiani, Coppi, the Campeonissimo, dying of malaria in Africa during a safari like Hemingway's sublime and laughable heroes, but I had stopped listening. Joe Louis, the Brown Bomber from Chicago, whose right hook reached fifty-five miles per hour, left Walcott bleeding in the middle of the ring, under that violent white glare that confers upon unforgettable matches a kind of inerasable aureole, and it faded from my head in a decrescendo of noise, further and further away, of cheers, whistles, the hoarse shouts of the seconds. Valdemiro, standing before me, smiling, as unreal as a drunken angel, like old-time bakers sprinkling an angelic dust on stairs, like a Christ in a trance walking on water in his filthy sandals, smiled and pointed to the dirty reddish smoke of Barreiro with a triumphant finger:

"I'm working with the stars again, doctor. Look how they obey me."

I was going home and I was tired, tired like Charlie Gaul after the Val d'Isère, tired like Georges Carpentier beaten by Jack Dempsey, tired from dozens and dozens of monotonous complaints in the medical clinic in Montijo, packed with exhausted people worn down by work at the slaughterhouse and cutting cork. My body ached, my shoulders ached, my head ached, a slight dizziness floated before my eyes like a cellophane veil, my stomach, liver, spleen, guts were tightening, complaining of hunger. In the distance, the city quavered on the opposite bank like a faded smile. I was going home by way of the bridge, in a long line of trucks, three-wheeled carts, motor scooters, tractor-trailers swaying and shaking like proud old ducks moving about on the short flattened thighs of their wheels. An eyelid-shadow descended diagonally over the trees, purple and blue, like melancholy. An unknown voice, a voice that wasn't mine, the rough voice of an executioner sprang from my mouth in a bitter exhalation of envy and rage:

"You ran away from Bombarda, Valdemiro."

I was envious, in the swampy Montijo afternoon, of Valdemiro's happiness, of his clear smile, his long hair, his unshaven face, his triumphal poverty. I was disgusted at finding myself exhausted and pale, eaten up by a profession that was destroying me, melting my bones, transforming me into a music-box figurine condemned to two or three unchanging movements, to the rhythm of hesitant schematic melodies. I lacked the courage to skip my shift at Bombarda, to go off down the street, removing the psychiatric Cheviot wool that covered me inside and out, to display before the stupefied faces of the swans at Campo de Santana, so silent, so polite, so stupid, so plastic on the green skin of the lake, the thirty-two teeth of a mighty roar. I didn't have the courage to drown in shit to keep from drowning in shit, to tell everything to fuck off, medicine, psychoanalysis, tranquilizers, antidepressants, psychotherapy, psychodrama, whatever the fuck. I got paid punctually every month and pretended to believe in my work. I pretended to believe in insulin, sleep cures, occupational therapy, pretended to believe in psychiatrists and ensconced myself behind my desk in the bank building in Montijo, near the school and the old mulberry trees in the square, prescribing pills to help the slaughterhouse workers, the cork-fac-

tory employees, the peasants immersed in the putrescent nauseating odor and plowing in vain the fog and humidity, who en-
dured without dreams until a new morning as pale and cold as
the blind vitreous gaze of the departed. So a voice that wasn't
mine, the rough voice of an executioner, leapt from my mouth in
a bitter exhalation of envy and rage:

"You're going back to the hospital with me, Valdemiro."

What year was it that Charlie Gaul, the Angel of the Mountains,
won at Val d'Isère? Is it true that Federico Bahamontes would sit
on top of the hills, his chin in his hands, smiling and silently waiting for the tardy pack? How did the shy, neutral Roger Walkowiak
manage a surprise victory? Jorge chatted with the gulls skimming
over the mud in flocks impatient with hunger, leaned out over the
chestnut-colored plants of the bank to explain Puy de Dôme to
them, adjusting his glasses with his ring finger like a math professor spouting a table of cosines. The motorbikes of the reporters
rattled on the pavement in search of the divine Eddy Merckx, who
was flying solo, bent over the handlebars, on his way to Príncipes
Park. Valdemiro's smile ceased to sway among the side streets, the
alleys, the narrow streets of Montijo, in the confusion of the
small, apparently deserted houses of Montijo, impregnated with
the putrefacient vapor rising from the river, and was replaced for
a moment, instantaneously, by the asylum patients' grimaces of
hollow panic as they begged under the sycamores for the pathetic
alms of cigarettes. Valdemiro began retreating along the dock,
skipping on the loose stones on the pavement. A slipper came

loose and slid into the mud, floated for a moment, then disappeared, a yellowish dog started barking next to an abandoned shop, Valdemiro begged, still retreating

"No no no no no no no"

and an unknown voice, a voice that wasn't mine, the rough voice of an executioner, sprang from my mouth in a bitter exhalation of envy and rage, clamoring

"You're going back to the hospital, you bastard."

Jorge, facing the distant city on the far bank, similar to a faded smile, was speaking of Fausto Coppi's mysterious white lady, who waited for him, exuberant and secretive, at the end of the stages, speaking of Jacques Anquetil, André Darrigade, Nencini, Luís Ocaña, of Poulidor as sad as a mongrel dog, and I began running desperately after the long hair, the unshaven face, the triumphant poverty of Valdemiro, who fled, stumbling, begging

"No no no no no"

in the rotten-fish smell of Montijo's cramped streets.

So when the orderly came to me with a loaded syringe and told me

"Drop your pants, artist man"

I undid the string of the pajamas and offered my buttocks to the needle as if trying to pay for an inexpiable sin.

The car seemed to drift, en route to Lisbon, in something warm, emotional, naked, as if across the body of a sleeping woman, lying prone, on night's sheet of silence and trees. The birds, transformed by darkness into monstrous insects, crept noisily in the blackness repelling and attracting one another, scraping the slate of the fields with the red-chalk drone of their antennae. The sky flickered like the roof of a basement in which voices and footsteps circulate on the floor above, rattling the stucco with their suddenly enormous weight, and I thought, I'm back in Beira, lying in bed, listening enviously to the laughter, the coughing, the grownups' commingled words up there, my grandfather's shoes creaking on the stairs the withdrawn, almost supplicant shyness of the deaf. I thought What oppresses me is Beira's weight against my chest, my temples, the swelling curve of my belly, that weight of interminable twilights and of the melancholies of childhood, above the immense silhouette of the mountains. It's my grandfather standing in the middle of the living room, his hand cupped to his ear, trying in vain to hear the murmured conversations of the figures in the pictures that gazed at him from behind glass with the eyes of a dying cat. But the well pump didn't squeak in the yard, no cup shone on the sideboard, the smell of the vineyard wasn't coming toward me in viscous sugary waves, in an oceanlike lurch. A different kind of odor, smooth, uniform, soft, abstracted, the odor of a womb, a limitless emptiness in which the olive trees shook gently in distressed restiveness, dragged along the ground like a sheet of fog, drowning out the cries of the crickets and the invisible whistling of the stars in the confused tangles of the trees. I didn't feel the tremor, the fear, the indefinable dread that nighttime in Beira invariably provoked in me, looming like vertical walls, impossible to demolish, before my sweating hands. I didn't feel the tortured anguish of the chestnut trees beckoning in the window frames with their green and black arms, calling me to roam with the specters of the dogs, the hens, the people, the specters of specters, through the undulating expanse of pines traversed by mute tumultuous rivers of shadow. I didn't feel the wind in the pale crown of the eucalyptuses, parting the narrow silvery leaves in search of something it had lost: I found myself at the entrance to Grândola, heading toward Lisbon, floating in the gigantic warm, moving, naked body of woman, the Alentejo stretched out upon the silent sheet of darkness. I found myself in the environs of Grândola, on my way to Canal-Caveira for dinner, and I crossed the town like the angel of death over doomed cities, leaving a carbonous trail of smoke in the deserted streets. Ahead of me, the headlights invented from nothingness doors, windows, a railroad station, scenes of gardens that summer withered just as the years empty a breast of its shiny denseness of milk, and I imagined myself traveling in a set constructed of wood and cardboard, behind which were surely hidden carpenter's tools, cans of paint, actors' wigs, humble like useless pubic hair. The set unfolded, ever the same, its tunnel of pictorial walls, a display window suddenly stared at me, illuminated by garlands of tenuous colored bulbs, a gasoline pump thrust toward me the curved trunk of its hose, and my bladder gently ached from the urge to urinate, bleating in my insides the low moans of a child, the moans of a feverish child crying softly in its sleep.

I'll take a piss at the restaurant in Canal-Caveira, he decided, in a nauseating toilet clogged with the immemorial shit of fellow diners that leaves in the porcelain the dirty smeared fingerprints of an ID file, which no amount of water will cleanse. I'll take a piss at the restaurant, where I'll sit before last year's steak with last year's lack of appetite in my guts, refusing the French fries on the tray with immense disgust. I'll sit down alone at the table, elbows on the cloth, and smile and nod my head at the people I know, waiting for company that doesn't arrive, drowning cigarette after cigarette in the remains of the coffee from the previous customer, who warmed the seat for me and left on the tablecloth a battlefield of devastated plates. And he remembered the patients' dinner at the hospital, at six or seven P.M., in damp and gloomy dining halls, among whose tables the orderlies, in aprons, circulated with the small plastic cups of medications, distributing drops and pills. The patients ate in silence like cows in stables, chained by unseen irons to the tiles on the wall, sunk like wax dolls into the rigid cotton molds of their pajamas. They ate from tin plates, from tin mugs, with tin utensils, ate and looked at me as they chewed with their chins almost touching the table, wearing the imploring and fearful expression of dogs hunched over bowls of rice beside the concrete wash tub in the yard. They're men, I thought, men destroyed by pills, by poverty, by their unhappy phantoms, men who little by little come to resemble strange animals, desperate, obedient, strange animals who circulate along the fence like animals behind the bars at the zoo, with expressions ground by apathy and fear. A kind of repugnance, of disgust, of anger grew in me like a tidal wave, Joanna, and I felt like pushing them, felt like beating them, felt like forcing them toward the gate, felt like insulting them until they regained insolence, defiance, pride, disdain, conviction, until they lifted their chins from the table and stared at me in the damp and nauseating dining hall, smiling arrogantly and sarcastically.

Sitting in the restaurant in Canal-Caveira, his face in his hands, he drowned cigarette after cigarette in the remains of the coffee from the previous customer, in the dark yellowish paste of the sugar from the previous customer, hearing without comprehension the shouting voices, the petty arguments, the conversations. He had passed through the fields of Grândola carved into the darkness like hollow eyes in whose belly trees and invisible insects moved with mysterious furor, and where the sky resembled a broad, limitless estuary simultaneously turbulent and static, had passed through the cardboard town that the headlights arranged into the rigidity of a completed play's set, and found himself in the asylum dining hall, standing among the tables, observing with alienated indulgence my flock of convicts, while other dinners, other places, other years, appeared and disappeared, jumbled in memory like the superimposition of images in a film that had suddenly abolished time and distance: a luxury to which the patients can't consent because we have amputated them from past and future and reduced them, through injections, shock treatment, insulin-induced comas, to obedient animals with expressions ground by apathy and fear.

Standing in the middle of the tables, I breathed the dampness of the nearby urinal in which you pissed against stone plaques along which ran, by means of a rusty system of tubes, a mossy slime of water that slowly dragged shit through a vein of cement toward an unlikely drain: and it seemed to me, staring at the feces that floated slowly by, that they were circling interminably in the asylum, through the four or five stories of the asylum, the vegetable garden, the pharmacy, the kitchen, the conference room, the chapel, circling and contaminating everything with their putrid odor, emanating the thick smell of a poisoned cavity identical to that of the dead men in Africa in their lead coffins, decomposing in the storeroom like spoiled food.

"Can we eat the dead?" I once asked the corporal who was trying to seal the cracks in a coffin with a blowtorch. If we eat the dead we'll get rid of the smell: we can finally sleep without the smell that wakes us up in the middle of the night and shakes our shoulders with its sticky noisome hands.

And I remembered a woman telling me that when she was a little girl she would be taken to her parents' gravesite on All Souls' Day. While the people placed flowers in the glass vases, the useless melancholy flowers that cadavers receive as gifts and accept without protest, on those November mornings of a grayish white like the lividness of scars, she would approach the caskets lined up on the marble shelves with their plastic handles and their rusted crucifixes, rap her knuckles on her mother's coffin, listen intently to the hollow sound of the wood, and think to herself, quite happily

"There's no one in there"
just as when we tap an empty bottle with a knife and the absence of liquid answers us.

"Can we eat the dead?" I asked the corporal, who closed his eyes to protect himself from the rain of sparks from the blowtorch, whose tongue of yellow-and-green fire, the approximate shape of an almond, slowly bent the metal. It was the coffin of Pereira, which had broken in a Unimoog accident at the end of twenty-four months of war, Pereira who had the innocent, wise smile of poor little boys.

"What if instead of giving them food," I suggested to the orderly who was handing out lunch, "why don't we make them devour one another? I'm sure they'd obey if we ordered them to devour one another: all animals obey their owners."

In the restaurant in Canal-Caveira the men and women feigned a type of amusement, of festive cheer, and I knew, drowning the fifth cigarette in the cup of coffee I hadn't drunk, that in reality they were chewing on themselves as if their teeth were turned inward to gnaw at their faces, their shoulders, their necks, the bit of skin their open shirts displayed. Little by little the Alentejo night, as sharp and clear as a face without clouds, gave way to the humid night of Sintra, draped like a wet veil on the paralyzed surface of things. The fogged windows of the automobiles took on the opaque reflections of teapots. From the leafless branches of the trees hung enormous translucent fruits of water that swung like light bulbs on wires. In the cloister of the town palace walked phosphorescent ghosts of pages, holding gigantic tin candelabras in their narrow hands. Doctors, orderlies, social workers, psychologists, occupational therapists met for one of those confused commemorations, a birthday, a farewell party, some promotion or other, that normally serve as pretext for an illusory sense of camaraderie, a sudden jubilation of prison guards on holiday, dressed as for a wedding without bride and groom, in which they seem to be awaiting the momentary arrival of a white veil.

Sintra is an aquarium, Joanna, the sea bottom peopled by old houses immersed in the undulation of the fog, in which pink and blue fishes float among the chests of drawers, the pictures, the geometric profile of the armoires, bleating softly like a flock of sheep, fusiform, with long fluttering and attentive lashes. The light comes not from the sun but from the oblique and unmoving trees, a glare that could be said to arise from our very bones, our very teeth, our hair, our gestures, the words we speak, and like some enormous leaf spreads in concentric circles whirling and vibrating into the air.

"Isn't it true you're sick and tired of the food and would rather chew on a piece of Pereira's shoulder?" I asked the corporal who was welding the coffin with a blowtorch, averting his head to protect himself from the rain of silvery sparks that leapt from the lead like minuscule petals of fire. "Why don't we open the casket and both of us have a piece of Pereira's shoulder? There should still be some beer left, warm beer, the type that leaves a kind of ballast of mud in your belly. Why don't you go look for some beer to go with Pereira's shoulder?"

"There's no one in there," repeated the little girl, rapping her knuckles on the wood, the way we tap an empty bottle with a knife and the absence of liquid answers us. There's no one in there, there can't be anyone in there, there never was anyone in there.

He touched the arm of a guy passing by carrying plates:

"Is the steak going to take long?"

You always used to fall asleep in the car somewhere around Tercena, near Cacém, and sometimes I would slow down to look back at you and see you stretched out on the seat, your brown curls scattered over your arms, and your lips in a kind of pout as if you were about to cry, or speak, or get angry at me. You would fall asleep near Cacém, and I would hear your breathing coming from behind me, rapid like that of a feverish puppy, and my shoulders shivered with tenderness for you. Then I would make my way through Sintra with my daughter motionless in the back seat, and her eyelashes cast upon her cheeks the same oblique and unmoving shadow of the trees of Sintra, which emerge suddenly along the side of the road like submerged coral. The corporal turned off the blowtorch with his blackened thumb:

"It's a sin to eat the dead, doctor."

"The blacks swear that you take on their qualities that way," I replied.

"One second," said the guy with the plates to justify himself, his sweaty forehead looking like the surface of a pot over a flame.

The doctors, the orderlies, the social workers, the psychologists, the occupational therapists were chatting among themselves as they cut into Pereira's corpse, smiling at one another with the mysterious incomprehensible gaiety of executioners. The women's perfume induced in me the beginnings of nausea, like a very light wine, and my body leaned imperceptibly in the direction of their breasts, as toward enormous fleshy and swollen flowers, hidden by the petals of cloth of their dresses, emitting a dusty fragrance of stamens.

"How do you like it at the hospital?" the wife of the head of the team asked me, pouring a golden drizzle of sauce onto the dead soldier's flesh. Two dangles clinked on a bracelet the thickness of a sommelier's chain. "Every time I go there with my husband I think it's a matter of habit, you know what I mean? We get used to anything."

"There's no one in there," said the little girl inside the family mausoleum on All Souls' Day, rapping her knuckles on the hollow wood. The aroma of rotting hyacinths filled the air in the small stone building and spilled out into the afternoon in a stain like a repulsive blot of fat, a cloud yellow and sticky like a drunkard's breath. The aroma of the hyacinths came to our children's bedroom and disturbed us like certain night dampness, certain inaudible sounds, certain dark menaces that upset horses in their stables, making them brush against the walls the distress in their haunches. My mother looked up from her crochet and, concerned, breathed the air of the living room: her brown eyes widened with a secret fear.

"It's easy to get used to the misery of others," I replied, chewing in turn the portion of Pereira that the worker had deposited on my plate, ringed with greens and potatoes: a thigh? the knee? the neck tendons? There's nothing more tender, he thought, than the flesh of a dead soldier.

"I detest the hospital," declared a chinless woman in back, dripping into her glass drops of a medicine that diffused into the liquid like one breath into another, clouding the water into the milky color of cataracts. "It's so dirty."

"The ill are normally dirty," explained the leader of the team, didactically, as he deposited a slab of butter on a fragment of bread: the bread disappeared instantly into his mouth like a bunch of carrots in an elephant's throat, with an easy gesture of his coat-sleeve trunk. "The ill are normally dirty and they love dirtiness. I sometimes wonder what would happen if they lived in a clean environment."

"Open the coffin," I told the corporal, who had begun resealing the lead with the blue-and-yellow hiss of the blowtorch. "Open the coffin and we'll split Pereira's body fifty-fifty. Once the guts are out you'll see he doesn't even smell bad."

The team leader rested his butter knife on the edge of his plate:

"We give them a bath once a week. It's all a question of not overdoing it."

"I feel good at the hospital," I stated, groping with my fingers for the glass of white wine. "Being able to bathe once a week is a luxury."

The naked patients became still more patient-like, more passive, slower, covered with soap foam, standing in the bathtub like gigantic babies, skinny and ugly, that the custodians quickly scrubbed, squatting on the tiles, and wrapped in ragged sheets like clowns' shrouds. The locks of hair plastered to their foreheads dribbled a hot sap of steam. The juice from the roast resembled the water in the tubs, equally oily, thick, dark.

"Do you like barbecued patient?"

It's not Pereira: it's Durand, Nobre, Luís, Agapito, Baleizão, Mr. Chambel chatting with the sycamores in the courtyard, it's Mário with his long white beard entangling himself in endless courtesies:

"And how is the good doctor today? May a thousand blessings always shower upon the good doctor. May you continue in good health for our happiness, doctor. You seem more and more vigorous, doctor. I have always contended that you are our salvation, doctor. Much obliged to you, great sir."

This meat isn't from Pereira, he thought, it doesn't have the fermented-clove smell of sea without sea, of the picture-less frame of the soldiers killed on the trail through the jungle, their noses in the sand like sleeping animals. This meat, he thought in the restaurant in Canal-Caveira, in the restaurant in Sintra, is the flesh of the man who thought he was an airplane and soared, arms spread, over the bathing area, shouted at from below by the desperate orderlies. I want to die, a small voice inside began clamoring in microscopic insistence: I want to die, I want to die, I want to die.

"We have close to fifteen patients taking part in sewing," said the therapist, who sat before him eating and manipulating the utensils as if they were needles: the sole was a sweater that she was constructing diligently, little by little.

"The sleeves are going to be too short, like always," I sighed.

"What?" the team leader asked, swallowing another bunch of carrots. He could have asked How? or When? He was totally distracted, occupied with his schematic trained-pachyderm tasks. Luckily, there was no trumpet at hand to be blown.

The Sintra night chilled his veins, chilled his bones. If he wiped the fog from the window with his handkerchief, he could make out the houses in the town unfocused by the myopia of the humidity, to which the streetlights imparted the unexpected depth of apparitions. At long intervals, the headlights of one or another automobile would fleetingly lick the facades and evaporate in the direction of Lisbon. A scarlet fire engine emerged from the illuminated fire station like an obscene tongue. You always went through Sintra asleep, and your lashes darkened your cheeks with the frightened tremor of the acacias. I want to die, insisted the small voice with tenacious obstinacy: I want to die I want to die I want to die. The workers came and went carrying pieces of patient smothered in roasted potatoes and salad.

"We have fifteen doing sewing," stated the therapist, "several others who paint, and seven or eight more who work with clay. Out of five hundred women that's not a lot, but we're getting there: in a year or two we'll flood the city with sculptures and watercolors."

"No one," murmured the girl, rapping her knuckles on the varnished mahogany surface. "There's no one in here."

"Just a second," said the guy in the restaurant in Canal-Caveira, balancing a pile of plates on his outstretched arms. "It's summer and we're working our asses off."

The fluorescent lights on the ceiling reduced shadows to small asymmetrical amoebas shrinking and expanding, beneath the chairs, their protoplasm arms.

"Soon," prophesied an assistant, "those suffering from mental disorders will once again be useful members of society."

And I recalled the elderly women sewing, in the office by the elevator, doing their macabre embroidering in the resigned silence that constituted the most unbearable of the asylum's noises: the silence of blank eyes, the silence of mouths, the silence of sluggish anemones of their gestures. At Christmas they would eat their slices of cake with expressionless lethargy: the assistant shook his fork menacingly in the direction of the occupational therapist, as if her eyes were a pair of olives from which he had difficulty in choosing:

"Open the coffin," I ordered the corporal. "We'll start the meal with the eyes."

"Useful to society in minor roles," rephrased the team leader, holding his knife with the limp trunk of his sleeve, like the elephant with the trumpet at the zoo. "My colleague mustn't forget about the destructuralization of personality. Janitor, doorman, cab driver is one thing. But a doctor, for example. Did you ever think about the danger of a destructured doctor, a schizophrenic doctor? A psychotic cannot go beyond, at most, a floor sweeper at city hall. Sewing, sculpture, painting, that sort of thing is fine. A psychotic can't go beyond, at most, a floor sweeper at city hall. Sewing, sculpture, painting, things of that nature, all well and good. Artistic activities, excellent: to be an artist you don't need a steady head. I give you my word that I've treated several and have seen what they are inside: so fragile that they commit suicide over nothing, become alcoholics, drug addicts. There's something of the feminine in them, something of the mad and the feminine, something profoundly morbid. The very fact of writing, if we look at it closely, is caricatural: adult people torturing themselves to create school compositions, imaginary intrigues, useless imbroglios. Novels are good for reading in bed before falling asleep: you dog-ear the page, turn out the light, and the next morning resume thinking about life."

"When I go to the movies," stated his wife, covering her brassiere strap with her sweater, "I tell my husband right away: choose a light little film that will put me in a good mood because there's enough sadness and trouble in everyday life."

"I like crime stories," said a patient from the corner of the table. His mustache, made of cardboard, appeared stuck with glue to the scarlet glass of his mouth. The stain of his tongue could be seen inside his nearly transparent cheeks, like the shadow of a silkworm moving inside its cocoon. The humidity of Sintra fogged the windows with its sticky breath: the trees emerged from the fog, sugary, like the bushes on the bottles of anise liqueur that leaves in our mouths the smooth delicate taste of childhood, drunk on Thursdays from Uncle Elói's blue chalices, while the clocks on the wall silently pealed the echo of infinite hours. The voice of Chaby Pinheiro still rose, in scratchy spirals, from the old gramophone. Through the attic window the afternoon could be seen reddening the trees of Monsanto, just as the cold of morning turns the beaches lilac in September, that mucous hue common to conchs and other shells, worn by the acid of the ebb tide foam.

"Have you ever thought of the danger of a schizophrenic doctor?" repeated the team leader, pointing his butter knife at the assistants, the occupational therapists, the psychologists, the patients, the orderlies, the small dining army of his subjects.

The workers attentively deposited before us roasted chunks of the ill, chunks of Durand, Baleizão, blind Lino, Marques, Mr. Chambel, buried under cones of vegetables and roasted potatoes. A vein throbbed, rhythmically, on the tray, perhaps the bush that pulsates obliquely in Nobre's pale brow when he stares at me from the opposite pole of the desk, with indignation and alarm. A social worker chewed, holding in her red nails one of Luís's ribs, and the bone emerged, white and smooth, from her gluttonous double row of teeth. The radishes looked like enormous molars sunk into the sour gums of their skin. The carrots were obscene boiled penises. Something of a biblical scene, biblical martyrdom, the slaughter of the innocents, the flogging of saints, something of the atrocious mystic scenes of church paintings, darkened by the humidity and smoke from candles, was reproduced in the restaurant in Canal-Caveira, in the Sintra restaurant, causing me to contemplate the other diners with an inexplicable mix of curiosity and terror. The lights flickered as if at a wake, enlarging noses, making caverns of eye sockets, extending gestures as if the phalanges were long thin flames of stearin.

"Open the coffin," ordered the team leader to the corporal who turned off the soot-covered blowtorch, placed it on the floor, and began hammering the lead seal on the casket, through which escaped a lukewarm, unpleasant stench. Overhead, the tall trees of Gago Coutinho murmured softly, combining the sound of their leaves with the monotonous drone of the conversations. In the distance the sky, stirred by thunder, rose and fell like an impatient Adam's apple: our hair, the earth, the sleeping body of my daughter in the backseat, en route to the beach, now smelled like the thick angry rain of Africa approaching, rolling over the Cambo, the river of crocodiles, in far-off fury. Chief Macau, kneeling in the sand, scrutinized the storm with the antique-porcelain eyes of the old. Alone on the porch of the house in Nelas as if at a command post, my grandfather, in the wind, wrapped his neck in a scarf of lightning bolts: an acid scent of sulfur came through the closed doors of the porch and illuminated our bones under the skin with its yellowish glare. The furniture, startled, groaned in the half-shadow. Dogs numb with fear dragged themselves along the terraces of the vineyard. Sometimes, for an instant, an inlet, a gulf, an abyss parted the clouds, silvered like a mirror, and the narrow scythe of the moon could be glimpsed beheading the colorless branches of the olive trees. The team leader pointed his butter knife at the casket placed on the table in the restaurant in Sintra like a gigantic wooden cake:

"Open the coffin," he ordered the corporal, who was hammering the lead seal. An unbearable stench seeped into the air.

The doctors, the orderlies, the social workers, the psychologists, the occupational therapists leaned forward toward the bier, gripping their silverware with anxious appetite. Collars and ties vibrated. Here and there silver incisors shone in their gigantic mouths. The battalion priest, in vestments at the rear of the restaurant, next to the cubicles of the bathrooms, solemnly blessed the diners, his aspergillum spurting viscous drops of sauce. The convex lenses of his glasses glittered with understanding indulgence.

"Hello, Honório," I said. We hadn't seen each other for several years, since Luanda, since March in Luanda before boarding for the trip home, in the last feverish days of war filled with bitterness, relief, and expectation.

"I'm going back to Africa," he had explained, but there he was in the restaurant in Sintra, in the restaurant in the Alentejo, drawing with the sleeve of his robe pious geometric arabesques in the nothingness. There he was, smiling, his soldier's boots visible under the skirt, like the sacristan off to the side holding the sauce dish with feigned unction.

"Honório," I called. My voice came out soundlessly from my mouth, a silent croaking identical to the screams of statues.

"Open the coffin," implored a fat social worker in whose neckline a breast swelled and shrank restlessly. She had introduced her fork into an opening in the lead and stirred the interior like one of those children's fishing games in which they use a magnet to try to catch numbered fishes inside a cardboard prism. The sugary trees, suspended in the humidity and fog, throbbed like bloodless veins.

"It won't be long now," the Canal-Caveira employee told me, thrusting a sweaty mustache against my ear. His expression had suddenly become mysterious, inexplicable: I had the obscure feeling that he harbored for me the kind of pity and repulsion that corpses evoke in us as they lie on sheets in the quiet dignity of things. The team leader's wife takes a handkerchief from her purse and comes toward me to cover my face the way one covers the face of the deceased.

"There can't be a schizophrenic doctor," I state in reply, desperately seeking, over the glasses, approbation that isn't forthcoming.

"Psychiatrists are humorless and crazy," my father's friend softly testifies, in a birch-wood whisper.

Psychiatrists who go crazy, he thought, stirring the remaining coffee with the extinguished butt of the cigarette, decay as quickly as a tooth with a cavity. They're sad, melancholy, sour crazies, gnawed by a deep rot of bitterness, ensconced behind their desks, hollow-eyed, staring with absent indifference at the opposite wall. I knew one who worked every day until three or four in the morning, seeing patients, prescribing medicine, signing commitment papers, very tall, very stooped, sunk into the cocoon of his smock as if in a chitinous carapace. On Saturdays he would fill the trunk of his car with bottles of brandy and spend the weekend in a viscous coma, beside the sea, sitting on a kitchen bench, leaning against the stove, his elbows resting on the stone sink which now and again regurgitated impatient gases. The waves smashed against the wooden fence in the yard, saltpeter gradually poisoned the walls of the house, the wisteria slowly dropped its leaves in a translucent rain of petals that the wind wafted through the open window and deposited on the cupboards, kettles, the broken refrigerator, as light and blue as snow in dreams. Some would touch the psychiatrist's forehead, his hair, his shoulders, others would stain with oval blotches the whiteness of his hands, still others would vanish whirling into the hallway, in the direction of the disorderly bedroom, its sheets brutally pulled apart like legs at the gynecologist. The doctor stared at the petals dancing in the air, listened to the sound of the inert body of the waves in the yard and extended his arm toward the glass (a blue flower, humid, had stuck to the rim) in order to expel the terrible phantasms of his loneliness, the loneliness he treated with pills in his patients, very tall, very stooped, sunk into the cocoon of his smock as if in a chitinous carapace.

"There's no one in there," repeated the little girl, scratching the gravestone with her fingernails. "No one's in there."

The corporal raised the lid of the coffin and an unbearable stench spread through the room, a stench of feces, of decomposing entrails, of rotten flesh, the repulsive stench of death, of the hospital nurses, on Sundays, after the visitors leave, when the silence drills an endless well at our feet, full of crumpled wrapping paper and cake crumbs, of the family meetings in which people age visibly, minute by minute, white hairs sprout in their heads, wrinkles multiply, backs hunch, voices take on grayish hollow tones without luster, the sad voices of bleating goats. The wisteria petals floated in the restaurant, onto the plates, transparent and blue like my brothers' irises, the wind gently stirred the curtains, flexing the rounded muscles of the cloth, the sea struggled against the slats of the broken fence in the yard. The doctors, the orderlies, the social workers, the psychologists, the occupational therapists, stood up, their plates raised toward the coffin, all speaking at once, all moving at once, all laughing at once, the team leader said to those around him

"There's enough for everyone, there's enough for everyone"

the corporal handed him the carpenter's saw we used to amputate the men injured by mines so he could carve up the deceased, the shattered, horribly burned body of Pereira, in the Unimoog accident twenty-four months after our arrival in Angola, near Belo, on the road to the Malanje highway, at the beginning of January 1973, A month from now I'll be there remembrances to all from me signed António. I had gone to take the internship exam in Luanda, with the pompous and rude whites in Luanda who observed me with sour mistrust, and when I returned to the barracks the chaplain, at the sentry post, pulled me behind the guardhouse by the arm (a slow, soft rain was falling from the smooth copper sheet of the sky) and whispered a shameful confession

"Three from your company bought it," and a murmur full of recrimination and shame escaped his lips. (It was at that time, Joanna, that I sired you, on a military bed of white metal just like those in the asylum, which with every movement groaned abominable raucous protests of rust. I sired you in the jungle, in Marimba, during the siesta, while my other daughter slept under the mosquito net and my body sank vegetative into your mother's the same way the mango trees next to the post office merged the dark green of their branches, ever heavy with night, a night dense as liquid shadow, in whose belly pulsated the anguish of the mourning of bats.)

"This is one enormous pile of shit," said the priest.

And I realized that he was indignant with fury, with piety, with horror, to use the word shit, because to him the word shit constituted a forbidden exclamation, a sin, a vulgar unburdening.

"There's enough for everyone," shouted the team leader, using the saw to shoo away the nearer orderlies, who were advancing with forks, spoons, glasses, their bare hands, toward the corpse, like a ravenous army of ants attacking a morsel of food. Dresses, coats, earrings shook with gluttonous fever, psychiatrists like the dead, I thought, they love the dead with the eager tenderness of vampires, they like to numb people with pills in order to then lean over them, chuckle silently, imagining them dead in the bedrooms of the clinics so they could suck out the happiness, sadness, enthusiasm, rage, the despondency from their veins, and transform them into sluggish stuffed animals with empty eyes, indifferent to everything, drooling in the common areas like the old people in Mitra, in front of a checkerboard where no one moves the pieces. The man who thought himself an airplane flew less and less, heavy from injections and pills: squatting on the steps of the first ward he raised toward me the sick, disheartened pigeon eyes of rudderless angels: when he was no longer capable of leaping even a single millimeter, he would be cured: cured the same way that toads are healthy.

I approached the casket and peered inside: the bulbs in the restaurant, amplified in the china and metal, suddenly curdled the light into a glare that blinded me, kept me from discerning the form lying with his hands across his chest, the shoes that directed their gleaming tips at the ceiling, pointed, the waxlike nose of a bird whose overly white wings seemed to extend the sugary mist of the anise trees in Sintra, drowned beyond the window of dampened felt that was the night. I approached the casket (the corporal smiled at me a timid smile of pardon) and looked inside over the shoulder of a patient who was energetically sinking his fork into a soft mass of cloth: it wasn't Pereira, it wasn't any of the war dead torn to pieces by booby traps, amputated by mines, shattered by bullets, that I would sometimes find when I returned home, lodged in the living room chairs, staring at me from a distance with ineffable anguish; they weren't my patients from the hospital, Durand, Nobre, Mário, Luís, Agapito, Sequeira, roaming about the courtyard in the harmless sleepwalking of circus beasts, poor castrated circus beasts snarling from time to time toothless yawns; it wasn't my daughter sleeping in the back seat of the car, breathing softly through her sulky mouth. Little by little I recognized the features, the shape of the shoulders, the hips, the shade of the hair tight against the forehead or in clusters over the ears, into which the team leader's wife stuck plastic toothpicks identical to the ones used for croquettes at birthday parties, encouraged by the shouts of enthusiasm from the occupational therapists.

"Try the loin steak first," advised a psychologist.

I was lying in the coffin, on my back, and I wasn't my war age, the twenty-eight of my war years, and the bandaged face with which I embarked for Africa one rainy morning already so long ago, wavering, unfocused in my memory. I had the face I have now, which I suddenly meet, surprised, in the mirror, stupid, melancholy, bovine, the soft and aged face of now, the mouth, the wrinkles, the broken locks of hair, the idiotically knowing face of a psychiatrist darkened by a mossy beard, my simpleton hangman's face.

(What brings you here, what brings you here?)

The opaque face listening eruditely in silence, speaking eruditely about the suffering of others, making me important to the suffering of others, indispensable to the suffering of others, the face behind which I hid and spied on the unhappiness of others, the happiness of others, the anxiety of others, the face that drained when the consultations ended and becomes grotesque and hollow like carnival masks in a shop window, walking to the elevator, after turning out the lights, with the hesitant steps of ghosts. The expression with which I leave work, Joanna, lay in the coffin in the restaurant in Sintra, patiently awaiting dinner in the restaurant in Canal-Caveira, and the night in the mountains and the night of the Alentejo, the humid and the dry, the small and the large, the narrow and the wide, the houses and the walnut palaces, and the enormous silence of the land, the silence that breathes like some wineskin of the land, approached and converged the way my breathing merges with yours if I kiss you while you sleep, and I feel under my fingers the soft bones of your chest.

"A slice of loin, well done," requested a social worker who looked like a porcelain Dutch doll. Her cheeks, red, glittered with makeup.

The team leader opened my coat, unbuttoned my shirt, exposing the white skin of my ribs.

"I haven't been to the beach this year," I thought, embarrassed and he began to slice open my belly using the saw with deep and precise blows. The smell of rotten blood, of rotten entrails, of rotten flesh, sickened me like the excessive perfume of old women at spas, playing mah-jongg in rooms full of potted cacti, with some hunchbacked bald guy playing the cello on a platform. The manager, hands behind his back, was bowing left and right obsequiously, while face powder rose like incense between the heavy damask curtains toward the stucco pergolas on the ceiling, the clusters of grapes on the ceiling, the chandeliers on the ceiling where the light leapt and scattered into fleeting colored beads, into tiny pieces of paper, scarlet, blue, and green, that came to rest in the dyed hair of the elderly women like those small furry windborne seeds that land, still fluttering, on the scarred parapet of porches.

"How did I die?" he asked, startled, searching inside his head for an agony he could not remember. The forks, the knives, the plastic toothpicks were stripping the bones of cartilage and muscle. Someone scraped the tendons of his legs with a carving knife, the porcelain social worker bit his fingers with her doll's incisors. "How did I die?" he asked the orderly in the patients' dining room.

"Shall we go to the apprentice bullfights *un día de éstos?*" the orderly proposed. He expressed himself in a singsong mixture of Portuguese and Spanish, and on Sundays he worked with bulls in the rings, on the team of one matador or another. The doctor enjoyed hearing him speak of Luís Miguel Dominguín, Paquirri, Curro Romero, Antonio Ordóñez, of his caprices, his terrors, his delicate and pathetic courage free of irony.

"Some people follow Curro Romero the whole season," the orderly related, "and Curro Romero runs away from the *toros*, full of fear. Sometimes he doesn't even enter the arena and stays behind the refuge fence, scared shitless. And then, one afternoon, a *toro* comes out that he likes, so he makes a *faena* and leaves the public gasping, captivated, *en éxtasis*, a wonderful *faena*. And people follow the whole season waiting for the *milagro* because they know that sooner or later Curro Romero will enter the *círculo* again like no one else and the animal will move under his hand like mercury. *Es un artista.*"

Curro Romero crosses diagonally through the dining room, slowly and proudly, with his heavy, hesitant grace, the mass of his testicles against his left thigh, his bullfighter's hat pulled down to his black eyebrows, his lips clenched in puerile vanity, as the patients observe him from head to toe, their chins in the aluminum plates, saliva dripping from the corners of their mouths like bulls after the second *tercio*, laden with the paper flowers of the *banderillas*, and he disappears behind them in the direction of the smell of piss from the urinals, from which comes the translucent glare, tinged by the sycamore leaves, of morning.

"Better than Curro Romero, *sólo Ordóñez*," explains the orderly. "Ordóñez's left hand was not of this world. Ordóñez embroidered with the *muleta*, doctor, embroidered passes like a tapestry: the arm moving, the feet steady, the body as slim as a vine, and what nobility, what *majestad*, what breeding, the serenity of death."

Ordóñez comes tumbling through the window like a flying flower, gilded and purple, whirling above the smoke from the lunch pails in evanescent spirals, rising to the ceiling, where he dissipates into the humidity stains of the plaster. His eyes, serious and heavy with shadow, still hover, alone, in the dining room, identical to a pair of fevered insects, and the patients seem to calm under their weight like vanquished foes, their beaks pointing to the floor before the motionless matador.

"Doctor," said the orderly, "*esto es* a pigsty of dying cattle."

"We're going to dynamize the asylum," declared the team leader, holding up a cardboard folder. "Open a day hospital, protected workshops, reactivate occupational therapy, increase psychotherapy and group sessions, create special departments for families, drug addicts, and alcoholics."

"*Esto es* a pigsty of dying cattle," said the orderly, pointing his finger at the dining room, the urinals, the decrepit buildings with the women under lock and key inside, the men stretched out in the sun smoking cigarettes made from newspapers.

"This is a pigsty of dying cattle," I added, "and we're the Curro Romeros of this piece of shit: the boss vowed that we were going to dynamize the asylum."

The orderly, aided by the custodian, began collecting the empty plates:

"Just try *boca* to *boca* with a dead person and see if it gets your ass anywhere. Dynamizing the asylum *significa* dying a different way. Instead of sucking on newspaper *cigarillos* they pass away making paper cones. Nobody wants the people who *están aquí*: they're worn-out *toros*, doctor, they're exhausted *toros*."

The waiter at the restaurant in Canal-Caveira deposited before me a gelatinous fragment of myself. The crazy people slowly abandoned the dining room, in single file, dragging their slippers on the wet cement of the floor. A guy in pajamas was crawling in the courtyard, barking. The orderly observed him pensively:

"In spite of everything, this is el único place that takes them. And, us, quién anywhere else will accept us?"

"We must de-dramatize mental illness," proclaimed the team leader, drawing arrows on a blackboard, "rationalize asylums, make them habitable, decent, even pleasant."

"How about planting flowerbeds around the cremation ovens?" I suggested. "The Nazis surrounded the gas chambers with gardens."

"You're always joking," asseverated the team leader, angrily pointing at me with a ballpoint pen. "Always joking."

The guy crawling around the courtyard suddenly began to writhe, shuddering, in an epileptic seizure, his legs and arms extended and retracted like metallic pistons, a rosy foam rising from his clenched teeth.

"You're mistaken," I replied.

The last interns, the last social workers, the last psychologists abandoned the empty casket. The corporal put the lid back, fitted it, took a strip of lead from his pocket and lit the blowtorch: a lilac-colored tulip spurted hissing from the iron nozzle. My daughter approached the coffin, rapped on the wood with her knuckles, listened attentively to the hollow sound in response, thought

"There's no one in there"

and moved away by herself through the restaurant toward the humid night of Sintra, which had drowned the final trees in anise mist.

"Yesterday afternoon I spent three hours in Carcavelos," said the psychoanalyst to the other doctors during the morning coffee break.

His heavy-lashed eyes looked around with feminine shyness, in a kind of compassionate and puerile abandon. He held the cup with the tips of his fingers as if the handle were a venomous grasshopper, and crossed his legs the way women do, in order to hide from us the improbable volume of his sex.

"I felt a desire to contact my mother and thus went to the beach, got undressed, and the waves were a great maternal breast that flooded me with milk."

"Bathing in the sea takes us back to the pregenital stage," added a guy dressed as if for some provincial ball, a rich clown whose enormous polka-dot tie resembled the hour hand of a wall clock paralyzed at six. His avian head moved in constant restlessness, famished, in search of an invisible saucer of birdseed.

"A milk full of tar," I suggested, "a shit-milk. Have you ever noticed the number of turds floating in the mother?"

And I thought:

"These guys are crazy, these guys are the ones who're really crazy."

"The conscious desire for oneness with the mother," continued the psychoanalyst, crossing and uncrossing his legs with an oily wriggle (There's nothing between his legs, I bet myself, nothing of anything, except maybe a safety pin holding up the flaps of his underwear), "signifies the non-neurotic resolution of the precocious, of primary narcissism. The mother becomes an object at once good and bad, loved in a healthy and critical fashion."

"The breast-penis disappears, the threatening nipple disappears," added the rich clown (I've always hated rich clowns, always detested the whiteface, the sequins, the coat-hanger shoulders, the accordion), "the omnipotent configuration of the all-powerful ghost, and the real woman emerges, sexual, to whom our patients, because of their inability to acknowledge their own genitalia, cannot relate."

"These guys are really crazy," I thought in the now-complete night on the highway to Alcácer, a night broad and hollow like an empty corridor in which the headlights revealed only the pale flesh-colored trees at the side of the road, reduced to profiles like faces on medals. The darkness had completely swallowed the fields and I glided shakily along a tunnel with faltering light. Through the open window the intense breath of the land ruffled my hair, as hot as the exhalation of fever, imbued with the minuscule drops of saliva from phosphorescent insects that smashed against the windshield, the colored butterflies of the Alentejo, silver, amianthus, sulfur, mercury emerged from the ground to precipitate toward the slightest brightness in a blind, disorderly plunge. From time to time I could make out the indistinct shape of a house (a wall, a roof, the eyeglass-arms of the shafts of a cart) spinning behind me like cutout targets at a fair. The steak at Canal-Caveira, resistant, vigorous, rose in my esophagus in its revenge of heartburn: When I get to Lisbon should I stop at a drugstore and get some Pepto-Bismol, one of those pills that taste like chalk and bird droppings intended to coat your stomach with nauseating newsprint? Do I wake up the clerk and negotiate sleepily over the counter, enveloped in the gentle complicitous aroma of the medicines, while the dark glasses of the display window watch me with spy-like suspicion? Or do I wait until I get home and look for my mother's pills in the straw bag dumped in a corner of the sofa, signaling its presence silently in the living room that we all deserted? Not the Carcavelos mother, with turds bobbing in the waves of the kidneys, but a concrete lady, small, serious, installed at the head of the table distributing the lunch-time salad.

"The problem of the threatening nipple persists forever," declared the psychoanalyst, asking the woman doctor on his left for a cigarette, a person of soft arched features from whom came only polar silence darkened now and then by an uneasy smile, as uncertain as the reflection of the cloud of an idea in her thick glacial interior. She sometimes says Good morning, he admitted, she says Good morning, but it could very well be some other person behind a screen speaking for her. The psychoanalyst flicked his cigarette lighter and brought it to his chicken's ass mouth in a precious gesture. He tugged desperately at his parted hair near the ear, with the intent of hiding an incipient but growing bald spot, and he emanated the same unmistakable sweetish odor of cologne and dead horse as the psychiatrists, an aroma both repugnant and mild, like that of a man buried with a vial of perfume in his pocket.

"The problem of the threatening nipple persists forever, yesterday in Carcavelos a strong wave almost dragged me under, and I immediately thought: I'm going to die drowned in maternal milk."

A female intern who resembled an insect moved about in distress, waving the skeletal antennae of her arms, and the psychoanalyst, turning to her, asked abruptly:

"What's disquieting about the orgasm?"

Of all the doctors, he thought with Alcácer in the distance, imprinted topsy-turvy against the belly of the river like the upside-down face, complete with eyes, of the queen of spades, surrounded by sparkles, scales, glitter, by unexpected nocturnal flames that the Sado river transported on its way to the sea (and therefore Alcácer is a town adrift, never anchored, eternally on the move like some enormous ship), of all the doctors I have known, psychoanalysts, a congregation of lay priests with bible, rites, and the faithful, constitute the most sinister, the most ridiculous, the most unwholesome of the species. While pill-psychiatrists are simple people, without detours, mere executioners reduced to the schematic guillotine of electroshock, the others come armed with a complex religion with couches for altars, a rigidly hierarchical religion with its cardinals, its bishops, its canons, its prematurely grave and aged seminarians, droning in the convents of institutes the clumsy Latin of apprentices. They divide people's worlds into two irreconcilable categories: the analyzed and the unanalyzed, which is to say Christians and the impious, and harbor for the latter the infinite aristocratic disdain reserved for the heathen, the as yet unbaptized and those who refuse baptism, lying on a bed to narrate to a silent prior their intimate and secret miseries, their shame, their fear, their sorrows. Nothing else exists for them in the universe beyond enormous mothers and fathers, colossal, almost cosmic, and a child reduced to anus, penis, and mouth who maintains with these two unbearable creatures a singular relationship from which are excluded spontaneity and joy. Social happenings are limited to the narrow surprises of the first six months of life, and psychoanalysts cling stubbornly to the outmoded Freudian microscope that allows them to observe one square centimeter of skin while the rest of the body, far removed from them, breathes, throbs, pulsates, shakes, protests, and moves.

"What's disquieting about the orgasm?"

The insect flicked her antennae back and forth like a distressed praying mantis holding in both hands the dying fly of a slice of cake. She had a rectangular lizard's face in which was concentrated an anguished stupidity beyond help, the submissive stupidity of dogs, the startled stupidity, filled with anxiety and amazement, of the soldiers when I would descend from the helicopter on the trail to pick up those wounded by mines and they would approach, unshaven and shouldering their weapons, their damp perplexity brushing against my nostrils. The black guides, squatting on the ground, resembled mural figures sketched on the brown-and-green panel of the trees, scratching the thick yellow toes of their feet with the paleness of their fingernails, or drawing random lines in the sand with pieces of wood. These bastards distrust us like the devil, I thought, our hearts don't beat with the same rhythm, we don't know what worries them, what interests them, what frightens them. We came with machine guns at the ready, we leave with machine guns at the ready, and we call them brothers while we screw their women on their mats and the guys wait outside, leaning against the stakes in the fields, hiding joints in their hands. We come out into the moonlight zipping up our pants and hear at the back of our necks

"Good evening, my soldier"

without anger or revolt, hear

"Good evening, my soldier"

and an oblique figure disappears into the darkness, startling the hens and dogs as we leave, tripping over roots like swimmers without fins, on our way to the barbed wire of the barracks.

"Orgasm in Carcavelos, submerged in mother's milk up to the neck, becomes less disturbing," I said. "You open your mouth to moan and a turd goes down your throat."

The psychoanalyst looked at me disdainfully (To this fool I'm hopelessly lost, I'm the epitome of the sinner beyond redemption) and accepted a slice of orange cake baked by the arched woman doctor, with all the pomp of someone receiving an Oscar:

"Adolescent phallicism, exhibitionism, unbridled competition with the father figure," he discoursed.

"Fear of castration," acknowledged the rich clown, raising one eyebrow heavy with make-up.

Alcácer drifted before me like a shipwrecked transatlantic liner, whose glare of lights in the September night, from streetlamps, from windows, from restaurants, from stores, took on the spectral tonality of a dead face inhabited from within by a hidden wick. A last bit of twilight, red, was still entangled in the crowns of the trees, awaiting the cold transparent lividity of morning, which confers on things the knitted, repulsive appearance of unwell cheeks: it's the time when gestures clink like milk bottles, and the hearty muscular whistle of ships brutally rousts us from bed toward an adventure already underway: dawn, in Alcácer, rises from the river like some great dripping beast, a large, green, shapeless dripping beast, and the town resembles a reef sub-

mersed in silence, wrapping the tentacles of its streets about itself in the manner of a dying octopus.

"Good evening, my soldier," said the black man, his breath
brushing against my shoulder. The woman lay stretched out inside, wrapped in the repugnance of my smell.

"Fear of castration," repeated the apprentice psychoanalysts, in
unison.

The hospital office became a kind of circus, a round circus arena
pitilessly illuminated by spotlights of various colors (a puddle of
pee from the trained dogs sparkled at my feet, empty trapezes
swung from side to side overhead, near the high cupola of the ceiling) and an immense audience of psychoanalysts dressed like rich
clowns gravely whispered their idiotic convictions. A distant or-
chestra played a noisy off-key *paso doble*, and I, with a float around
my waist, waited patiently for the consoling wave of maternal
milk through the animals' door, behind which seals groaned,
ponies with plumes on their backs neighed, the shy doves of magicians cooed.

"After finishing your analyses you'll see the world in a different
way," prophesied the lover of Carcavelos, flicking with his pinky
a cake crumb from his chin: in his gesture was something of the
compassionate and feminine abandon of my childhood, in which
elderly ladies drank tea and ate cookies under hats with veils, in a
tepid setting saturated with porcelain and place mats, in whose
shadow swung giant pendulums of grandfather clocks.

I began to cough and fidget in my chair until everyone turned
around in surprise and looked at me:

"After finishing analysis I'll stop seeing the eighth ward?" I asked.

The eighth men's ward of Miguel Bombarda Hospital, set away from the rest, near the garage, the workshops and the high dark wall going to Avenida Gomes Freire, near the anemic greens of the vegetable garden and the neglected bushes, is an odd building in the shape of a bullring, bearing the words Security Ward above an iron door. Inside are enclosed, in cubicles sealed with enormous latches, the patients that the police, the courts, the doctors consider dangerous, poor slow and obtuse creatures with fingers like fat smashed worms, shuffling about under a sky that falls on their heads like some gigantic cube of blue lead, with edges sharpened by the blind, empty, white eye of the sun. The doors open with large keys, misery is obvious, lamentable, tragic, the orderlies' offices uncomfortable and melancholy. There were patients who stayed there for thirty or forty years, who stayed there until they died, who died there in those abject and icy cubicles, which a rickety bed almost filled completely, coughing into their tattered sheets their humble condition as animals. An indefinable odor of rot and filth, the odor of the dead and of dogs put to flight, floated like a cloud over the muddy sea of faces.

"Yes, we have to put an end to it," the doctors replied solemnly, "better conditions have to be afforded these people."

And we forgot in the next moment our promises in order to continue discussing fine and ingenious theories imported from France, England, Italy, Germany, the United States, about Social Psychiatry, community interventions, protected workshops, halfway houses, and the sinister concentrative wonders that clinicians invent to prolong insanity, transforming them into acceptable massacres in the name of ludicrous, obscure, deeply flawed standards of health.

"Once analysis is over, the eighth ward will disappear?" I asked. "Will the disgraceful, repugnant, hateful scandal of the madhouse disappear and will I occupy myself exclusively, enchanted, with mother's milk in Carcavelos? Will I come to bathe from the generous breast in Carcavelos?"

"Good evening, soldier," the black man whispered to me. I was pissing against some reeds behind the huts (pissing after fucking is the best way of preventing venereal diseases) beneath an immense flock of unfamiliar stars encrusted in black velvet like tiny pointed diamonds. I could still feel her hands on my neck, my chest, a passive aroma, an obedient aroma of woman. Hair like wool and a mouth that constantly avoided mine, neither brusque nor aggressive, merely obstinate. A mouth that avoided and an inert body, legs spread on the mat, with the baby at her side moaning in its dream.

"What's disquieting about the orgasm?" inquired the psychoanalyst with the smile of the chosen, the smile of a bishop.

The patients in the eighth ward, for lack of women, secretly fucked the others in the ass, or masturbated in the dining room, their mouths open, manipulating with awkward wrists the sparse bulges from their flies. The orgasm rose like a wave, a wave of shit, and receded, leaving behind on the sands of the thighs a yellowish foam of sperm. I had my orgasms at home, after dinner and the nightclub, with Shirley Bassey singing softly in my ear the complicities of violins. I would have a smoke, lying on my back on the sheets, reaching out my hand for the Jim Beam without water that the mother, or the wife, or the children of a patient had offered days before, wrapped in tissue paper, in hopes of softening the question

"How is he, doctor?"

that they didn't dare ask because doctors are important people, people too important for them, they are their bosses, their foremen, their jailers, and it is necessary, it is convenient, it is imperative to achieve the good will of the masters at the cost of a vassal's apologetic submissiveness.

"Yes, we have to put an end to it," said the doctors, "these people must be given better conditions. They have to wait less time for consultations, be better dealt with, observed more attentively, with more care, the families listened to, treatment provided," declared the doctors and in the next moment forgot their promises, entertained in discussing the latest psychiatric novelty from Paris, London, Chicago, New York, and the latest theory, the latest medication intended to eliminate the disquietude of the orgasm. They ended at lunchtime, got into their cars, left, the cars would disappear at the corner of the building down below, and the next morning at ten or eleven park again under the sycamores (the shade of the leaves quivered on the hoods, ran along the hoods like the summer breeze) and the doctors, their heads oscillating like censers filled with shaving lotion, would direct themselves to the offices, scattering about them the Dior of science.

"Good evening, soldier," murmured the patients of the first, second, fifth, and sixth wards, sitting on the steps like the old people on thresholds in the villages, like the black men crouching on the grass waiting for them to leave their wives, for them to leave their houses so they could go to sleep, to stretch out their dark bodies in our sticky odor of invaders. I urinated leaning against a patch of reeds, slathered my penis with anti-venereal cream, and went back cross-country to the barbed wire, tripping over roots, stones, pieces of tree trunks, as if treading on the hard bellies of cadavers at every step.

Sometimes, near dawn, when I was beginning to drift into the dense delta of sleep like a rudderless ship, when my head would break free from me and rise vertically in the bedroom like a paper balloon wafted by an oblique stearin flame, when my limbs stretched out on the mattress with the gentle creeping of lizards, a voice suddenly booming, imperative, accusatory, the huge voice of a man waking somewhere else in the superimposed darkness of the asylum, would call me on the phone to come certify a death. To many doctors there is something comforting in death, something of validation, of recompense, of sweet victory in death: there are doctors who more than anything else study medicine to witness the death of others, not to treat them: they enjoy the wounds, the sores, the pustules, they enjoy the smooth thick smell of blood, enjoy the moans of distress of the dying, enjoy suffering and fever, but above all enjoy death's immobility, its dignified quietness, its taste of green apples, of gum, of paper flowers, and they hover over the moribund with the funereal cruelty of large birds in the field, which at twilight observe with cruel jubilation the homes of the sick, rowing their dark wings in lilac waters. They would call me on the phone to certify a death, my head would descend from the ceiling to my shoulders, my arms would reattach themselves to my thorax, I would gather up pieces of myself from the rug, on the bed, hidden under the newspaper, lost in the hollows inside of shoes, or rolled up in the tangle of my socks, and head for the hallway, to the deceased, running my fingers through my tousled hair.

There are doctors, Joanna, as cruel and tragic as dwarfs, as cripples, as hunchbacks, as musicians blowing trombones at the end of corteges, amid crying angels and ugly paper Christs. Cruel, tragic, and reserved, they fly with the remiges of their white smocks around the serum-balloon of the sun. Whenever someone is about to die, they gather, guided by some strange insect response, around a pale, emaciated patient, happily ordering x-rays, analyses, biopsies, ready to discuss what they euphemistically refer to as a *pretty* case: complicated cancers, bizarre leukemias, incurable infections, radiantly sniffing out an imminent corpse. I would go toward the hallway

"Good evening, our soldier"

running my fingers through my tousled hair or feeling with my hand the sandpaper beard on my cheeks, and the sycamores outside swelled in the moonlight like large melons of shadow, occasionally releasing clouds of pollen similar to silvered discharges. In profile the eighth ward looked like a fallen cake, next to the wall on Avenida Gomes Freire where the electric trolley plucked from the wires sudden blue sparks that dissolved against the fronts of buildings in dull flashes coating the skin of the tiles with unexpected wrinkles. In Mr. Carlos's workshop rang the eternal echo of daytime hammering, amid twisted metal and pieces of bidets. The river was a horizontal band of black glass buoyed by the motionless lights of boats, a lacquered plate squeezed between the outlines of houses. The custodian was waiting for me at the door, his eyelids greasy with sleep like toads in October.

"We gave him a shot but he died all of a sudden. His wife and son were here just yesterday."

"How is he, doctor?"

And the bottle of Jim Beam in a plastic bag in the humble attempt to not offend the boss, the foreman, the jailer, the owner, the bottle wrapped in tissue paper with small stars, the bottle in a plastic bag

"Please don't take it wrong if I offer you this"

which I drank naked, lying on my back in the muddled sheets, looking through the window at the enormous mass of the neighboring building under construction, whose cement would take on, before dawn, the milky spectral appearance of white wax. The custodian opened the door of the arena with an enormous key (the bolt creaked and protested its hemorrhoidal outrage) and led me into one of the narrow nauseating cubicles of the bullring of the Security Ward, where the orderly was waiting for me with a stethoscope in his pocket, also running his fingers through his tousled hair. A corpse was pointing its sharp nose at the ceiling, and its gray teeth reflected, like tiny mirrors, the filament of the light bulb. The teeth of the dead, he thought, change into small mosaic pieces embedded in the brick of the gums, into decayed stones, into dirty fragments of plaster: if we touch them with our fingers they break, fall apart, crumble into a kind of repugnant lump, the cheeks slowly start to pucker, the ears disappear into the interior of the head, the forehead sinks, the temples evaporate, and only the eyelids endure in the empty face, like two gelatinous purple flowers.

"Do you think he's maybe a little bit better, doctor?"

"It smells awful in here," I told the orderly, who was uncovering the chest of the cadaver so I could confirm the absence of heartbeat. We were in June and the grass around the garage whispered and laughed as if inhabited by a band of children.

"We all smell awful here," the other man replied. "One of these days my wife's going to stop sleeping beside me."

"Maybe that's why I sleep alone," he thought, looking at the dead man's prominent ribs, covered with a grayish down that his death throes had coagulated. He took the stethoscope from the orderly, plugged it into his ears, tested the diaphragm by scratching it with the nail of his index finger, and as soon as he applied it to the chest of the patient there came into memory the day October 13, 1972, in Marimba, in Baixa do Cassanje, Angola, when the officers dragged the three blacks to the medical station and forced them to lie on the ground, side by side, in the narrow space between the marquise and the wall. They were the three blacks who stole the clothes, the money, the personal effects of the lieutenant in the course of that long second year of the war, during which the rains destroyed the trails, cut off communications, opened deep trenches in the highways, falling ragingly in thick fuzzy streaks onto the saturated earth. Lightning flashed continuously in an acrid stench of sulfur. The new administrator observed through the window the lake of aluminum into which the football field had been transformed, and the place where the mango trees huddled the high muscular shoulders of their crowns, in which could be spotted the myopic pupils of bats. The three had been beaten for hours for stealing the clothes, the money, the personal effects of the lieutenant, punches, lashes, insults from the entire company, exhausted from many months of war, from the soldiers whose weapons had been taken away so they wouldn't kill one another in the barracks after the last beer, down there under a bamboo awning next to the cannon protected by an oilcloth. There was a shortage of money, of pants, of shirts, we were rotting away from parasites, malaria, stagnant water, fear, and the three blacks, with their features swollen beyond recognition from the beating, were to blame for the gunfire, the anguish, the injustice, the stupidity of the war, and so we began dropping onto their chests, their bellies, their thighs, burning cigarette butts, lit matches, glowing ashes that pleated their skin with translucent blisters that swelled and burst. Clouds accumulated to the north, far away, like the wall of some devastated village, a village of granite and basalt whose walls sometimes retreated unexpectedly, revealing the steps, the attics, the blue porches of the endless sky. I closed the medical post by force (all the men wanted to take part in the massacre, to avenge their anguish, their rage, their fear of the three blacks who were howling in panic and pain as they writhed on the floorboards).

"Shut up," we screamed as we kicked them, and I placed the stethoscope against the ribs of the dead man as years before I had stubbed out a cigarette in a terrified navel. The orderly and the custodian, standing in the rain in Marimba, watched the formality speaking quietly to each other: morning was emerging slowly in the tense worn veins of their faces, emerging in the wrinkles of their sleeplessness like the quivering melancholy happiness of alcohol, the row of rooftops was underlined by a hint of light, and the cold wind of dawn rustled the grass near the cannon by the garage, shook with its gaseous ghostly hands the shoulders of the sleeping patients, calling them from afar with the gravelly voice of fever.

"What's disquieting about the orgasm?"

I handed the apparatus back to the orderly while the custodian covered the dead man with a sheet as if covering a sleeping son with his own coat, in a sudden, unexpected, fragile and crystal moment of kindness:

"How is he, doctor?"

He's better, he's always better, they're all better here and your father is cured once and for all, in fact I've just come from verifying his cure, if you'd like to take a look, please, he's in there, yes, a bit too pale, excessively immobile, I grant that, but perfectly fine, no fright, no delirium, no agitation, no illness, I'm going to write it all down on paper in detail and give it to you in no time, and afterward all you have to do is contact your funeral home of choice, you don't even have to bother with the telephone because they show up, efficient, fast, reasonably priced, a bargain, you can pay in installments and sign the fine print, six, twelve, eighteen payments deducted automatically from your salary, you won't even notice it, one of the lieutenants pulled me by the arm, uneasy:

"Did you see the condition they're in? What do we do with them now?"

"Call a coffee planter to shoot them," I answered, shaking myself free.

The thunderclaps came toward us like grand pianos thumping down a staircase, the rain smashed violently against the tin, spat by a chestnut-colored mouth, flat, oblique, raveled in steam, where the mango trees buried like nails the thick cones of their branches. The rich clown tapped an American cigarette against his thumb and pointed his definitive index finger at me:

"Adolescent phallicism."

The psychoanalyst, absorbed, cleaned the crumbs from his fingers with a paper napkin. Through his thin graying hair could be seen his cue-ball colored scalp:

"Seriously exhibitionist personality factors. He can't understand that the relationship between individuals is purely mental."

"These idiots have gone berserk," I thought. "Now they're just fucking with their heads."

And they truly were fucking with their heads: they would gather in a group and whisper to one another about Freud, reducing hunger, hatred, cowardice, contentment, hope, to an empty game of words, to an obstacle course of disconnected phrases, to a kind of checkmate-in-three of the emotions. It was like this that I learned that whispering constitutes for them the only possible form of making love: the mouth in the ear sensually salivating the sputterings of Oedipus.

"Are you going to fill out the certificate in your office?" asked the orderly. The custodian closed the cell on the stretched-out form of the dead man.

"You can always ask the PIDE guys," suggested a fat officer who wore a paratrooper's camouflage uniform patched with tape and covered with insignias: those months of war had transformed us into people we weren't before, that we'd never been, into poor cornered animals filled with evil and terror. In the depths of our yellow eyes wailed a panicked childhood fear, a mute timid panic clouded by hesitation and shame.

"Get up, you bastards," I said. I thought We're screwed, when I saw the lesions on their bodies, the wounds, the swelling: your father is much better, madam: a milk bath in Carcavelos, a swig from the nipple and he'll be like new.

"His pulse suddenly disappeared under my finger," the orderly explained. "I did everything I could to find the vein."

"What's disquieting about the orgasm?"

Through the office window of the eighth it was dawning: the gray of the buildings, the grass, the parked cars, the workshop sheds, separated little by little into a sheath of ever brighter colors, more vivid, more pulsating. The cold and acid sun, edible, hovered like a fruit on the shelf of the rooftops, spreading around itself a tenuous chestnut-colored aroma. Sitting in the wooden chair in the office to fill out the death certificate, I felt my exhausted eyes aching like twin tumors of pus. A small cat vanished into the bushes. From the lit porch of the emergency room a form, numb, leaned out toward the street.

"How is he, doctor?"

Cause of death, the printed sheet of paper demanded. I wrote down Cardiac Arrest instead of writing he died from being here, died from being fed up with dying here. Take it easy, you have to make a living, I repeated to myself, and a government job is a government job, a guaranteed pension, the assurance of not having to beg in the square at the end of the afternoon, appealing to people's emotions through diplomas: Please help a psychiatrist in poverty. And them with their noses in suddenly interesting newspapers. It was dawning: the orderly put away the stethoscope in the drawer. The stains on his smock had increased in size. His beard was growing freely on his cheeks with the impetuosity of grass. Bags of dirty clothes were accumulating in a corner, soft like bellies swollen and empty at the same time. He smelled of medicine, disinfectant, and cold tobacco. A bubble of gas escaped from my mouth.

"It's going to be a hot day."

The first patients were beginning to awaken and peer outside their cells, drowsy, with the tame stupidity of cattle. Valentim, a former dancer, dressed as a girl, came past us, swinging his hips on his way outside. He served as woman for the others and would exhibit his withered buttocks behind the bushes, emitting sub-missive and pathetic little lamblike cries, observing with lollipop gluttony the penises that came out of the pajama flies at the pull of a string, like the pee-pees of toy friars in clay robes. He usually embroidered or crocheted in his cubicle stuffed with shawls, flasks of varnish, old high-heel shoes in which his too-large feet were deformed and twisted. A damp odor floated in the air like a curtain fluttering in the humid wind. Cardiac Arrest is a simple solution, free of problems: don't make waves, don't become a nuisance. And, after all, apparently it's true: the heart really did stop beating, so you don't even feel bad about yourself. The colors take on consistency, edges sharpen. The custodian, with a slow gesture of sleepiness, turned out the light in the office.

"Good morning," he said.

It's Saturday morning and it's going to rain, I thought. It's going to rain all day Saturday, monotonously, the smooth, un-changing silent rain of May, light and melancholy like the memory of my grandfather, whom I sometimes recall when I'm alone, rebuilding on the ceiling the fragile architecture of the past. It's Saturday morning, and a funnel of despairing hours awaits me.

"You should've been more careful," the PIDE agent offered am-icably, examining the blacks' ulcerated bodies. "There's ways of doing things without leaving marks."

He smiled at our naïveté, our inexperience: There's ways of doing things without leaving marks. Electroshock, for example, doesn't leave marks. An insulin-induced coma doesn't leave marks. Ten years of psychoanalysis doesn't leave marks: they're polite forms of killing people, decent acceptable forms. Not a single scar, and the cadavers go on talking, working, having children, definitively murdered but completely fine.

"Watch what you write," said a friend at the beach house, after lunch, looking at the sea through the picture window. "Sooner or later they'll descend on you, for revenge. You'll have a bunch of bastards after your scalp."

"Next time," suggested the PIDE, "give it to them on the soles of the feet. The effect's the same and nobody can tell."

The orderly took off his smock and got his coat from the hanger in the closet. His eyes, hollow from fatigue, lingered absently on the dusky tunnel of the rain:

"I'm getting out of here. The Carnaxide clinic."

"The place for rich crazies," I laughed. "It's only on the soles of the feet that it doesn't show. And a garden for the deceased to walk around in."

The psychoanalyst shook his head in consternation: all the works of Freud were rattling around in there, making the sound of rotten eggs.

"Neurotic aggressivity," he sighed.

"Adolescent phallicism," added the insect.

"Exhibitionism," completed the others in unison, their mouths full of orange cake.

Alcácer was approaching me along the bridge, lightly veiled by the heat of night as if seen through a sheet of cellophane that made the houses and lights shimmer. The battlements of the castle glided slowly down the hill toward the river, whose waters slipped by with the tepid pang of a varicose vein. I was beginning to make out the esplanades by the docks, the arches of cafés from whose windows diffused a brightness without brilliance. On a small boat a man was pumping a kerosene lamp: the flickering flame underlined his profile similar to a La Tour painting, a curved alert profile drawn in yellow against the slate of the river.

"Don't give it another thought," said the PIDE. "Who cares about the blacks?"

"The rain's not going to stop," advised the administrator, moving away from the window. "Not a single trail is passable."

In an hour I'll be home, I realized. When I returned to the doctor's room morning had broken out as completely as an open flower, a dun-colored flower over a dun-colored day. Workers were taking the breakfast coffee-with-milk to the patients' dining room. My shoulders were shaking from cold and lack of sleep, my head ached, a light buzz droned in my ears, the buzzing of weariness and fever: I must have caught a cold somewhere, my nose must be stopped up, my throat raw, my bronchial tubes obstructed. I dropped my clothes on a table and lay down in bed, first on one side then the other, then on my back, finally with my legs tucked up against my stomach like a fetus: I couldn't fall asleep. The arteries in my temples were beating like drums: it's the dead man in the eighth, I thought, I still haven't gotten used to dead people, to their unusual statue-like calm, to the way they rot, I still haven't gotten used to this misery, to this senseless cruelty, to Valentim with his little cries among the bushes, his withered ass in the air, to the patients' clay-friar pee-pees. Dawn was infiltrating through the metal slits of the blinds faltering beams of light that crossed the compartment obliquely like the bellows of headlights in the fog to imprint on the wall a pale staff of lines. As my body grew heavier, my neck sank further into the pillow, my feet ceased exploring restlessly for the cool spots in the sheets, something (my head, my ears, my nose, my gradually closing eyes) broke loose from me to roam by itself in the hospital, and I realized that I was no longer nude on the mattress but wearing a tie in the room where the analysts' meetings were normally held. Dozens of rich clowns and women who owned pet poodles were examining me reprovingly, uttering to one another astonished comments that I couldn't hear and from which I perceived only a vague whisper of indignation. Finally the guy in glasses who was presiding and whose lenses sparked with sharp authoritarian flashes, pointed forcefully at my genitals and roared

"Show it"

in a tremulous soprano fury. The poodle owners leaned forward to get a better look. The creatures in back eagerly stood up on their chairs. Near me the mother's-milk psychoanalyst whispered an indistinct secret to an elderly lady sitting in an armchair with the humble pomp of invalids, who quickly changed glasses, fumbling with shaky fingers through the trash of tissues and papers in her purse.

"Show it," the guy in glasses repeated, in gooselike indignation. He himself stood up in rapture, undid my zipper, and pulled from my underwear the dark cylinder of my penis, surrounded by a thicket of copper-colored hairs.

"As you can see for yourselves," he told the outraged audience, "it clearly goes against the first paragraph of the bylaws. I move for his immediate expulsion from the Society."

"Maybe he doesn't use it," suggested a fat young woman who refused to believe in such horrible betrayal. She resembled the moles in animated cartoons, and her enormous nose sniffed myopically at the air around her.

"That's not how it seems," said the old lady, as she scrutinized me closely. "He used it this afternoon: just smell it."

A little man in a goatee hastened to open the window so the repugnant odor could evaporate from the room. "Relationships are in the mind," he bellowed as he struggled with the latch, "there's a sign at the entrance that says Relationships Are in the Mind. I drew it myself with a T-square the other day."

"Either expel him or castrate him," the one in glasses said decisively.

"I move for both, to serve as an example for the future," howled a young woman who fidgeted incessantly in her seat.

"Clara, did you bring the cake knife?" the psychoanalyst asked his blank female colleague, who quickly handed him, wordlessly as always, a blade encrusted with sugar and crumbs.

"Step forward," the soprano ordered me brusquely. And to the old lady, as friendly as could be: "Care to do the honors?"

Two Freuds helped the octogenarian up from the depths of the soft armchair, where her body disappeared in a quicksand of print pillows. The deacon of adolescent phallicism took hold of my prepuce with two disgusted fingers. The mummy shook her tremulous knife-wielding arm in the air:

"Down with the penis," she bleated.

And in a single blow, to the support of a vengeful and enthusiastic clapping of hands, she relieved me of three useless ounces.

I turned on the lamp: my body twisted, greasy, into a sticky pasty sweat, as when a fever breaks and objects little by little reacquire their normal consistency and shape. They must have already taken the patient to the funeral home and informed the family:

"Just to let you know your father is cured."

I got out of bed, went into the bathroom and wrapped a towel around my thighs to stop the blood. Thick warm drops ran from my fingers

"Good evening, my soldier," murmured a breath in my ear.

And fallen over the wash basin I saw the three blacks from Marimba, smiling gently at me in the reverberation from the tiles.

9

I'm arriving home, he thought after passing Setúbal, recognizing the smell, the breathing of the countryside, the tumescent and damp tone of the air. Upon returning from the war he had spent some difficult years in small hospitals in towns on the southern bank of the Tagus, which the river's marshes putrefied, where he had seen the waters dragging dead seagulls whose eyes still flew, clear and sharp, in a sky filled with a network of fractures like a broken mirror. In Alcochete, in Coina, in Barreiro, in Montijo, thousands of birds' eyes floated above the trees, the houses, the dirty smoke of factories, brandishing their muddled wings in distressed spirals, next to bandstands surrounded by mulberry trees whose leaves are sixty-fourth notes stirred by the waltz of the wind. I'm arriving home, he thought, I'm smelling my land, I know that smell by heart, that breathing of the countryside, that tumescent and damp tone of the air, know by heart these nights spent on horseback on the witch's broom of a brandy bottle, hearing the garbage trucks in the streets that announce the coming of day, with lights that whirl on their roofs until an invisible wind blows them out. For months, because I needed to eat, I had worked in emergency rooms at the Misericórdia hospital in Montijo, and in the intervals between consultations watched television in the room of an old man who never moved, never spoke, no longer listened, panting into the sheets the arid cough of the dying: when the old man would shake in the pillows, like a mane, the long wisps of his white hair, I was afraid he would stand up and fall down, like a blind centaur, into the autoclaves and buckets of medications, knocking over in turn the beauty products with which sickness embellishes itself, compresses, tinctures, surgical clips, bandages, which confer on the sick the pathetic makeup of misfortune. I'm arriving home, I thought, remembering the gigantic, obese, frightening woman who took the x-rays of accident victims and called me into the darkroom, protected by a thick gray curtain, to show me the blurry result of her work. A red bulb lit the trays, provoking from the solutions vibrations pulsating like fish scales. I was bending over to observe the outline of a skull, a tibia, the fanlike bones of the hand similar to the rigid wiry crest of a crane, when she grabbed me from behind with her enormous arm (my ribs cracked, I could hardly breathe, my shoes lifted off the floor) and planted on the back of my neck a kiss capable of sucking me bodily down her endless esophagus. She must have swallowed dozens of doctors with those lips, in that room populated by scarlet scintillations, which crept up the walls, the ceiling, the metal cabinets, like unexpected worms, like insects, like rats, identical to the strange animals that people hallucinate with horrible and derisive menace. The gigantic woman advanced toward me smiling (she was missing several teeth in front), the floor shook, the shelves rattled, and I fled in vain from the kisses that were being thrust into my neck, the ring of spit from that stormy sucking. Whenever I go through Montijo, whenever anyone mentions Montijo to me, whenever on the highway I encounter a sign pointing to Montijo, there always comes to mind that monstrous creature from the darkroom devouring me in the red glare of the cement cocoon, softly whispering the ferocious endearments one uses to call dogs before killing them.

When I get out of this madhouse, I told myself, the beams of sunset shining in the distance with the exuberance of a local fair, and beyond them the stain of shadow sown by hundreds of sparks and the crackling transparent sky that lightly touches it like a burning leaf, like a piece of porcelain veined with minuscule wrinkles, like a gaze fogged with sleep or with happiness, when I leave the madhouse will I remember the inmates' Christmas party, in front of the office of the general orderlies, near the bar and their cakes sticky as dried-up breasts? Will I remember the faded paper garlands, the patients sitting on benches, the curtain that opened lopsided, to the insipid sound of the piano? The people declared

"Something has to be done"

so they were dancing on the stage, at the Christmas party, with the gramophone needle skipping in the grooves of the record and thrusting the couples against one another in a muddle of knees. The people declared

"Something has to be done"

and didn't realize that the only thing to do was to destroy the hospital, destroy the hospital physically, the leprous walls, the cloisters, the clubs, the vegetable garden, the sinister concentrative organization of madness, the ponderous and hideous bureaucratizing of anguish, and start over from the beginning, in another place, in another way, to combat the suffering, the anxiety, the depression, the mania.

I watched the party leaning against a stone column, the curtain about to open obliquely to the rhythm of the gramophone or the piano, and I thought about how happiness is so often sad, a sad, painful, false imitation of pleasure, and how, as a child, laughing eyes frightened me like the mechanical toys in shop windows, swaggering spasmodically behind the glass in jerky gestures of rage. I'm afraid of toys, I thought, I'm afraid of turning into a teddy bear clapping cymbals, into a crying wind-up clown, into an electric doll bumping its stubborn humming against the furniture, I'm afraid of the patient tenacity of things that neither scream nor bleed, that go ferociously about their futile task until a screw, a spring, a wheel in the motor goes bad: then, in the middle of a movement, a nod, a step, they become motionless and silent and stare at us fixedly with the disturbing, alarmed expression of the dead.

I watched the party at the hospital, seeing the rain fall on the arch at the end of the corridor, oblique and cold, the endless rain of December with its smell of attic, of underclothes, of old dentures, and thought that we, those who worked in the asylum, the doctors, the orderlies, the custodians, were starting to look like bears, like clowns, like broken dolls, that little by little we were, like them, taking on the desperate, empty appearance of superficial things, worn out by hundreds and hundreds of convulsions without cause.

"Mr. Valentim is going to recite a poem of his own authorship," declared a chubby young woman at the microphone, holding a piece of paper, while behind the curtain a stumbling change of scenery was noisily taking place.

What year will I be reciting on that stage poems of my own authorship? he wondered. There comes a time, there always comes a time, when without warning others start looking at us strangely, treating us with odd benevolence, taking a sudden interest in us, whispering tiny plots behind our backs, suggesting we see the doctor because we're tired (I'm not tired), because we perhaps need more sleep (I sleep as much as ever), because maybe a vacation (I don't want a vacation), because maybe a leave (I don't want a leave), you know I've always been your friend but you strike me as nervous, suspicious, irritable, different. The director of personnel reduces our work load. We're overloaded with staff, we can afford to redistribute assignments, you're going to be in charge of a new area, our colleagues speak to us with excessive friendliness, with excessive care, your family insists at dinner He's not a psychiatrist, a doctor for crazies, for loonies, he's a specialist in nervous exhaustion, he'll give you vitamins, you'll be fine, and you reply But I feel fine now, and they smile patiently, affectionately, with unexpected tenderness, Look, it's not really like that, you've lost weight, you're pale, you've become a bit more nervous, isn't that right João that he's just a tiny bit more nervous than usual, it's not at all important, some tonic is what you need, you've always recovered quick as a flash, you're a real lucky guy, and what does it cost to humor us a little, go there, it's nothing and it'll be over before you know it. And always the whispers, the plotting, the sideways glances, the little secrets. The doctor, as nice as can be, licks an envelope with a letter in it, There's nothing abnormal about you but with this life we lead sooner or later all of us need a rest, a week or two at most, just rest, treatments are out of the question, your head is fine, just take a look at yourself, your wife your husband your father your son will bring you here to this hospital I don't even know if it's called a hospital to call it a hospital you'd have to call hospitals the places where athletes go to train before competitions, there you have it, that's what you need, a time-out, a brief period of rest to revitalize, everything's explained in the note all you have to do is deliver it to my colleague and he'll set things up, just to be on the safe side I'm asking your relative to take care of the missive, relatives have to be useful for something don't you think, now keep it in your pocket and don't forget. His hands, very white, rest fraternally on our shoulders It's been a great pleasure meeting you. He smells of shaving cream and dead mare but we haven't yet distinguished that odor, the true profound meaning of the odor. His mouth opens and closes like a porgy Very glad to meet you, very glad to meet you. The woman at the desk in the outer office takes the money for the consultation with a lipstick smile as red as a compound fracture, her scarlet nails put the bills in the drawer the way workers in circus ticket booths do, the lace of her bra can be seen in the gap of her smock, the smooth flesh of her breast, clear, rounded, soft to the touch, the crossed legs that spill tenderly onto the chair. The athletic training facility in fact bears a resemblance to a prison, but perhaps it's only in appearance, there are luxury hotels like that to fool nouveau-riche suckers, we cross corridor after tiled corridor where our steps echo loudly as in an empty church in which the images have been replaced by posters assuring us that smoking is very harmful, the bell is rung in front of a glass door, there are two stretchers with women who writhe and scream, firemen, a policeman with a drunk gypsy, his clothes in tatters, protesting, guys in pajamas dragging their feet in the background. The colleague behind the secretary scribbles down appointments without looking at people, he reads the letter, calls the orderly Today is World Schizophrenia Day, go see if there's a bed for this one. Did they bring his pajamas, asks the orderly. Miraculously the pajamas appear, starched in a plastic bag, the pajamas, the toothbrush, toothpaste, slippers, it distresses me to see my slippers there in a strange place, an impression of spied-upon nakedness, of timid modesty, I'm ashamed of the slippers, I'm ashamed of the pajamas I don't want to stay here. Calm down, says the doctor with a gesture of his hand, calmness. Listen doctor it's been hell lately, whispers the husband or the wife or the father or the son, keep him here because we can't take any more at home. The gypsy starts to sing an *espagnolade* in the corridor, For God's sake shut that pest up, the doctor tells the orderly. One of the guys dragging his feet appears at the door and smiles Good evening everyone and Happy New Year, please have a seat, the doctor stops him. What a lousy night, he sighs, if I can function tomorrow it'll be a miracle. The orderly shows up with a syringe and in a short time the gypsy falls silent. A regular customer, explains the orderly. Why can't they stand me at home, I ask. Someone is about to say something but the doctor cuts him off with a gesture. There's no point in talking about it now, he says. Good evening everyone, repeats the other man. The custodian shoos him away. Doctor, please see us right away 'cause we have to get back to Beja, requests one of the firemen. I don't have four hands, replies the doctor, irritated, if it were up to me you wouldn't even have left there. Or to me either, adds the fireman. I want the slippers in my room, I shout, this isn't the place for my slippers. Does he have any valuables with him, asks the orderly. They take away my wallet, my money, my watch, my key ring. It's better if you give us your wedding ring, suggests the doctor, we can't be responsible for such items. The ring won't come off my finger. If it won't come off, leave it, says the custodian expeditiously. It'll come off, says the husband or the wife or the father or the son, do you have some soap? Who authorized them to bring my toothbrush? I ask, its place is in the bathroom in the chrome holder over the washbowl, you've been pulling the wool over my eyes for a long time, what the hell is this conspiracy against me, I have the right to know what's going on, give me back my slippers, who gave you permission to take them from my closet. The orderly grabs my arms from behind, Hey you, what's this, he asks, nobody's taken your slippers. Three needles to see if the guy calms down, says the doctor. We haven't slowed down since two o'clock, the custodian complains to the policeman about the gypsy who nods his head, now that ambulance I hear outside. The number of crazies in the city keeps on growing, at this rate we'll all end up nuts, philosophizes the policeman, who for a policeman has a sensible air about him, he doesn't seem like the usual policemen. All of you deceived me treacherously, I say, now I want you to explain what this shit is. Someone in the corridor begins to cry in the convulsive shrieks of a child. The man who drags his feet reappears. A drop of water, he requests. The orderly pulls me by the arm to a compartment with a high stretcher, with wheels, two glassed-in cabinets filled with vials of medicines, a metal box on top of a kerosene stove, a footstool. Lower your pants, he says using the syringe to suck the contents from a large number of vials, which he flicks, without missing a single one, into an enameled bucket, lower your pants asshole, while he takes a piece of cotton from a plastic container and wets it in a jug of alcohol. Are they vitamins, I ask full of hope, specialists don't lie, the thought comes into my mind of the woman with the red fingernails putting away the money in the drawer, I have the desire to lay my head on her soft pink breast, touch with my fingers the space between her thighs, breathe her thick perfume, her hair, the injection stings as if a wire had been shoved into my buttocks, a thin burning wire, into the muscle. Relax, it'll go easier for you, advises the orderly. Why are they doing this to me, I ask, what's going on for them to do this to me? You can pull up your little shorts now, says the orderly. I drag myself to the corridor with my left leg paralyzed, the gypsy has fallen asleep on a bench and is snoring with a whistling sound like lighthouses, the doctor is squatting beside the stretchers to parley with the women on them, This one stays, that one goes, there's too much light and I'm sleepy, the wire has become the center, the axis of my body. He's getting groggy, the orderly tells the custodian, get him to a bed before he passes out on us. They take me by the armpits to the room, it smells like a barracks, of unwashed skin, of vomit. My pajamas, I say, and my voice seems to float away from me, alien to my ears, a voice in which I don't recognize myself, a voice that doesn't belong to me, small, distant, ashamed. We'll talk about it tomorrow, says the custodian, unbuttoning my shirt. The guy with the dragging feet stretches out on the next mattress Good evening everyone, he says. Give me a hand 'cause this one's already out of it, requests the custodian of someone I can't see, and the words rattle around like stones in my head, Already out of it, already out of it, already out of it, the pillow is the tender body of the secretary, the red fingernails caress my back, I feel her belly against mine, the valves of her thighs opening to me, the custodian moves away, silently watching me, if I had my slippers with me my happiness would be complete, there are women who unfold themselves like sailing ships, whose hair unfurls, whose breasts undulate, women damp as shells, as conchs, I slowly disappear, return to the surface, dive, an ochre light enters on a slant through the window, dusty, cheerless, the light of rainfall, a vacuum cleaner drones somewhere or other, the gypsy sleeps with his teeth buried in the pillow, an awakened man stares silently at the ceiling, the absence of my wedding ring leaves a lighter mark on my finger, I don't know this bed, don't know this mattress, my back aches, I hear the rain on the pavement, the metallic gurgling of gutters, I try to get up and my body refuses, my muscles obey with painful slowness, the gypsy changes positions and goes on sleeping, the vials distort my vision because his dirty fingernails appear enormous, square, the size of windowpanes, I manage to slide off the mattress, drag my legs into the corridor, I feel the need to urinate and suddenly, as when I was small, my bladder drains into my pants, my damp groin makes me uncomfortable, the wet contact of clothing, nurses hurriedly pass by me, everything is happening so fast now, there's no fireman, no stretcher, no policeman, only people running this way and that with papers in their hands, somebody pushes me into a kind of dining hall with colored Formica tables, they pour coffee-with-milk into tin cups, women in chemises, their hair uncombed, eat wordlessly, with trembling gestures, their lips hesitant, a man in a white smock appears distributing pills, three, four, five pills to each one, Why doesn't someone from the family come get me out of here, take me home, bathe me, the gypsy drops the bread, rests his chin on the tabletop, goes to sleep again, on his feet are shoes larger than Grandma Duck's, his ankles are very thin, his pajamas torn.

"Mr. Valentim will recite a poem of his own authorship"

An orderly asks How many have we got here today. Half are for release, replies a short, fat, ill-tempered man, he cut a corner of his lip shaving and constantly touches the gash with a finger. From a barred porch I see the rain falling, the houses refracted like spoons in water, the mushroom of a glossy umbrella trots down a tree-lined street, the faded colors overlap,

"of his own authorship"

I sit on a sofa in front of a lifeless television, the antenna is an aluminum bush, the only trees that will soon populate the city, the country, the entire continent, the Amazon will be a virgin forest of antennas, an elderly guy installs himself on my left, loosens his pajamas, rests his hand on my knee. I like this program, he informs me, what comes at the end after the national anthem with the flag is what I like best. The imageless screen resembles the day outside, viscous and soft like the sweaty back of an animal. My wife wants to kill me, the elderly guy whispers in my ear, every time she starches my clothes she puts poison on the iron, all you have to do is smell the shirts to see what she's up to, he shakes his balding head in disillusionment, They're all bitches, they're all bitches. One of the unkempt women plops into a chair in front of us, her gaze as cold and unmoving as eyes of glass, her hairy legs give me shivers, her hairy arms, her mustache, a tendon or vein throbs in her neck. Look at her, whispers the old man, she's part of the gang too. The telephone starts ringing, intermittently, distressing and imperative. Didn't I tell you? the old man asks me triumphantly, following in his head reasoning that escaped me, the only solution is to turn off the refrigerator before going to bed. An orderly picks up the phone, Emergency room, he says and listens silently, trying with difficulty to clean a stain on his smock, As soon as I can, he says, wetting his thumb with his tongue and rubbing. Mr. Orderly, announces the elderly man, this woman wants to kill us. The sky looks like a milky brow, a uniformly milky brow. The orderly leaves without replying, He's going to take care of it, concludes the elderly man with great satisfaction. A custodian comes for me, not the same one as the night before. Go see the doctor, he says. I have a conspiracy to denounce, reveals the elderly man. You're going to have to put up with the conspiracy a while longer, the custodian replies, C'mere you, with the wet pants. The hairy woman suddenly opens her mouth, The guy pissed himself, she says and immediately returns to her vacant muteness. The guy pissed himself, the guy pissed himself, the guy pissed himself, protest my legs dragging along the tiles, the doctor is a different one too unless it's the same one with a fake gray beard and a pipe smoking Gama tobacco like a freighter. Which one is this, asks the doctor going through a series of index cards. Sit there, says a nurse. The family brought him in last night with a letter, very agitated, explains a voice behind me. I'm never agitated, I say, I'm the picture of calmness. The Gama lets out a complacent puff. So then, in your mind what happened? We're here by mistake, my slippers and me. Your slippers, the pipe says, surprised. Whenever I go to the bathroom barefoot at night I always catch a cold, I say, doesn't the same thing happen to you. What do you think, he asks me. I don't think I like you, I say, that tobacco gives off a smell of shit. The orderly quickly removes the glass ashtray from the top of the desk and places it on a cabinet, very far from me. Why is it you're angry, asks the doctor with foreboding gentleness. Because all of you are busting my balls and I see it, I complain, you're busting my balls with me watching and apologizing. I don't understand anything of what you're saying, groans the Gama, I still don't know what went on. Then we're even, I don't know either, I answer him, and can't you smoke some other brand of straw. The orderly who was on the telephone taps me on the back How did you get along at home with your family. At home with my family, I think, it was always the same thing, wake up go to work go to bed, wake up go to work go to bed, and on Sundays a drive to Cruz Quebrada, but instead of that I say None of your business, your business is to return my slippers to me and send me away from here as quickly as you can, I don't have to answer to anyone, to justify myself, to give explanations, to tell you how it is, I'm the picture of calmness, the picture of calmness in calmness, you bust my balls and tame as a dead sheep I don't protest, I don't accuse, I don't lodge complaints against anybody, all I want is to get out of here, open the door. Has he been given the medicine we specified, the Gama asks the orderly, the guy laughs at that dosage, better hit him with a couple more to see. A couple more what, I yell. Rain strong enough to fade colors has turned the day completely white like a ruined roll of photos where you can see the vague outline of houses or what you assume are the outline of houses, a complex of indistinct horizontal and vertical lines that fade away. Vitamins, man, the doctor says, vitamins to unbust your balls, to get you in shape, make you healthy as a pig. I'm not falling for the same thing twice, I say, you won't catch me napping. The orderly grabs me on one side, the custodian on the other, a second orderly who was arranging vials in a cabinet undoes my trousers. He stinks of piss, he says, he stinks of rotten piss. I feel the cold cotton on my buttocks and then the burning wire piercing my flesh, they take me to my room, undress me, lay me out on the bed and I begin to disappear slow-

"Recite a poem of"

ly from myself, to become diluted, to evaporate. I still moan for my slippers, if I want to pee during the night I'm sure to catch a cold, I'll sneeze all week at work

(There's a part of the bridge where you drive without making any noise and another part where the car's tires go trrrrrrrrrrrr, a kind of steel grid, Joanna, that you like to cross: we come from Caparica, covered with sand, dazzled from the sun, feel the vibration under our feet, in our entire bodies, in our heads, you see the river below through the little holes, deep blue and wrinkled like the enamel of the thermos bottle and the city before us, the docks, the squares, the cemeteries full of dark green flames, unmoving, the cypresses that make the sky duller and paler around us, more and more pale around us, more veiled, as if the shadow of a mystery inhabited it, and you think: It's terrific. No, seriously, precisely that, you see the city, the light of Alcântara, Amoreiras, and think: It's terrific)

and then I begin waking up again under the same rain, doubtless the same drops as yesterday and the day before, the same endlessly white morning, the same absence of color, I'm in an enormous room full of empty beds, the stucco on the ceiling is brown from tobacco and humidity, there's another room on one side and a hallway on the other, a guy in pajamas and holding a broom is sweeping up the trash in a whirl of dust, cigarette butts, pieces of paper, at the same time a young man sitting on the floor against the wall winches his body back and forth to the rhythm, I have an iron night table with an aluminum plate on it serving as ashtray, I push aside the bedclothes to rise, the sheets, the blanket, the broken-down mattress, and start to get up, my unyielding body refuses to move, doesn't obey me, I try to support myself on the rails, my hand slips, the floor suddenly rushes toward me, I must have hit it with my face but I don't feel the pain, something hot wets my nose, I try to get to my knees, crawl, a pair of shoes appears at the level of my eyes, You fell off the shelf for God's sake. I'm lifted up, set on the mattress, my head spins, whirls, ideas become confused, What's my name, what day is it, how old am I? I vaguely recall the specialist's secretary putting the money in the drawer, the fireman impatient to get back to Beja, the smell of Gama irritating my throat. The shoes have a white smock above them and my face is wiped with a cloth You smacked the floor with your face, friend. The wire they stuck into my buttocks continues to hurt, two filaments of acid that clutch my muscles, a conservative type in pajamas watches, smoking a newspaper cigar. The one in the smock tells him Bring me more compresses and the bottle of alcohol, and to me Lift your chin in the air like a seal. I want to go home, I say, I want to go home now, to take a bath, change clothes, brush my teeth, wait in the office for you to arrive reading Stefan Zweig, hear the noise of dishes in the kitchen, sniff the smell of food, bury my face in the sauna of the vegetable soup, feel like singing. A few more days in the suite and you'll be released, the smock promises. Why can't I go now, I ask, and I notice that my voice sounds sluggish and slurred, my tongue rolls around in my salivaless mouth, sticks to my cheeks, to my teeth, folds viscously over my gums. Hey point your chin at the ceiling, grumbles the smock

(Sometimes in childhood, for no reason, I would get nosebleeds in Mr. André's school. There was Mr. André, Miss Adelaide with her pockmarked face, her aunt who had raised her since she was a small girl, and a dog named Pirate. A house on Avenida Gomes Pereira, on the right side as you go uphill, with a yard in back with greens and vegetables, the Simões factory across the street, the second floor of the Frias house right next door. Frias's father was a barber on the Benfica highway and never smiled. I was feeling fine in the middle of class when my nose started to bleed. None of those small buildings from back then exist anymore, those small buildings with a garden and sunlight filtered through the sycamores, and under whose marquees women bent over to wash clothes in stone tubs. And there was the Benfica movie theater and the skating rink, Barata, Luís Lopes, Cruzeiro, Lisboa and Perdigão, the fat, enormous sewer rats, the map of the mountains, Mr. André plucking the hairs from his ears and the peacefulness of afternoon)

the young man sitting on the floor is asleep with his chin on his chest, the rain, unchanging, seems the only thing alive, real, around me. For some unknown reason I dwell in a made-up dream with real rain in it: the rain is going to fade my face, fade my eyes, fade my hair like everything here is faded, people, walls, sheets, words. So, how's it going, says a jovial voice behind me. A clap on the shoulder. I begin the difficult maneuver of turning around. That's what I call resting you've had more than enough sleep, the voice insists, we've brought you a little something to sweeten your mouth. I succeed in turning my body and there's my family standing by the bed, smiling, amiable, obliging, tender, How wonderful you look. I try to answer and the words won't come out, trapped on the roof of my mouth like toffee, Take me home. My brother says Didn't we tell you that you needed the rest, just take a look in the mirror and you'll see the difference. They all nod vigorously in agreement. We found a pound of French pears for you. They hold up like a trophy a plastic bag with fruit in it, the fruit appears to be leaking. In case the food's not all that great, you know. My sister-in-law says, I never thought the facilities could be so good. My brother claps me on the shoulder again. I'll be damned if I'm not jealous, a good-for-nothing like this in a five-star hotel. My father says Don't worry about your job they've sent a form there so they won't deduct a penny from your salary. When you're released, says my brother, you've got a bundle of money waiting for you without lifting a finger. I think: Somebody's missing. My sister-in-law reads my look Your wife couldn't come, she's got a sore throat, she sends a kiss and maybe she'll come tomorrow. Everybody sends their best, adds my brother. As far as I know she's never had a sore throat, what kind of fucking excuse is that, I shout, agitated, without making a sound, there's some kind of conspiracy going on that I don't understand, a threat, a plot, it's the way they've found to kill me, but kill me why, I don't have anything that matters, that would be of any use to them, old furniture, appliances out of warranty, no cash in the bank, what do they hope to gain at my expense, why did they make up the story that I'm upset, that I'm sick. We'll be back on Sunday, says my brother as he leaves. My stove has one more burner than his is that the reason, I ask myself staring suspiciously at his smile. We'll bring the kids to see you, promises my sister-in-law wearing a necklace I've never seen before, a necklace with large yellow rings and a silver clasp. Maybe they pawned my vacuum cleaner to pay for it: in addition, they all seem plumper, happier, jollier, they leave through the ward talking among themselves. I think: What are they putting together now, maybe the guy was right about the wife, this isn't a hospital it's an annihilation center, a slaughterhouse, people pay to be rid of us. I start to tremble with fear, panic, a black man stretches out in the bed to my left, his cheekbones swollen, a dressing on his forehead, his right hand wrapped in bandages.

Why do they torture people, I ask. The black man looks at me in silence, turns away his clouded, sad dark-gray eyes.

"Mr. Valentim is going to recite a poem of his own authorship."

The orderly comes to get me The doctor wants to talk to you. I don't want to see the doctor, I say, I don't want them to do to me what they did to him. I'm very weak, my body won't obey me, my unsteady limbs oscillate, I stumble into a dark damp corridor where there are people whispering softly as they lean against the wall. They must be witnesses against me, I think. My soles slip on the wet floor, the orderly opens a door painted green, we go in, this time it's a woman doctor leafing through papers behind a massive desk, at least they claim she's a doctor, an agent of the slaughterhouse directorate, a policeman in drag, through the half-open window it's always raining, the rain has finally diluted, like acid, the last remaining shape of things, the city has disappeared, no longer exists, isn't there, the orderly who isn't an orderly motions me to a chair, I sit down, the simple act of bending my knees has become difficult, slow, painful, my joints have been replaced by warped hinges, the doctor picks up a stethoscope and a pad of paper, asks me my age, marital status, the names of my parents. What medicine did they give me, I inquire. You were agitated and we were obliged to sedate you a bit, she says. I was the same as always, I say, and I still don't understand why I was brought here. Just another day or two and it's over, she says, you'll leave. I don't believe you, I say, they locked me up here to kill me. What a notion, she says, this is a hospital not a gas chamber. Gas chambers never look like gas chambers, I say, do you think I'm an idiot. I don't think you're an idiot, she says, you're disturbed: it would be good if we could discover the reason you're disturbed, don't you agree. I'm not disturbed, I say, I just want them to let me out of here. You find it difficult to talk to me, she says. I don't feel like talking to anyone as long as I'm in here, I say. The doctor scratches her head with her pen: her nails are almost as long as those of the woman who hid the money in the drawer. It's still difficult to establish a relationship with this patient, she tells the orderly. I'm not sick, I say. Yes you are, says the orderly, at home you made scenes with your family. Made scenes my ass, I say, I'm a peaceful guy, ask the neighbors, my co-workers, anybody. What kind of scenes, the doctor asks the orderly. Hitting, breaking things, I don't know what else, explains the orderly. How much are they paying you to spread these lies, I say. The doctor scratches her head with the pen again: He's still delirious, she says, we're going to have to wait a while longer. In any case the medication lays him pretty low, says the orderly, he slept forty-eight hours from a single syringe. Families don't detect these things at first, she says, and later it all blows up in our hands. And he's nothing but skin and bone, the orderly says, you could knock him over with a feather. Even so, says the doctor, he should be better. Maybe changing his chart, says the orderly, hit him with a different drug. More than anything I find him anxious, says the doctor. I'm not anxious, I say, I just want out of here. Has the family been here, asks the doctor, they come every day, says the orderly, no problem there. Good, says the doctor, now I'd like to see Martins.

The orderly opens the door, yells outside for Martins and a little man with a red nose enters greeting everyone effusively. Let Martins sit down, says the orderly. I see you're still drinking, Mr. Martins, the doctor complains, that way no treatment will do any good. Stand up, the orderly tells me, we're going back to beddy-bye. The people in the corridor come forward a step when they see us. Hold on a minute, says the orderly. One of them is an old woman with white hair, she has in her hand a parasol with a bone handle, an apologetic smile hovers before her lips like a halo. Sorry, sorry, says the old woman. The orderly helps me lie down, pulls the sheet over me, I stare at the ceiling, the large globes of dingy glass, the archipelago of stains in the stucco, my pupils wander like insects along the bright surface, from time to time a prisoner passes by dragging his feet along the floor, his wrinkled pajamas float on his body like a priest's vestments, a young man with hair down to his shoulders watches me. Hello, he says. I think: You must really smell bad. The guy approaches, stands there with his head almost touching the spherical light bulbs. Do you believe in God, he asks. I believe in gluttons, I answer. Maybe they grabbed you in bad faith too, he says, they swore to me it was for detox from the drugs. I notice that his mouth is older than the rest of his face, wiser, I notice the acne scars on his cheeks, in the poorly sown beard, still sprouting, in the furious pensive docility of his gestures, the odor of putrefaction that envelops him like a veil. You're perishing in life, I think, you look like a dying hare. He offers me a cigarette. It's probably poisoned, I presume, I'll bet you're part of the gang. The youth looks like an ugly Christ, a brooding and sick Christ: in twenty years the world will be inhabited by that sad race, by that gaunt, humble, wounded race. Can I sit down, he asks. He smokes in silence at my feet and forces phlegm from his throat, and stamps it on the floor. I upholster cars, he says, they want to release me but I'm not up for it: you can always score a pill here and there, they're sold out there outside Camões: the trick is for a guy to get permission to leave and the rest is pure profit: no putting up with a boss, free room and board, if you're out for a trial week they save your bed, they save your place, you scam the doctor. He heaves up a powerful ball of phlegm, twirls it from one cheek to the other, shoots it onto the black man from a distance. Wear this! he shouts. I want to get out of here, I think, I want to get out of here as fast as possible. Then a guy in pajamas starts to fly, arms spread, very close to the iron headboards, screaming in imitation of the sound of a propeller, followed by four or five decrepit creatures who bump randomly into the wall like blind quail, knocking over tables, buzzing their wasp-like impatience against the window frames. I haven't worked in two years, the hawking youth says very rapidly, and in his expression appears childlike embarrassment, an unexpected shyness and shamefacedness. The flying man disappears with a jolt through the open window. The rain's going to melt him, I think, the way quicklime does the bones of corpses, only the spitting guy and I still resist, my family melted away, the house I haven't finished paying for melted away, the appliances for which I still owe installments melted away, the mortgaged car melted away, the office melted away, the Sunday morning football games with friends melted away, Christmas

"Mr. Valentim is going to recite a poem of his own authorship"

Easter and the seasons of the year melted away, everything melted away, what good does it do to leave if I have nowhere to go, if outside this room the rain falls monotonously, endlessly on a monotonous gray plain populated with ruins. After all, I always accept a cigarette, I say. The youth searches for the pack in his pockets while he loudly readies another expectoration

"Mr. Valentim is going to recite a poem of his own authorship" and finally extracts the burnt butt of a piece of silvery paper. This is one of the good ones, I swiped it just a while ago from a doctor. Where's the bathroom, I say. Baths are on Friday, he informs me in the solemn tone of a hotel manager. It's just to urinate, I say. The urinals are there to the left, he says, just follow the smell. My car must surely be a small stain of water under the water, I think, my house a little pile of gray stones in the gray morning, my family a group of indistinct forms like the portraits of grandparents. I slowly slip to the floor and trip dragging my legs, clutching the bedrails, in the direction of the urinals

"Mr. Valentim is going to recite a poem of his own authorship" the *piano* of rain in the gutters becomes more of a *forte*, more insistent, higher, crueler, identical to a dozen drums hammering in unison their sour rage: soon the rain will destroy the roof of the ward and dump on the beds its weight of pebbles, its weight of bullets, the ceiling is already starting to bulge, oscillate, it's going to collapse, the bathroom is a complex of dividers with a door at the far end for the toilet and a Paleolithic flushing device overhead, the wind has broken one of the window frames and water spilled onto the tiles like some spreading skin disease

"Mr. Valentim is going to recite a poem of his own authorship" we brought you these French pears, these smiles, these claps on the shoulder, this hypocritical tenderness, I slip along the wall until my buttocks squash against the tiles, the rain falls onto my neck, the nape of my neck, my shoulder blades, I can feel it running down the hollow of my back, sliding down my sides, my groin, spreading out onto my thighs, my hand touches a triangular piece of the window glass

"Mr. Valentim is going to recite a poem of his own authorship" I lift it to eye level and observe through it the beds, the round lamp, the black man lying in his bed, observe the distorted world, the white world, the dead world of the slaughterhouse, the dead white world of the slaughterhouse, the youth with long hair who settles down beside me in the rain, without speaking, and whose aged mouth looks like a pale sealed scar, a fold of flesh, I observe through the glass my own melted face, without substance, the diffuse almost nonexistent features of my face, my eyes, the thick curve of my nose, the young man with long hair will also disappear little by little, his feet, for example, evaporate and now it's the ankles, the legs, the knees that slowly dissolve, the water will carry the ruined testicles far away, the navel vanishes, the bulge of his belly disintegrates, its softened contents spatter on the floor,

"Mr. Valentim is going to recite a poem of his own authorship" the very eyes with which he stares at me take on the dull and wrinkled tone of plaster, I rest the piece of glass lightly against my wrist, the prominent tender tendons and veins of my wrist

"Mr. Valentim is going to recite a poem of his own authorship" I feel his arm against mine, his shoulder against mine, family doesn't exist, job doesn't exist, house doesn't exist. Help me, I say, pointing to the glass with my chin, help me, I can't do it by my- self.

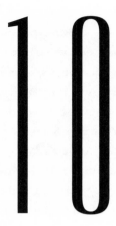

"Why do people kill themselves?" asked the second lieutenant.

We were in the barracks in Mangando, in the shabby barracks in Mangando on the Congo border: a few more kilometers and you could see, across the river, the MPLA camp on the other side, further down, the buildings that distance rendered minute, one or another microscopic van whose fenders gleamed in the sun, painfully climbing the rounded crest of a hillock. Mangando is a small unimportant settlement, so unimportant that no map, no chart mentions it, composed of miserable native dwellings, a row of ragged bald palm trees, the house where the commandant hid his black lover (no one ever saw her), and the barbed-wire fence around the troops' wooden shacks, where a half-naked platoon, trembling from malaria, was rotting away. It was five A.M. and the suicide had just died after a drawn-out series of convulsions before our terror-stricken eyes. Soon the troops' limping, skinny dogs would start barking restlessly in the courtyard, announcing the turbid glare of the humid mist, in which the sun rose dampened by the juice of the fog like a crushed orange. The glass in the jeeps was covered with a film of tears, the trees were wrapped in steamy cellophane, bright and mysterious like the pupils of sick people who stare up at us from their pillows with the cruel humility of children. The suicide had just died and lay, covered in a sheet, in a nearby cubicle, among empty beer crates and boxes of canned preserves that retained, if we smelled them, a strange, thick, concentrated aroma of the sea. They were cans of sardines and anchovies, cans of tuna and mackerel, and the odor surrounded the dead man the way water does the wooden bodies of the drowned, who little by little assume the tortured porous texture of roots. We could feel his presence like a gaze embedded in our backs, a transparent gaze full of indifference and rancor, a gaze of heedless and calm hatred, the gaze of an enemy who loathes and disdains us and toward whom the lamp turned the solitary petal of its flame with the agitation of a tongue in search of a missing tooth.

"Why do people kill themselves?" asked the second lieutenant.

We were in the barracks in Mangando, sitting at the table, the lieutenant, the quartermaster medic and I, a bottle of beer in my hand, and our faces translated in each wrinkle, each feature, each crease around eyebrows or mouth, months upon months of perplexity and suffering. A cloud of mosquitoes, indistinguishable from a rain of silvery sequins, swarmed furiously around the light, from time to time smashing themselves against the burning grill with a tiny, frying, crackling sound. A few plates and glasses were piled on a shelf. The vehicles outside were acquiring the phantasmagoric shape of dreams, and the shadow of the palms, of the commandant's house, the surrounding jungle, possessed the limitless depth of sorrow. The gaze of the suicide, full of indifference and rancor, pierced the partition of the wall and descended on us like the soft, oblique, alert footsteps of a cat.

Maybe we'd had too much to drink (there were several empty bottles within reach), maybe the prolonged dying agony of the soldier and the tragic accompanying death-rattle and vomiting awoke in us the secret feverish anguish that we concealed every day, maybe so many months of war had transformed us into indecisive, useless creatures, into pitiful drunkards waiting for the paleness of dawn, to later wait for afternoon and night in the same disinterested surrender. The lieutenant was naked from the waist up, in shorts and espadrilles, and his fat breasts, yellow and pendulous, reminded us of those old women that at the end of his life Goya drew with passionate and furious repugnance. The quartermaster medic and I had arrived at sunset, in the jeep belonging to the PIDE (the intelligence officer who had driven us and was now snoring in a corner, his mouth agape), and our memory still held the image of owls perching immobile in the pass, staring at the headlights with the gigantic red coals of their eyes. A greasy smell of kerosene and cold food hovered in the room.

"Why do people kill themselves?" asked the lieutenant, a mustache of beer foam whitening his lip.

"Caged animals," I said, "often prefer to die and we're nothing more than caged animals: they'll never let us out of here. In Luanda they're afraid we'll get out: how would those guys, who dress well, eat well, and sleep well, face us? We're their remorse."

"Suppose," said the quartermaster medic, "that we went into general headquarters with the coffins on our backs: the majors and colonels would go nuts, screaming in terror and jingling their shiny medals."

"There's no danger of us getting into general headquarters," sighed the lieutenant, glancing out of the corner of his eye at the PIDE sleeping in the corner. "We stay at the entrance, berets in hand like beggars."

"People kill themselves because we're the beggars of this war," I said. "Even those who are already dead kill themselves."

The lieutenant got up (the chair fell backwards and the PIDE stirred in his sleep), took an oval mirror from the nail on the wall, one of those small cheap mirrors with a metal frame, and scrutinized himself, running his disillusioned hand over his soft cheeks:

"I'm already dead," he said. "I died at Mussuma, in the east, when I put my finger to my head and fired. You can't imagine the noise a finger makes when it fires."

I was familiar with Mussuma, six miles from Zambia. I had been there often, in a small plane, taking fresh food and medicine to a ragged group of men, armed with rifles and stuck in a hole like rats. From a distance, the tin roofs shone in the sun. It didn't have eucalyptus trees like Cessa or Ninda, or the limitless horizon of clearings, red and blue, in Chiúme: it was a grave the size of an inert body, a weary body. You went in through the barbed wire and your mouth filled with dirt like the dead, who feed on themselves in the mahogany silence of coffins.

"In any case," said the quartermaster medic, "for that guy over there it's the second time he died. I didn't know dead people killed themselves."

"The dead like to die," I said, "they like feeling the desperate fright of agony again."

"We dead people are very strange," declared the lieutenant, hanging the mirror back on its nail. "One of these days I'm going to raise my finger to my temple again and fire."

And he added quietly as he groped for a bottle beneath the table:

"It's the same as using a rifle."

The first skinny, limping dog stuck its snout into the open door and lightly breathed in the dark rust-colored smoke of the kerosene: its wide humble head stared at us with an expression of dolorous piety, of commiserative and melancholy understanding. The shacks became clearer, more defined, the vehicles in the dirt courtyard little by little lost their odd density, a damp and sticky fog, a kitchen fog, clung to the sweaty skin of our necks. The palm trees leaned their haunches toward the east like great surprising sunflowers.

"People kill themselves because they've had enough," said the quartermaster medic, opening a bottle cap with his teeth. "Enough of not understanding why they die."

He was an excellent medic and we got along well: normally we would work without talking because we each understood what the other wanted, what the other needed, whether dealing with the wounded, the child-bearing, or the ill. Before the war he sold insurance, but he had the gentle and agile hands, infinitely delicate, of a surgeon. Objects vibrated in his fingers as if in them beat a tiny, hidden, anxious heart.

"We've had enough of being dead," proclaimed the lieutenant, making with his tongue the sound of a pistol being loaded and raising it slowly to the level of his neck.

"Bang," he said, smiling.

I extinguished the lamp. A murky light like dirty water penetrated the space obliquely, revealing to us our wrinkled, exhausted faces, knotted with folds, prominent veins, small creases: none of us had reached thirty and yet we looked like ancient beings, of unknown age, worn down by interminable and terrible days.

"Bang," said the quartermaster medic, imitating his gesture.

"Bang," I said, pointing my thumb at my left ear, the one that from time to time they operated on to remove from the lobe cysts as round and white as the eggs of insects.

"Bang to him," said the lieutenant, pointing his chin toward the sleeping PIDE.

"Bang," we repeated, looking at the little man contorted in the uncomfortable wooden chair, revolver at his waist, blowing through his open mouth the unprotected rosy whistle of small children.

Without meaning to, I raised my head and looked into the mirror: it reflected the ailing morning, the miserable morning, the dun-colored morning of Mangando, the veil of the dank mist becoming entangled in the trees like a web of water. It reflected the huts of the native quarter from whose interior, one by one, emerged tiny African hens, scrawny and long-legged, whose feet hesitate a moment before touching the ground, as if threatened by some kind of danger. It also reflected the suicide laid out in the next compartment, among the boxes of sardine cans that emanated the violent acid perfume of the sea, the sea motionless above the palm trees, suspended over our heads like the flat sheet of water of autumn, without ebbs or flows, gliding in the sky like a cloud of milk. A soldier had rested his weapon against a bench to wash in a pail of water, and three, four, five, six ravenous dogs, six old, lame dogs, sitting on their hind legs, followed his slightest movement in humble wonder. The cold tangerine of colored paper, the sun, would not succeed in breaking through the dull plaster of the mist.

"I don't feel right with that PIDE here," said the lieutenant, standing up. The shadow of a beard darkened his face, hollowing the cheeks and stretching his yellowish skin over the bones. I noticed that lack of sleep had thickened his eyelids like round tumors, with the bluish lump of his pupils inside. On the unmowed airstrip, the red and white windsock hung limply on its pole. The lieutenant slapped his thigh with his leather swagger stick:

"No one's yet explained to me why people kill themselves," he protested. Now the soldier was drying himself with a lilac-colored towel, which he ran over his arms as if shining his stiff armpits. On his head was the camouflage beret, its bill almost touching his nose, and I thought suddenly, seeing the hoops of his ribs covered by knots of muscle that lengthened and thickened with the movement of his shoulders, We're drunk. I thought, We're drunk as hell after three straight hours of beer under the smoky light of the lamp, which from time to time spat small irritated blazes of kerosene.

I thought, We're drunk, and the Mangando morning spread its anemic damp vapor in the courtyard, in the trees, in the lopsided wooden barracks. It was no light, happy binge, gaseous like the weightless wind of August in the pines: there was something melancholy, unpleasant, dense, to which the closeness of the dead soldier lent the acidic, repugnant taste of vomit, something agitated, restive, profoundly terrifying. I thought that the only thing left us in the war was the wait for death and beer, sitting at the table with the sleeping PIDE, pistol at his waist, snoring in the corner, while the bonelike clarity of morning penetrated obliquely through the open door. The lieutenant took some steps into the courtyard, scaring away the dogs. His shoulders, covered with boils, shook:

"Anybody else want to commit suicide?" he shouted in the direction of the barracks, the ammunition depot, the mess hall, the storeroom, the tangled bushes in the forest. "Anybody else want to commit suicide?" he repeated to us, the intruders from Marimba, an empty bottle in his hand like the drunks in cartoons, arriving at twilight with our useless art. The dwellers in the native huts carefully approached the wire, intrigued. The quartermaster medic tried to grab him by the elbow:

"Lieutenant."

The lieutenant shook off the arm with such force that he almost tumbled to the ground:

"Lieutenant my ass."

And shouting into the foggy silence of morning, which the misty silhouettes of soldiers little by little peopled with indistinct greenish blots with neither limbs nor heads, identical to the mossy stains on the moon:

"Whoever wants to be the next suicide, step forward."

In the commandant's house, a secret shadow watched from behind the curtains, as the changing of the guard proceeded slowly.

"Lieutenant," warned the quartermaster medic, "you'll wake up the PIDE."

With some difficulty the lieutenant straightened up and directed at him the most regal and profound look of disdain:

"The PIDE can go fuck himself."

And beating his flattened hands indignantly against his chest: "That dead man belongs to me."

There's no arguing with a drunk, I thought, when you're drunk yourself, when your legs give out from under you, your body fights itself looking for the balance to remain upright, your head drifts in a kind of cloud like an out-of-control balloon. I pushed a door, went inside, sat down on a crate: an unbearable smell of fish and ocean hovered in the compartment, and as my eyes became accustomed to the half-shadow I saw that I was almost leaning against the dead man (the sheet covering him brushed against my hand) among crates of empty beer bottles and cans of preserves. The voice of the lieutenant howled in the yard

"Whoever wants to be the next suicide, step forward"

but I was beginning to feel very far from there, far away from Mangando, from Angola, from the war, very tired of the morning that pierced my skin with its thousand sharp needles of mist, tired of the dead and the living and especially tired of myself, of my sleeplessness, my anguish, my indignant and bitter expectation. I leaned my head back against the wall and closed my eyes: colored disks whirled before my nose, my brain was spinning like a wheel inside my skull. There was still a little beer in the bottle: I offered it to the soldier laid out at my feet, but since he said nothing, I drank it in one gulp.

I entered Lisbon coming from the Algarve, and my body ached

like that dawn in Mangando, filled with rage and acrimony. I ought to go to Praia das Maçãs to get my books, my clothes, my papers, and return the next day to the hospital and my job as jailer, monotonous and useless. The city's hundreds of street lights, folding and unfolding before me in capricious spirals, unnerved me. People moved about on the esplanades, talking with the vehement gestures of deaf-mutes. The illuminated store windows approached me with their enormous mouths, neon spilled onto the walkway in volatile blotches of mercury. Sometimes, at a corner, a somber street would menace me like the hollow black opening of a well. The luminous signs of pedestrian passageways (little scarlet and green men in small metal frames) declared

"Whoever wants to be the next suicide, step forward"

in the minutely clear voice of telephone interlocutors. I stopped the car in front of the bar where from time to time, in the breaks from writing, I would sip on vodka as I pensively chewed on a phase, an idea, the alteration of a chapter, I rang the bell and waited.

It must have been midnight or one o'clock but the smoke hanging over the tables or next to the ceiling resembled the viscous haze of the humid dawn mist, which clings to objects, to gestures, to facial features, like opaque liquid glue. The bottles on the shelves behind the counter, identical to the dim trees unfocused by the fog, trickled the slow resin of whiskey down the damp walls. Voices assumed the sharp, dilacerating tonality of early morning, slashing my ears like tiny cruel knives. Faces os-cillated like fat anemic moons imprisoned by the branch of an oak. I groped for a bench: my fingers unwittingly touched the edge of a table, and for an instant I thought I was being sought out by the smell of fish and sea.

"Doctor sir," came a murmur from my left.

The dead soldier was smiling at me. He was holding a glass of beer and smiling at me: whenever he tilted his head back to drink, the round bullet hole appeared next to his Adam's apple, ringed by crystallized scales of blood. He had gotten a bit thin-ner in the last nine years, a few white hairs fell over his ears. But he smiled. Installed in front of him, pistol at his waist, the PIDE went on sleeping.

"We're all here," informed the soldier. And in fact the unclear silhouettes at the bar were little by little taking on the shape, the form, the way of walking or the tics of the men in the Mangando platoon, speaking softly in the artificial morning of light bulbs whose lamps lent them a tint of apparitions. The quartermaster medic was distributing anti-malaria medicine surrounded by the limping skinny dogs from the barracks, the troops' humble old dogs, squatting on their hind legs, with the sluggish spittle of hunger dripping from their lips.

"Doctor sir doctor sir," they said, smiling.

The smell of the sea, the smell of canned tuna and sardines, ad-vanced and withdrew from me rhythmically like the breathing of an abandoned body. It was a toy sea contained in the yellow-green oil in the cans, a sea without waves, without gulls, without boats, reduced to the salty sweetness of the perfume that escaped from the crates like the echo of the wind in the concentric ears of conch shells.

"Why do people kill themselves?" the lieutenant suddenly asked me.

Leaning his naked trunk toward me, he shook his empty beer under my nose. He too had aged: large parentheses of creases split his soft cheeks, his navel fell over his shorts like a wilted apron of fat. Only the eyes remained red and sharp like before, the frightened pupils of a man agonizing without knowing why.

"You never did explain to me why people kill themselves," he insisted, poking me in the chest with his leather swagger stick.

To make it to Praia das Maçãs would just take a moment, I thought, stick the key in the door and find myself dead in the living room, my wrists slashed, like the guy who committed suicide using a piece of glass in the bathroom of the ward, while downstairs everyone was attending the asylum's Christmas party: the blood, diluted by the rain coming in through the window, was advancing on the floor like some kind of snake seeking its path through the spaces between the boards. A young man was smoking peacefully, in silence, beside the deceased, not looking at us, as if he hated us, a hatred composed of indifference and disgust.

"That guy has contempt for us," said the orderly. At the door to the urinals our shoes bathed in a rose-colored puddle that was growing, we stared stupefied at the cadaver with its head tilted, as if in a religious image, toward the drenched shoulder of the other man.

"All the guys have contempt for us," I said. "Every guy here has more than enough reason to hold us in contempt."

"What good does it do for you to be a doctor?" bellowed the lieutenant, swaying lightly on his unsteady legs. The swagger stick brushed my chest with a rough caress of leather. "What good does it do for you to be a doctor if you don't understand the first thing about us?"

"He didn't want to stay here," explained the orderly. "He didn't want to stay here for all the money in the world. Every time he reared his head we had to stick another needle in him."

"If it was because of that," I replied, "he's gone so far away that nobody can keep him here."

The young man who was smoking put his arm around the other man's shoulders. Then he gathered phlegm in his mouth and spat with all his might onto the floor tiles, in the direction of our legs: the blood immediately began to dissolve the darkened amoeba of saliva.

"Doctor sir doctor sir," exclaimed the soldiers of Mangando, smiling. The morning brightness seemed to increase in intensity, the row of palm trees could be made out in back, sharply defined against the coffee-and-cream color of the mist, the huts resembled strange adobe nipples, nipples of straw and earth grouped around the chieftain's light-colored dwelling. From the chimney of the commandant rose the white smoke of a papal election. The PIDE appeared in the yard, stretching:

"Shitty weather," he said.

He was a man of indeterminate age like all executioners, like doctors, psychologists, the social workers at the hospital, those who suicide their prisoners with shards of glass, with pieces of rope, those who help them hurtle, floundering, from the highest windows of the asylum. The rain fell violently on the two stretched-out corpses. The odor of the sea, a sea without waves, without gulls, without boats, rose from the soaked pajamas.

"Let's get them out of here," I suggested to the orderly.

From time to time the wind brought us fragments of music and voices at a party, distorted by the bucket-echo of the microphones and the anger of the rain. The sycamores bent in the courtyard, stripped of leaves like bald skulls. The buildings in Lisbon were reduced to the empty geometry of their outlines like uninhabited carnival masks and seemed to move away from us, slowly, along the hard skeletal rivers of the deserted avenues. The lieutenant beat his chest with the defiant pride of a turkey:

"The next one to kill himself, raise your hand."

The orderly lifted the corpse by the armpits, I grabbed its thighs. The fabric of the pajamas came apart in our hands in sopping clumps. The young man's cigarette had gone out and he tossed it away, silently, as if he hadn't seen us, as if we didn't actually exist, as if we were completely alien, transparent: his disdain pained me like an infected wound, like the cruel confirmation of my job as guard, vigilante, policeman. I wanted to talk to the soldiers, respond to their smiles, their words, I opened my mouth and the sleepy voice of the PIDE came out, stretching, from my throat:

"Shitty weather."

"Shitty weather," I told the orderly.

We lifted the dead man and transported him to an empty bed, a bed that could be concealed behind the steel-and-cloth screens with which hospitals shamefully hide the proof of our impotence, the sad uselessness of our machines, our medications, our techniques. The body, which was beginning to stiffen, resembled a rigid, twisted piece of root, rough and porous, very light, with neither blood nor shadow, a leaf dried between the pages of a book. The rain ran down my back, my elbows, my knees, drenching my socks, flooding into my shoes, plastering to our foreheads the viscous slime of our hair. A pinkish liquid came from us as well, slowly forming around our heels a growing oval puddle.

"Why do people kill themselves?" asked the lieutenant, adjusting the wick of the lamp. He had removed the glass chimney and a billow of soot disseminated into the compartment in small carbonous particles that floated near the ceiling for an instant, hesitating, then fell on us like a kind of snow. The foam on the beer acquired a peculiar burnt taste.

"Doctor sir," said the dead soldier, smiling at me. The bullet hole looked like a pierced eye, with no pupil, that seemed to stare at me with a melancholy grievance or silent remorse.

"Let's go find the other one," I suggested to the orderly.

The young man, sitting on the floor, spat into the flooded urinal. He had lit a cigarette butt that hung disdainfully, challengingly, from his lips, and he coughed from time to time to prepare his future mucus. The prominent bones of his shins emerged from the shapeless cardboard of his shoes.

"Move it, man," said the orderly. "Nothing you can do for him now."

"Shitty weather," said the PIDE, stretching.

"You want to catch pneumonia?" I asked.

From the main building of the asylum a shrill dialogue of marionettes came in blasts, howling like the puppets in the square, hysterically clubbing each other on the head. A white mouse ran across the neck of the bit player, who from outside the canvas curtain talked with the puppets, advising them, praising them, insulting them, at the end holding out the tin saucer to the audience, his cigarette politely hidden in his cupped hand. After the spectators dispersed, a second guy emerged from the stall, shabbily dressed and with a vulgar appearance, with a box under his arm, who began dismantling the tent, conferred with his colleague, pocketed the money, and, a hundred yards further down, resumed his noisy carnage.

"Come on, buddy," said the orderly. "You don't want us to be here all day, do you?"

Squatting in the tiny compartment in Mangando, almost rubbing legs with the dead man, I heard the lieutenant's bellows as if the shouts were very far away, somewhere else, in another world, on a morning when the beer shut me out, rising inside my head in a smooth dizziness, a childish contentment. I had worked for hours and hours, I felt like sleeping, and the marine odor of the preserves enveloped me like a shroud in a veil of foam, the curtain of water a reef raises and curls, gray and blue, around the shattered body of a shipwrecked man. The grass softly whispered its mysterious harp, the yellow earth stank with the sugary sweat of weariness.

"Get up," I told the patient. "The orderly will bring you a towel to dry off with: you can't bring anyone back to life by staying here."

Will this damned rain ever stop? I wondered. The asylum courtyard had become filled with mud, a bluish-green soup in which legs buried themselves, a swamp into which buildings imperceptibly submerged like sinking ships, disappearing window by window, floor by floor, roof by roof, noiselessly, the way clouds dissolve into the smooth, limitless watercolor of the sky.

"Do something before I get mad," said the orderly, a towel hanging from his arm like an impatient waiter in a café.

The lieutenant leaned closer toward me. His pendulous breasts shook. Our faces were so near that I could make out, one by one, the flaws in his skin, the pimples, the moles, the blackheads, the dilated pores of his nose:

"Why do people kill themselves?" he insisted. His anguished question, formulated in the sharp voice of a child, reminded me of the time when, at fourteen or fifteen, desperate in my hateful loneliness, I lay in bed, my fever-swollen eyes fixed on the ceiling, and repeated furiously to myself, I want to die, thus enjoying a strange sort of revenge. Or I would sit on the stone steps in the yard under the milky fruit of the fig tree (my arms clotted with its green reflections of cream) and imagine myself pointing my brothers' small air rifle at my forehead, the one we used to scare away the cats that jumped over the wall in light silky leaps. The puppets had given way, without transition, to the screeching tremors of a fado: Surely the custodian's in the front row, I calculated, we'll have to handle it ourselves. Herculano came into the hospital's consultation room with his wife and said:

"We haven't seen each other since the war, doctor sir, since Mangando."

"A shitty season," repeated the PIDE. "This mist frays my nerves."

The commandant locked the door so the cloistered woman wouldn't get out: from time to time, behind the curtains, glided the indistinct outline of an apparition.

"I'm a subway conductor now, doctor sir," explained Herculano from the other side of the desk, pointing his large bird-nose at me. "But you're still doing the same thing, doctor."

The morning fog made the trees, the huts, the wooden shacks, float like fishes drifting in an unreal atmosphere, flashing the tarnished, muddy brilliance of their scales.

"My wife loses her head over everything and nothing," Herculano offered. "We live in one room and the other guests complain."

"Well," I told the orderly, "you take care of the dead man and I'll handle the matter of our friend here."

"A week ago tomorrow she had a fight with the landlord. With the cost of living what it is, I don't make enough to rent a house, you know how it is, doctor."

I stretched out in bed, affixed my fever-swollen eyes on the ceiling, and repeated furiously to myself, I want to die. The rain had completely obliterated the rosy bloodstain and continued to come down on us through the broken window frames. The patient closed one eye, took aim at his own shoes, and spat a wad at the toe.

"That's not the least bit funny," I said. "Come have a talk with me in my office."

"I slugged him, pulled him by the hair, I felt like banging his head against the wall. He's an old man, he reported me to the police."

"Stick your office up your ass," said the young man.

The orderly undressed the corpse, tied his wrists together, wrapped him carefully in the sheet like a birthday present: With a little blue bow he'd be perfect, I thought, a little blue bow and paper with tiny stars: To my dear psychiatrists with lots of kisses and best wishes for a merry Christmas.

"I can't sleep," said Herculano's wife. "I can't sleep and don't know what's going on in my head."

The lieutenant gestured to me to slide over on the bench and sat down ponderously beside me: he smelled of the sea also, the oily, motionless sea of the preserves.

"I'm going to raise my finger to my temple someday," he whispered to me. "You'll see what fireworks my brains make."

"Bang," said the dead soldier, smiling.

My face suddenly contorted in a strangled fit of coughing: the smoke accumulating in the bar, the rain, the Mangando morning.

"If you don't beat it I'll bust your face," I told the patient.

"A good kick in the balls never hurt anybody," clarified the

PIDE over lunch. "Nothing like a nice calling card to make yourself understood."

We're going to return to Marimba with the dead soldier in the back of the jeep, jolting along the trail, and through the open door we could see the fog of May. The lieutenant, quite pale, was dissolving in a spoon the aspirin for his hangover. The dogs lying in the courtyard waited humbly for scraps of food, the bits of rice and meat the soldiers gave them, scraping their aluminum plates with the metal teeth of their forks. The presence of the dead man, however, bothered them: they beat their tails in the sand, pricked their ears in the direction of the jeep, and from time to time raised their snouts to howl: hoarse, sad laments, as brief as the alarmed, rotting pleas of owls.

"Ah, the dogs," sighed the lieutenant, wiping the sweat from his brow with his arm.

The sweetish odor, the mysterious odor of blood frightened and attracted them: whenever the wounded arrived at the barracks the dogs would fearfully approach, circling, and the round gelatinous wheels of their eyes were cloaked in interest and terror: they would sniff the men on the cots, lick their arms, their necks, their faces, then move away, support their bodies on their hind legs, raise their snouts and begin to bark in the strepitous and terrible silence of war.

"Ah, the dogs," we sighed, wiping the sweat from our brows with our arms.

The PIDE headed toward the door, took the pistol from his belt, fired: a flock of small black birds scattered from the palm trees, traced an erratic hyperbola in the air, then disappeared in the direction of the native quarter. The echo of the shot rose and fell in the fields like a shout reverberated and amplified by countless walls, fragmenting it into an infinity of sounds. But the dogs remained motionless in the yard, beating their tails in the sand and looking sidelong, melancholic and intrigued, at the white silhouette of the dead man. The PIDE, annoyed, holstered his weapon, sat down, and resumed eating.

"Everything's afraid of the PIDE," I said. "Men, women, the natives, birds. Even the birds are afraid, afraid of your prisons, your tortures, your pistols, your courts, your henchmen. Everyone's afraid of you except the dogs. When we become a nation of dogs we'll stop being slaves."

"Dogs are afraid of ghosts," said the lieutenant softly. "When we're dogs the PIDE will no doubt organize an army of ghosts. They'll go around cemeteries at night, recruiting the ghosts that float up from the tombs and wander about at random in the city, looking for the houses they lived in."

"Ghosts are easy to buy," said the PIDE. "As easy to buy as people."

"Ghosts are unhappy and funereal like dogs," I contradicted. "They have no fear of suffering or of death. They don't even fear themselves. You can't buy someone who has no fear of himself."

"We'll see who wins the battle," said the PIDE, gently depositing a bone on the edge of his plate. "Us or the ghosts."

"So far the ghosts have never lost one," replied the quartermaster medic. "If we sent companies of ghosts to Angola we'd have ended this war a long time ago."

"I can't sleep," said Herculano's wife. "I can't sleep and then all I have in my head are bad thoughts."

I grabbed the guy by the collar of his pajamas and tried to drag him over the tiles and out of the urinal. The young man clung tightly to the stone partitions. The cigarette butt hanging from his mouth was a limp little cylinder of mud.

"You murdering bastard," he hissed.

"Mr. Valentim will now recite poetry of his own authorship," declared a hollow voice, far off, wafting in the wind just as water in the gutters drags straw, small pieces of wood, sheets of newspapers, jumbled useless, floating things.

"Doctor sir," said the dead soldier, smiling.

"Get the hell out of here, you son of a bitch," I yelled, out of my head, trying to stamp on his hands with my shoes.

"We're already ghosts," said the lieutenant. "We're the most disgusting kind, the most pathetic, the most wretched of ghosts. The boat carrying us back to Lisbon is carrying a pile of cadavers so well embalmed that our families won't even notice the difference."

"Of his own authorship," repeated the wind in the broken bevel of the window frames.

One of my legs slipped, I lost my balance, tried to regain it with a windmill motion of my arms, and finally fell helplessly body to body, face to face, eye to eye, onto the patient's rigid outstretched form. I couldn't move, and the rain that came down on me, furious and violent, full of hatred, disgust, disdain, seemed like a ceaseless jet of phlegm.

So, Joanna, I left Lisbon for the beach like Margarida of Miguel Bombarda Hospital for the hairdresser's where she worked. The trees and houses resembled the unreal animals of dreams, which at morning hide like rats, under the furniture, to reappear when the lights are turned out, the way the unfamiliar birds that inhabit the sea do, if we turn our heads. The automobile headlights brushed the smooth skin of night, which stirred in slow protest like a body roused from sleep. It must have been three A.M. and the sky in the east, opposite the sea, was taking on the depth, the restlessness, the transparency of water that precedes the dawn, something of the ecstatic, almost painful shine of the eyes of women when desire or happiness illuminates them. A train ran for a few moments parallel to me, and I was assaulted by the sensation of being pursued by a building of countless windows, mooing like a cement steer along its path of rails. When I was little I would sleep like you, in the back seat around Cacém, or stare at the back of my father's neck with eyes round as plates until he would crouch in annoyance over the wheel, scratching his neck, besieged by an unexplainable itch. In São Pedro the gentle brightness of the town would slowly paralyze me and my eyelids would descend on a setting of palaces and deserted residences like a curtain on a stage where nothing has happened. And my clenched child's hands found twenty years later, in yours, an emotional perpetuation that conferred on me an unexpected sense of eternity.

Three in the morning was his Cape of Good Hope, especially without the life jacket of whiskey that would help him to float, on the surface, in the black mire of anguish. At home, he would usually turn off the lamps, disconnect the record player and the telephone, and crouch in the corner of the living room like Incan mummies, which in the color photographs in encyclopedias swallow their knees with toothless mouths, and remain in silence near a vase of innocent plants whose suddenly carnivorous breathing he imagined he could hear in the darkness, watching the river, whose apparent hidden tranquility concealed tumultuous agitation, as did his own, beyond any possible calm. It was the hour when freedom and solidity forcibly won over hard years of fierce altercations and prideful separations seemed petty victories as empty as the kitchen cabinets that, in the absence of food, accumulated dust, the neglected dust of bachelors used to eating standing up, like horses, eating sandwiches that held a poignant nostalgia for delicate croquettes and soup mixes. In the buildings of Sintra, to all appearances uninhabited, with untended gardens and rusted iron gates, ran, as in himself, the fleeting sound of past footsteps, amplified by the echo of remorse. And only your clenched hands in the back seat and the shadow of eyelashes on your cheek reassured me of the possibility, albeit problematic, of some kind of future. So I always carried your memory in my pocket, like a rabbit's foot, which from time to time I would touch to ensure a happiness in which I didn't believe, for the same reason, perhaps, that led Margarida to return to the beauty parlor when she ran away from the hospital, in the wondrous hope of a nonexistent reencounter in a room whose key and street names have been lost.

One couldn't see the ocean, yet it surely existed somewhere, to the left, stirring the bushes of Galamares in long conciliabula of leaves in the mist, branches of climbing plants beckoning in rhythm above leprous walls, exhausted by a far-off breath of ebb tides. The trolley line suddenly crossed the roadway, though no car rattled its weary turkey-haunches on the asphalt. In the deserted chalets, with windows as blind as the eyes of the dead, ghosts of old women spied from behind curtains, clutching to their chests the swift metallic hearts of crochet needles, preparing a hemorrhage of napkins. In my antediluvian childhood old bald men would play chess at tables in cafés, with pensive creases in their brows as deep as the folds of a groin. The headlights brutally wrested gates from the shadows as closed as a cop's grimace while he writes a ticket. And the sky was getting brighter on the morning side, rounded and pink like a swimmer's bare buttocks.

In Colares a tongue of the river flows past mediocre boarding-houses in which breasts half a century old murmur over teabags as bland as a priest's kiss. In bedrooms, couples united by thirty years of patient mutual hatred undress without looking at each other, aware that over time their bodies have acquired the strange similarity that makes, for example, dogs resemble their owners, splitting cream puffs between them at pastry shops, in a cooing dialogue of barks. The bedsprings sigh with resignation when two gray heads share the newspaper under a lamp that resembles an oil lantern destined to illuminate the resigned faces of departed relatives. The heads come together for the crossword, separate again for international politics, unite once more for an airplane crash, if the number of bodies warrants that apparent kindness, in reality done out of a common taste for dead passengers. The robes hung side-by-side on hooks on the door, beneath the daily rental rates framed like a family portrait, prolong an illusion of life together that the dentures, sitting unabashedly on the night table, cruelly belie with their plastic grins. And whoever is closer to the switch suddenly turns out the light, leaving the other in the middle of the romantic plights of a Greek shipping magnate or a British princess, grumbling in the dark of the sheets like an annoyed gorilla in an unfamiliar jungle.

At that time of night, however, Colares offered him the uniformly opaque face of a psychoanalyst during a session, staring at his client with the lucid sharpness of an Oedipal Sherlock Holmes, who simplifies his task by always considering the murderer the one who's paying, and the innocent suspects the father and mother from a Viennese mythology dating to the waltz age, corseted by the rigidity of waxed-mustache customs. The tongue of the river, without brilliance or reflections, glided slowly below the houses like a root of darkness, insignificant among the tresses of the reeds. Through the windows of the closed pastry shops appeared chairs inverted on tables, awaiting the morning sawdust. The town seemed more insignificant, smaller, shriveled like a withered fruit in the pantry. One stubborn and solitary fisherman had left hanging from the porch railing the umbilical cord of a nylon line that tied him to the unlikely baby of an eel. Trees whose names he didn't know formed overhead a mobile cupola of shadows. The road to the mountains serpentined to the left like the coil of a still, to where the sea's smooth perpendicular sheet, made of varnish, could be glimpsed. A large gray bird skimmed over the rooftops in the direction of morning. And he felt like a foreigner in relation to himself, like Margarida when she went beyond the hospital gate and suddenly found herself in the city to which she had become dishabituated and which responded to her anxious obliquities with the impenetrable austerity of its facades.

Leaving aside the statues, quiet on their pedestals in their heroic cramps, no one paid any attention at three in the afternoon to a nightgown, which, given the cyclical whims of fashion and a bit of myopia or benevolence, could pass for a summer dress whose unstitched hem added another surprisingly modern note of carelessness. The swans at Campo de Santana continued to float, sailing on the miniature lake, and the bronze statue of Sousa Martins beckoned spirits to the Morgue, where in refrigeration chambers the deceased awaited the formal convoking of a séance to be able to express their gloomy complaints to a circle of the faithful, scrupulously respectful like lovers of chamber music. Leaning against the door, at the end of a spiral staircase, the guard at the underground urinals was smoking his miner's cigarette: the city navigated its way through the afternoon in an imperturbable rhythm on its way to family dinners and tedious evenings at home, courageously borne in front of the perpetual prayer of the television, absorbing program after program the same way that ostriches swallow screws and monkey wrenches with monotonous appetite. People trickled before Margarida their hollow serious faces, made of cardboard, with eyes replaced by orifices identical to those left by nails in the plaster of walls, and she measured her loneliness by that carrousel of features empty as black masks balanced on the single foot of collars. In her room the alarm clock divided time impiously into small slices that scattered on the floor like checkers lost in corners, obliging her to resort to her button box in order to confront with relative hypotheses the tricks and subterfuges of the future. The immobility of the Spanish doll on the bed, resting on the pillow, its arms open in a papal celluloid blessing, alarmed her like the pictures from childhood in which smiles are prolonged indefinitely like the diapason of a choral group. On the bookshelf, a small porcelain dog, a velvet ribbon around its neck, lowered its cracked nose in her direction in an entreaty impossible to decode, like the anguish that sometimes, for no reason, began to swell inside her, from bottom to top, like the water in toilets, until it exploded violently in fireworks of tears. The wrappings from candy boxes that she glued above the bed (hunting scenes, the Moulin Rouge, waves lifting their skirts of foam so as not to wet the sand) pained her like the never-healed wounds of disappointment from early childhood. There was a photograph of a man by the headboard, with an incongruently jovial smile barely contained by the frame, that overpowered the room, from the hairbrush to the piggy bank, immobile on its table mat on the camphor chest intended for a nonexistent trousseau. She descended the stairs and took a taxi to the beauty parlor, in the hope that the tepid steam that rises, in concentric circles, from the washed heads would awaken the feelings of illusory complicity that one ordinarily associates with tureens of soup.

Inside the taxi various small handwritten signs in India ink, placed in strategic spots (on the dashboard, on the sun visors, on the back of the driver's seat, on the upholstery of the doors, and even on the ceiling, to the right of the mirror) asked passengers not to smoke, with a sour insistence in which could be discerned the meticulous ill humor of the driver, who embraced the steering wheel in a raging coitus. The taximeter shook at regular intervals in jerking sobs, and the numbers mounted on the small dial like metallic eyelids blinking over ever-increasing pupils of

$ signs. The tobacco hater, small, thin, nervous, worked the gear-shift like someone picking at earwax with an angry Q-Tip, and from time to time he would roll down the window to insult the family of the pedestrians in sharp poodle yelps. The liquid buildings slid from both sides of the hood like water cloven by a ship's bow: Lisbon resembled a Venice in bad taste, which an orchard of traffic lights planted at intersections embellished in vain: the driver ignored the lemons of the yellow and stopped, outraged, at the oranges of the red, quivering in his gasoline gondolier's impatience. The car's horn, in solidarity with its owner's bitterness like a well-trained animal, lowed dark threats at the facades. A huge van rumbled ahead of them, supported on the tremulous crutches of its tires.

"Wish I had a machine gun," the driver said suddenly, indicating something or other with a dirty fingernail, perhaps the maternity hospital on his left that was producing, with the silence of an incubator, an immense litter of pedestrians.

Local beauty parlors, Joanna, are a mixture of bathroom and living room, on which the astronaut's helmets of the dryers confer a false interplanetary coloration that the fashion magazines belie, reducing the grandeur of the galaxies to comic-strip misadventures. Young women in blue smocks secretly feed senseless television dreams ("Our program today has come to an end: tomorrow we present...") by attaching rollers, as if for a brain scan, to the half-bald skulls of the neighborhood ladies, the wives of minor officials who no longer inhabit any dream. The owner's husband, a retired railroad worker, to avoid the bad company from the sweet-shop, was bound to the cash register by the leash of his wife's imperious gaze, while his friends, in the shadow of cans of cookies and bottles of rosé, well boozed up, played cards. The pictures of hairdos glued to the windows have faded like old enthusiasms, of which remains a sepia recollection in some forgotten drawer of memory. The smell of shampoo transforms the afternoon into a sweet perfumed aquarium where one navigates amid the divorces of princesses, the marriages of actresses, and interviews with singers that the Venezuelan immigrants, in a laudable lurch of patriotism, tend to confuse with Sinatra.

"Dead, all of 'em," insisted the driver, distributing frenetic obscene gestures to traffic as indifferent as a herd. And she remembered that she normally excused taxi drivers, imagining that they suffered from congenital infected boils in the groin.

"Dona Carmo," said one of the employees in a panic, "Margarida's down there in the street looking up here."

The owner, up to her elbows in suds, rubbing a submissive nape energetically as if washing clothes in a tub, took the frightening information in stride: for twenty years she had taken the bull of marital boozing by the horns and had managed to turn him into a dour but abstemious steer, staring sidelong at her from the cash register with the fearful look of a vassal: that protracted combat afforded him the cold blood of deep-sea fishes, accustomed to the darkness filled with sharp edges of day-to-day contingencies.

"Margarida is in the hospital," she grumbled. "You saw the firemen take her away from here when she tried to recreate the miracle of the roses by changing the scissors into feather dusters. She was wrapped in a sheet, with a silvery paper crown on her head."

The taxi driver roared off without looking at her, with a precarious vomiting of the engine: the car bucked three times, belched, coughed its ancient bronchitis of a dinosaur on wheels, and disappeared around the corner, exhaling sickening fumes through the nostrils of its tailpipe.

"A machine gun," bellowed the guy from inside, pointing his dirty nail at the blind, gray, opaque face of the buildings, the thrift store, the fruit market, the pastry shop on the corner where some old guy was serving coffee with the delicate spindly hands of a spider, covered with the spots of old age.

"Dona Carmo," the employee said, "Margarida is coming upstairs."

The nape that the owner was washing trembled in terror under the suds, rising from the water in a cloud of weightless flakes that floated about the establishment like the contents of a punctured comforter:

"Dona Carmo, for God's sake call the firemen."

The housewives under the dryers put the princess's divorce on hold at the exact moment the deadly bullfighter appeared on the royal yacht, rolling his irresistible bovine eyes.

"She's a crazy person from the Bombarda who used to work here," the widow of a lieutenant, extremely alarmed, informed a lady wearing a hearing aid, who answered with the vague smile of the deaf.

"If she's in a rage she'll kill us all," groaned the woman who owned the butcher shop and understood knives and blood. "I don't want anything to do with lunatics."

Two catechists who were waiting their turn began to pray the Lord's prayer aloud. A fat woman, bristling with hairpins, got on her knees, knocking over the manicurist's tray, whose glass cover shattered with a bang.

"Call the firemen, Dona Carmo," begged the nape, close to fainting.

"Her eyes must glow like the hands of an alarm clock," said the lieutenant's widow, looking in her purse for her chaplet. "I saw it in a film the other day."

"I hear footsteps on the stairs," whispered an elderly lady with exuberant hair, clutching to her chest a tiny dog that already had a lavish tombstone waiting for it at the zoological garden's cemetery.

The entire establishment huddled in a tense silence that the mirrors seemed to share, amplifying with exaggerated sharpness the faces distorted by fear.

"They don't rest until they get someone in their hands and strangle them," murmured the pedicurist, her cheek resting against the pillow of a motionless ankle.

The clocks avidly knitted the endless time, weaving an anxious shawl of seconds. Objects (brushes, nail files, tweezers, combs, dryers) assumed the strange, almost painful importance of horror or hope in which the shapes of things possess the shadowless precision of grand moments. Only the husband, in the rear at the register, was removed from the common terror, dreaming of dry martinis drunk in manly fashion beside the sweet-shop's cookies: someone was shuffling the dominoes at the usual table, the janitor from the school was belching through his cupped hand in an effort to keep his enthusiasm about the game within tolerable limits of a whiff of garlic. The tavern owner was watching the game over the hunched shoulders of the athletes, masticating the chewing gum of his toothpick with the nervous paternalism of coaches. The onlookers, glasses in hand, maintained the well-bred reserve of spectators at a tennis match, underlining a posteriori the most significant plays with friendly pats on the shoulder blades of the dominoes virtuosi, who received these tributes by spitting modestly into their handkerchiefs the sweat from their bronchia. During the break they would reminisce about the feats of famous sportsmen who had graced the store with the glow of their unforgettable inspiration. And they approached dinnertime with the slightly giddy state of excitement of schoolboys on vacation, for whom the present possesses the miraculous elasticity of immaculate joy. Anchored in his chair by the watchful eye of his wife, the reformed man punched into the machine's keys the humble resignation of one sentenced to life imprisonment in that shampoo Sing-Sing.

"I can't leave the hospital, doctor," said Hélder. "Who's waiting for me out there?"

"We need your bed," I said. "There's a whole crowd around here a lot worse off than you."

"Don't do this to me, doctor," said Hélder. "Nobody at home wants me. They look at me like I was an animal."

"I'm working with the stars again, doctor," said Valdemiro, breaking into a huge smile.

"If I'm sent out there I'll get sick," said Hélder. "I'll start hearing the Israelites speaking into my ear."

"Either admit me here or I'll ask for political asylum at São José," said the groom.

I have a secretary, an appointment book, and a horrible feeling of the uselessness of all this, he thought at the crossroads to Mucifal, where up there, among the pines, he had once seen the first roosters crow in the morning: their voices, which called and responded, ripped the tissue paper of the sky and alarmed the dogs hiding in the dark, behind the gates of houses reduced to massive cubes of blackness, throbbing to the accelerated rhythm of their blood. The wind produced in the treetops the protest of a large bird, an enormous gull, slow, affectionate, and sad.

"I'm going back to work," Margarida said joyfully at the entrance to the building.

"Look at this," demanded Hélder. "Who is it buys fast bandages?"

"Call the firemen, Dona Carmo," shouted the nape, standing in the middle of the room with foam running down her neck, her arms, her back. "Call the firemen before we all die here!"

"I hear her," said an employee, as still as a statue, tilted to one side like a manikin in a display window.

The lieutenant's widow tried to open a window to call for help, but the latch was broken and came off in her hands. She rapped with her knuckles on the glass: the men delivering canisters of gas in the street, hoisting them to their shoulders with ease, didn't even look up: the neighborhood slumbered in the peaceful climate that precedes tragedy: FUGITIVE FROM PSYCHIATRIC HOSPITAL KILLS TWELVE IN BEAUTY PARLOR.

"Oh God," whispered the pedicurist, holding onto her customer's ankle like a talisman.

"If I'm sent out of here, where am I supposed to go?" asked Hélder. His lips were dry from the medications, his tongue fuzzy, slack, without saliva. The shadow of his formless anguish vibrated like a butterfly in the absence of brightness in his face.

"Call the firemen," Dona Carmo ordered her husband, quickly rounding up scissors, tweezers, nail files, hairpins, metallic instruments that she placed in the pocket of her floral apron. "Call the firemen, I don't want this place in the newspapers."

The people's faces turned into the paralyzed black-and-white features of the victims of railway disasters, who observe the viewer with the globular and hollow eyes of the dead.

The husband picked up the phone with a limp gesture, as if his wrist were the trunk of a bored elephant: the contents of a bottle of booze glittered, transparent, in his mind.

"I'm releasing you next week," I decided. "You have till then to find a room."

"The luxury hotels are full of vacancies," replied Hélder. "Are you paying?"

Margarida climbed the stairs very slowly: Dona Carmo, her fellow workers, the customers smiled at her in unison, enchanted, from the landing.

"Not even the sweet little dog will escape," squealed the lady with the tiny animal, trying to hide the rare species of rat in her neckline: the sharp muzzle of the animal stuck out, suffocating, from the space between her breasts, and she pushed him inside with her index finger as if ringing a doorbell of fur.

"They serve breakfast in bed and everything," insisted Hélder with a fierce little laugh. "Will Welfare advance the dough?"

"It's not the same here without you," Dona Carmo told Margarida. "I'd like to offer you a share in the establishment."

The catechists put into gear the final entreaty of the prayer to the Christ Child of Prague, accompanied by the fat woman and the butcher shop owner: the backlit sinking of the Titanic was sketched in the mirrors, conferring on Benfica a dimension of Greek drama cruelly deflated by the rattling of gas canisters in the street. On the porch across the street a woman was beating carpets with a wicker racket.

"The firemen?" Dona Carmo asked anxiously.

"I must've called the wrong number," stammered her husband from the rear. "A funeral home answered. Burial costs are enough to kill you."

"Oh God," whispered the pedicurist, climbing up the leg as if it were a lifeline.

"Try the Divine Holy Spirit," the lieutenant's widow advised the catechists. The deaf woman smiled without understanding, mildly intrigued by the unusual frenzy.

"Is there a problem?" she asked.

"We're all going to die here," the woman next to her screamed in her ear, red in the face from the effort of shouting.

"Personally, I prefer the Ritz," said Hélder. "You can have them prepare my bags."

"What's going on?" asked the deaf woman, adjusting the device in her ear.

"A crazy woman wants to kill us all," bellowed the neighbor again, almost purple, with the veins of her neck throbbing under the skin.

"Call the firemen for God's sake," ordered Dona Carmo, tossing the scissors into the sink. Plop plop plop went the instruments as they fell into the water.

Margarida arrived at the top of the stairs, in front of the parlor's milky glass door on which were written in blue, diagonally, the words: Flower of Benfica Beauty Institute, of which the second F had long since fallen off, and with a sense of gratification she breathed in the smell of shampoo, hairspray, perfume, lotions and nail polish that came over the glass in a delicate and light exhalation. Her clients must be lined up in the waiting room, someone had put soft, sweet violin music on the record player. After the neutral indifference of the asylum and its terrifying white ghosts, after the room that had expelled her and the alien, opaque, hostile city, the Flower of Benfica Beauty Institute appeared before

"Piss on the Ritz," I told Hélder. "And on your way there go fuck yourself."

her like a pleasant dock where she could anchor the anguish of so many days, the gloomy and funereal boat of her delirium inhabited by strange and antiquated images, of bizarre wild eyes like the irises of the dead that watch us from the depths of coffins, beneath their shrouds, with bitter envy. Lying in her bed at the madhouse she would see, at night, large black dogs leaping on the wall, their mouths open, silently devouring one another, and scream for the nurse, who would come from her lit cubicle armed with a hypodermic filled with tranquilizers. During the day she would watch the river through the window, the houses, the trees,

"You got to understand things," the custodian told Hélder. "We can't keep you here anymore."
the birds whose names she didn't know and the blue-green afternoon around her, and thought They're waiting for me at the beauty parlor, I'm going back to the beauty parlor because they're waiting for me there, so she opened the door with a piece of wire, left by melting into a group of visitors, made it to the iron gate flanked by twin stone pillars, and now found herself before the Flower of Benfica Beauty Institute, her hand reaching for the doorknob.

"Nobody answers at the fire station," her husband said.

"She cut the wire, you can bet on that," said the owner of the butcher shop. "That's how crazy people are: they don't do things by halves."

"Isn't there another way out of here, Dona Carmo?" asked the fat woman, towel around her neck and purse in hand, trembling like a mare before the final gallop.

"Only if we all hide in my house," said Dona Carmo, opening a ruffled curtain to reveal a Queen Anne dining room with an enormous television set on the sideboard, and a vase of flowers on top of that. The edge of a tablemat with tassels hung majestically over half of the screen.

"In any case," said Hélder, "even if I had suitcases I wouldn't have anything to put in them."

"Stick your spare socks in your pockets and get out," I ordered. "We need your bed today."

Margarida pushed open the door and entered the deserted establishment. Behind the curtain a frightened bunch of customers, their hair in rollers, painstakingly tried not to breathe. Suds from their tresses dripped onto the carpet. The deaf lady continued to smile vaguely at her surroundings, without understanding.

"Cover her mouth," whispered Dona Carmo. "If she asks what's going on again, we've had it."

"You really think there's nothing you can do, doctor?" asked Hélder.

If it were a little earlier, I'd go watch the sea at Praia Grande, he thought, the lilac waves, blood-colored, of morning, the cold wind that stirs and ruffles the reeds, the silver sand before dawn, forming something like a mirror that reflects the cloudy grayness, ever brighter, of the sky, where one by one the stars are extinguished like burned-out light bulbs. I'd see the fog that rises from the water and spreads like a tenuous web over the humid shivering skin of the houses. If it were just a bit earlier I could take the car, go down the steps to the beach and sit at the exact spot where the dry sand and the wet sand touch and become one, listening to the docile, faraway, faintly alarmed sound of the waves. Or I'd install myself outside the small deserted café, smoking silently, the thought of a beer within reach and my head full of old memories both happy and sad, while the last birds of the night graze the black treetops on their way to the pine forest, where the frightened darkness huddles. I sat outside the small deserted café as once I had leaned out over the wall, near the restaurant, dreaming of the great trips I would never take and the powerful force of departures beating, trapped, in my chest: down below, the bustle of Sundays bubbled on the beach, the ruddy, sweaty, weary bustle of Sunday swimmers, who at the end of the afternoon formed long lines near the parking lot, red and exhausted. They were fat, flabby men and women, in slippers, undershirts, and ridiculous straw hats that made them resemble poor clowns in some provincial fair, hurrying home after their antiquated, insipid act. Sitting outside the small deserted café, smoking in silence, I imagined a crowd of fat, flabby men and women eating mussels at neighboring tables, with the liquid from the shellfish running down the viscous flaccidity of their chins, or pounding at crabs with wooden mallets to extract the tender and mildly fibrous white flesh of the sea. Because the flesh of the sea is like the meat of its strange animals, its crustaceans and its mollusks, its unimaginable animals that converse with us through the spirals of conchs, the musical language of a breath hollow and blunted like that of people who've undergone a throat operation, who talk to us through small metal tubes implanted in their necks, eyes wide with some unspeakable terror.

No one was waiting for her in the empty beauty parlor. Margarida looked at the overturned tables, the broken glass, the mirrors as empty as the endless nights at the hospital, the abandoned objects lying randomly on the floor. No smile hovered in the room like a forgotten flower, the shadow of a forgotten flower waiting for her. The dryers were lined up against the wall like the helmets of some interrupted space voyage, rollers and hairpins were scattered about in disorder on the floor. Hangers for smocks swung in the open closet.

"Everything will go well, you'll see," I told Hélder, pushing him by the back. "Come by now and then to say hello."

"As soon as you leave you forget all about us," joked the orderly. "I don't know anybody who sticks by you through thick and thin."

Hélder proceeded down the corridor toward the door. He dragged his laceless shoes on the floorboards and carried, hanging from his hand, the small bag of bandages. His neck was stuck onto his massive shoulders as if it had been screwed on too tight. Dirty feathery hair rubbed against the greasy collar of his coat. When he disappeared at the corner and into the courtyard, I returned to my office and closed the door:

"We're free of that one," I said. "Who's the next gentleman?"

The hospital, Margarida thought, changed the world: it tossed out smiling, cooperative, friendly people who looked out for one another and replaced them with a bitter, opaque, enemy city, a city that wasn't hers, that she didn't know, that wherever she went chased her away in a sick rage, chased her away, to where she didn't know, because there was no place for her. She felt walled in

"We have a man here who attempted suicide two days after being released from your ward," explained the voice on the telephone. "He swallowed in one gulp the pills they gave him to take home."

inside herself as if in a tiny cell, it was difficult to breathe, a kind of discomfort, distress, a prickling pain, clutched at her chest, the veins of her throat, her brain.

"What's she doing?" whispered the butcher store owner to the fat woman, who at the same time she was covering the deaf woman's mouth with her hand was bent down spying through the gap in the curtains.

"Nothing," the other woman answered, looking. "Her expression is scary."

"He's getting out of the emergency room tomorrow," the voice insisted. "Can't you send someone here?"

"I hope to God she doesn't break everything," Dona Carmo told the bas-relief Last Supper that concealed the gas meter. A picture of her, much younger, in a dress with small polka dots, stared suspiciously at her husband who through the window was observing with great interest the comings and goings at the sweetshop: one by one, cigarettes in their lips, the athletes were entering the stadium. An old man in a beret and carrying a cane, an undisputed champion, approached, limping, and was greeted by the man from the fruit store, standing under the awning among the crates of melons and peaches. The catechists were attacking their ninth Hail Mary in a row without taking a breath, releasing through their mouths pale little bubbles like a scuba diver, aided by the oxygen tank of last night's novena.

"Hélder found a nice little way to give us a hard time," I told the orderly. "He gulped down I don't know how many pills."

Margarida, in the empty beauty parlor, continued to look around, not knowing what to do: What's the answer when not even the beauty parlors are operating? In the lavatories the last of the suds were disappearing down the drains, whirling slowly. A dryer droned on the floor. Something somewhere was murmuring but so softly that she couldn't make out the sentences, the words, the syllables. It seemed that several people were talking in a muffled voice behind the ruffled curtain, but this was what the doctors at the asylum called her illness, an unusual product, unreal, unimportant, of her imagination. There didn't exist, had never existed, couldn't exist, any conspiracy: no one, they had proved to her, was persecuting her,

"Are you going there, doctor?" asked the orderly

so she made herself comfortable in one of the chairs in the deserted establishment

"What now?" whispered the butcher shop owner, trembling with fear

leaned back her head, closed her eyes, and waited. However long it took, she would wait.

"Hélder can go to hell," I said.

12

When I was small and there were hockey games at the Praia das Maçãs skating rink and the public gathered to wait on the only grandstand overlooking the sea, a stone bench facing into the afternoon sun as it set into the water, a man wearing an enormous coat with an idiotic expression and limbs disjointed like those of dolls, started dashing around the cement, waving his arms in his gigantic sleeves, whistling and applauding at the people, who laughed in derision among themselves and encouraged him with exclamations, hisses, cries, guffaws, bellowing

"Go, Rui! Faster, Rui!"

in cruel, perverse joy. The oblong sun descended toward the sea enveloped in a fine cellophane of mist, the houses, illuminated by sidelight, seemed ablaze with reddish flames that faded little by little, and on the windows, where already dwelled a delicate film of shadow foretelling nightfall, the waves were colored the pale purple of dark eye-circles as if the skin of the water, weary, no longer saw, no longer pursued us with its attentive and forlorn face gripped in the fists of the rocks, in the reeds behind the rink, in the small hill of sand next to the traveling circuses with their hidden poverty of makeup and accordions, while the leaves, dry as teeth, rustled restlessly in whispers, and Rui went on running, exhausted, on the cement, egged on by the ferocious scorn of his audience:

"You'll play for Benfica yet, Rui!"

When he came past me I noticed his open mouth, his dilated pupils, the sweat that dripped from his chin onto his tattered shirt, as dirty as the feathers that turkeys drag, clucking, in the dust of henhouses, his heels flapping in his oversized shoes, and I too laughed in mockery at his pathetic innocence, at his abandon, his pointless and desperate effort, I laughed to encourage him, applauding him, jeering him, and shouted like the others

"You're a perfect fit for Benfica, Rui!"

until the teams entered the rink, attention diverted to the skaters who maneuvered in slow ellipses on the tiled surface, the oblong fruit of the sun touched the horizon like an apple on a silver wire, making the water look like the lilac and green scales of a huge dead fish (as if an immense olive grove swayed, in successive waves, in the silence), and Rui, forgotten, staggered randomly into the night, dragging his shapeless shoes along the empty grandstand. Whenever I go to Praia, whenever I glimpse, to the right of the highway, against the wall of a house, the sign that says Praia das Maçãs, I think that Rui is still running, in the dark, around the cement, with an expression of humble stupidity, of pathetic innocence, on his exhausted face.

Praia das Maçãs, coming immediately after Banzão, is an agglomeration of leprous dwellings perched over the raging ocean, howling from toothache and heartburn, beating in vain against the seawall as if at an eternally closed door. The shopkeepers are known by their nicknames and the summer visitors by the bathrobes that fade year by year just as eyes age, and flutter in the perpetual mist from café to café with the frightened lightness of apparitions. The family, courageously planted on the sand amid the humidity and cold, under concentric layers of undershirts for polar expeditions, listening resignedly to the foghorn from the lighthouse, a voice without a mouth that occupies the mist with its lowing of a wounded bull, makes out with difficulty the red flag that forbids swimming in waters where icebergs drift, and listens without hope to encouraging phrases from the mother, who under her Arctic fur promises in a murmur that the wind transforms into a tangle of syllables:

"After one o'clock it lifts."

But the foghorn blares all day, the unreal specter of a beach attendant, attenuated as though seen through out-of-focus binoculars, passes by them carrying on his shoulders the useless canvas of sunscreens, the position of nearby umbrella poles must be guessed, and they end up groping their way home, recognizing one another by the sound of their sneezes, while the mother, a heroic straw hat on her head, repeats

"After one o'clock it lifts."

preparing to hand out aspirin.

At lunch the crowns of pines that loom in the fog can be made out like black spots on unwell skin, and they leaf through disconsolate magazines all afternoon, stretched out in front of the heater with the tropism of sunflowers that have caught a cold. In bed the damp sheets afflict us with pneumonia chilblains, and when our bodies begin to melt into the nothingness of sleep the plaint of the foghorn brutally wrenches from us the painfully won peace in our bones, like yanking a bandage from the injured hairs of one's arm. And even then, in the middle of the night in which trees sway and irately brandished waves pound, one could believe he hears the insistent small voice of the mother repeating her monotonous promise

"After one o'clock it lifts"

with scornful tenacity.

From time to time, however, August dawns without rain, with a foggy brightness that confers on people and gestures a hint of shadow. One's limbs reacquire the consistency of flesh, clouds the color of military uniforms pile up over the mountains like poorly filled sacks, steam from Basque berets on the heads of castle battlements, a sliver of blue fills with ducks above the sea and dozens of robes converge, shuffling toward the beach, wonder-struck, exclaiming to one another with a smile of ecstatic happiness the indescribable joy of that miracle:

"It lifted!"

Zé, Filícia's husband, a whistle around his neck, attempts the supreme audacity of raising the yellow flag, victorious towels are laid out on the sand, he rubs a vengeance of creams on his belly, a few suicidal types venture a toe, in the posture of a suspended stork, into the frigid wave of foam, confirming to one another

"What a beautiful day"

to the rhythm of teeth chattering from the cold, until the clouds from the mountains start to fill, to swell and advance headlong toward them in the disordered confusion of soft things that plummet, and the waves darken like the roots of undyed hair, the fog swallows up the buildings in the humid whirlwind of its breath, the first drops of rain fall with the weight of tons of nocturnal drips from faucets, and towels and lotions are quickly gathered up on the way home, with the mother asking behind them

"Didn't I tell you it would lift?"

recalling, in the circumstance, the equatorial epic of other identical days, lived in the happy time of a sunny youth.

He had grown accustomed to Praia das Maçãs and to its corteges of vacation sites decked with unhappy orphans, policed by nuns in whose gestures could be discerned the angular movements of bats. He had grown accustomed to slow glasses of orangeade outside the café, smoking his cigarette in solitary melancholy amid a group of crocheting ladies and a stooped old couple waiting silently for an aneurism to save them. He had grown accustomed to Mr. Alves's pharmacy and Mr. Café's shoe store the way others grow accustomed to a wife without surprises. Above all, he had grown accustomed to the unquestioned decrees of his mother, who during the summer, in the midst of the fog, the bronchitis, and the cold, seemed to expand in size and assurance with a firmness that confused him: one of his brothers would show up at breakfast with a cough, pale from flu, dragging along the floor the heavy weariness of his feet, and immediately, disdaining a thermometer, she would place two expeditious fingers on his neck and decide

"You're as cool as can be"

and send him off into the street in the direction of a triumphant pleurisy, which would be explained to astonished visitors with the smile of one emitting a disarmingly self-evident truth:

"They're not used to the bracing air, you know? In just a little I'll smear some VapoRub on him and he'll be like new."

Praia das Maçãs, he thought as he passed the pool and its unpleasant odor of a small domesticated sea, passed the turned-off lights of the nightclub and, farther ahead, the bright ugly mass of the casino and the large advertisement for Nivea Crème, Praia das Maçãs by itself in the gray plain of the sand, to me is the rice pudding of the boardinghouse, my father's admiral's pipe giving orders to the waves from the command post of the esplanade, the cowlike breathing of the maid from the other side of the wall, awakening in my body a heated mixture of desires. But every time I arrive in Praia, every time I see the sign to the right of the

road, by the wall of a house, there comes into my head that man
wearing an enormous coat, with an idiotic expression and the disjointed limbs of a doll, running exhausted on the cement, egged
on by the people's scorn:

"You'll play for Benfica yet, Rui!"

I went up the street where the gate to my parents' was, with its
fountain, its chapel up above, and the pine grove that extends to
Azenhas, to Janas, to the foot of the mountains and maybe beyond, crossing fields, in the direction opposite the city, an earth-
colored pine grove, mysterious and gloomy, phosphorescent in
the stagnant glare of morning, in the oleaginous glassy glare of
morning, the car's engine, smooth and submissive, purred gently
beneath my feet, and he thought he had come a long way, like Rui,
that like Rui he galloped meaninglessly, obstinate and ridiculous,
before the merriment or the indifference of a deserted pit. Morning conferred on the buildings the hue of brown paper, of edges
as fleshless and sharp as bones, the roofs, darker, resembled scabs
of unhealed wounds, the cube of the garage grew in volume as if
someone from inside were inflating it, inflating the useless objects resting there, ruptured mattresses, broken bicycles, crippled
pieces of furniture, cobwebs, trash, dust, and he set the hand-
brake after aligning the fender with the edge of the flowerbed (the
sea breeze reduced plants to delicate wiry stalks that rang, rubbed
against one another like antennas, like the mandibles of insects,
like eliters), opened the door and went out into the milky clinging fog of morning, in which his movements seemed to dissolve
into that type of lukewarm blood, poisoned, that covers Septem-

ber dawns with a thick coating of pus. I thought: Rui finished his run and no one applauds him from the empty grandstand, no one pats him on the back, no one laughs at him, no one whistles at him from the empty grandstand, only the sea that steamed like a laundry tub and the inquietude of the reeds observed him, the lizards that awaited the day concealed in orifices in the wall, and the first birds, the first tiny anonymous birds, hidden, trembling with cold, in the green and yellow curtain of the bushes. There was an enormous blackbird in front of the house: sometimes, in the afternoon, when we were all sitting out here in canvas chairs, a loud sound of feathers would suddenly pierce the air, as straight and spindlelike as an arrow, conversations would stop, people would raise their heads, intrigued, my father would take the pipe out of his mouth, lean forward and say

"It's the blackbird"

in his tranquil voice in which every syllable constituted an element (a lake, a river, a mill, distant mountains) of one of those Italian or Dutch landscapes that form the background in oil paintings of nobles and church dignitaries, of the nameless men and women who cross the centuries to stare at us from their carved frames with a haughty indifference both atemporal and melancholy.

"It's the blackbird," my father would say, and the people would tilt their heads in the direction of its flight, touching with their nostrils the diminishing noise of its wings, which evaporated behind us, toward the vicinity of the school, with the sound of a tulle curtain against glass or the wrinkling of fine paper.

"The blackbird," they repeated, and for a moment their frozen attentive faces, listening, seemed to me features imprinted on cracked canvases like skin in poor condition, and from whose solitary and strange serenity emanates something like an inaudible echo of death.

I approached the flower bed, opened my fly and began to urinate: the stream was an ochre braid, a glass snake, a black stain that rattled the metallic antennas of the plants, the leaves identical to small shells or copper coins, the flowers withered like dead lips: my coat, too large, floated on my shoulders, my hands disappeared in the sleeves, my naked shins, very skinny, had chilblains in my shoes. I could hear the laughter and the shouts from the grandstand, the rink, the vociferous enthusiasm of the public. A vestige of the pale-lemon setting sun wrapped itself in the translucent cloths of the fog.

"The blackbird," informed my father, pointing with the stem of his pipe to the pines by the school, where a pure and solitary whistle, in two notes, identical to a bamboo flute, sounded sharply in the glassy air of afternoon.

"The blackbird," we repeated, trying to make out the black gloss of its body in the tree branches: and perhaps at that point we may really have resembled the characters of Rembrandt, Van Dyck, Lucas Cranach the Elder, and like them impregnated with dignity and the modesty of death, perhaps in our circle of canvas chairs, amid the pine leaves, were born the mustaches, the chin whiskers, the broad-brimmed hats, the impalpable ageless smiles that gaze gravely at us from museum walls with the severe eyebrows of some obscure accusation.

Rui began looking through his pockets for the key to the house, for the key tied on a string that his mother had given him to open the door on the ground floor, under a wrought-iron lantern, near the area where the nephews' bicycles and tricycles were stored. The equinox was approaching and with it the migration of ducks along the coast in great majestic triangles, fleeing from the insidious and treacherous heat, the color of cured tobacco, of October, and also from the rain, the hail, the cold that the heat transported concealed in its paunch like a glacial fetus, a misshapen hostile beast whose twisted branching of veins the lightning bolts suddenly revealed between the curtains of clouds.

"I'm a doctor, I've come from the Algarve, I'm in Praia das Maçãs, tomorrow I return to the hospital," he said to himself aloud in order to dispel the image of Rui staggering along the deserted cement: morning had come and the tattered shirt flapped in the wind. The indistinct shapes of campers moved about at the far end of the sand, near the lagoon of the sewer (or something that resembled a sewer) that empties into the sea. Clothes were drying on lines next to the tents, blue, green, white, red clothes that fluttered in the damp breeze from the water. I'll take the books, he said, the papers, the shirts, the socks that always get mixed up, and tomorrow I'll return to the hospital. The cliffs that separate Praia das Maçãs from Praia Grande bore a resemblance to a body outstretched on its stomach, its head drawn up into its shoulder blades, a massive, inert, unconscious body. A man pushing a kind of teacart passed by in the street, causing him to recall the patients at the asylum who pushed the lunch carts from the kitchen to the dining room, the pails from which escaped the soup's incense, evaporating through a gap in the aluminum lids, to recall Vasco weeping before him from the other side of the desk, wiping the snot on the sleeve of his striped pajamas:

"I don't understand what's happening I don't understand what's happening I don't understand what's happening."

He didn't understand what was happening, he explained to me, because everything was mixed up, strange, different, because familiar faces, the people he knew best, his brother, his uncles, the godfather with whom he lived, had suddenly changed, because even the house itself had been altered despite the furniture being the same and the odors identical, the floorboards creaked like before, groaning their protest in the middle of the night. Something indefinable (a curl of a lip, the coloration of the air, certain ostensibly innocuous words) threatened him, was surely poisoning his blood when he went to sleep, with tiny needles whose marks he found when he woke up, on his left arm, in the form of small freckles, small marks that didn't exist the night before, they whispered in his ears, in an unknown language, warnings he couldn't understand. In order to force an answer of some kind, he set fire to the mattress after slashing its belly with a knife, and now there he was before me, in the asylum, on the other side of the desk, repeating

"I don't understand what's happening I don't understand what's happening I don't understand what's happening"
wiping his snot the way children do, on the sleeve of his striped pajamas. Around him, their gestures frozen in an attitude of attention, the people heard the blackbird, its two-note song, the bible-paper sound of its wings.

Nor did I understand what was happening: I was in Praia das Maçãs, in my parents' large old house that emerged from the night of pines like an enormous decorated boat, and something different, strange, unusual, disturbed me. It was a subtle, imperceptible alteration, perhaps related to my exhaustion, my fatigue, to the flaccid waxy brightness of dawn, the bizarre damp fever of morning, something unexpected, odd, absurd that I couldn't elucidate, a different odor, a hue, of the plaintive bleat of a sheep, of the sea. I put the key into the lock, pushed open the door, and groped my way to the bedroom: the breathing of my nephews rose and fell, in cadence, in the darkness, and I divined their clenched hands, their bodies shrunk into the sheets like caterpillars in cocoons, their blond hair tousled by the fingers of sleep, their eyelids stitched and taut like the lashes of the dead. I tripped over a doll, a ball, over indistinct toys that groaned if I stepped on them, on the chrome tube of a bicycle pump that rolled away from me, emitting dented gleams of silver. I felt my way haltingly around the sides of the mattress, found the lamp and turned on the light: the bulb, held in a yellow cone, suddenly revealed the fringes of the carpet, the blankets, a dresser with a mirror in which my face, drawn and naked, was reflected as if lit by the sickly flame of a candle. As I got undressed, there appeared my chest, my belly, arms, thighs, and finally the reddish bristles of my genitals and my flaccid pendulous sex, my present body, strangely vulnerable, suspended by the clavicles in successive folds like a wrinkled raincoat on a hanger. I stretched out in the sheets (the morning glued onto the blinds the gelatinous white underbelly of a frog, a white underbelly striated with the green of the bushes, panting), and I was about to turn out the light when someone said distinctly

"Good evening"

from a corner of the room, the exact corner where I had tossed my coat, my shirt, my shoes, my socks, my underwear, and where I imagined I could distinguish in the shadow the geometric outline of a chair, or what looked like a chair, against the wall paint as cold, bright, and tense as a diaphragm.

It's the journey, I thought, I've driven for miles and miles, all too alone, throughout the day, it's the vodka from the bar in Lisbon at work on my head, it's my ears buzzing from weariness, it's protest, complaint, anger, my body's rebellion. It's the Algarve wind, the murmur from the fields of the Alentejo, the sound of the leaves and the sea that mix, merge, combine, in a beckoning like a whispered summons, and I imagine hearing it now, lying on the mattress, half asleep in the growing morning, in the form of a voice that awakens me.

"Good evening," someone said again.

I sat up in bed and turned the lamp toward the voice: my father was looking at me and smiling, sitting in the red chair of the bedroom: my clothes, turned inside out, tossed there haphazardly, hung from his shoulders, his knees, his arms. One of the socks had fallen onto his head and formed a kind of ridiculous hat of blue cotton resting on the brilliantine of his hair. He held the unlit pipe in his hand, the mouthpiece upright, and stared at me. It was the first time he'd been in my room, but he seemed completely familiar with my books, my papers, my suitcase, my look of incredulity and astonishment. I calculated that he didn't even feel the sock that fell across his forehead like a curious toupee, almost comical, above the grave, lean features. I allowed myself to slide down the pillow until the back of my neck was resting against the headboard of the bed.

"Listen," he whispered, pointing with his finger to a nonexistent sound, which little by little changed into the erratic breathing of Rui staggering on the cement, panting around the rink in the growing morning. The only spectator in the stands, alone on the stone steps, was Vasco, wiping the snot from his nose on the sleeve of his pajamas, repeating

"I don't understand what's happening I don't understand what's happening I don't understand what's happening"
with his features deranged by an ineffable anguish. The sound of the sea down below merged with the confused speech of the pines, the kind of strange, indefinable prayer of the crowns of the trees, which prolongs, in its restless and mournful respiration, the attenuated echo of the waves.

"I don't understand what's happening," I said aloud, and there was something like a croaking of gulls in the sound that came from my throat, the rancorous, surprised, disappointed croaking of gulls in September when the threat of the first rains approaches.

My father's pipe traced a vague ellipse in the air: the smell of burnt tobacco, of stale tobacco, came to my nostrils like a memory of childhood, a forgotten memory revisited with melancholic surprise. A slow torpor ran through my limbs, along the bones, saturating my muscles with an inert lethargy. I heard the cries, the jeers, the hisses, the encouragements, the sarcasm, the laughter from the public without paying any attention to them. I went on running, again and again, around the cement and little by little began to feel free from exhaustion, from an oppressed heart, from the dirty cocoon of my clothes, as if the soles of my shoes no longer touched the ground and I floated, weightless, in the free and abstract atmosphere of dreams, so I barely noticed it when my father rose, turned out the light, said

"The blackbird"

in his tranquil voice in which every syllable constituted an element (a lake, a river, a mill, distant mountains) of one of those Italian or Dutch landscapes that form the background in oil paintings of nobles and church dignitaries, of the nameless men and women who cross the centuries to stare at us from their carved frames with a haughty indifference both atemporal and melancholy, and pulled the sheet over my head like a shroud.

ANTÓNIO LOBO ANTUNES is the internationally acclaimed author of *Act of the Damned*, *An Explanation of the Birds*, *The Natural Order of Things*, and *Fado Alexandrino*, among others. Born in Lisbon in 1942, Antunes was trained as a psychiatrist and served in the Portuguese Army during the Angolan War. He lives in Portugal where he continues to write.

CLIFFORD E. LANDERS has translated from Brazilian Portuguese novels by Rubem Fonseca, Jorge Amado, João Ubaldo Ribeiro, Patrícia Melo, Jô Soares, Chico Buarque, Marcos Rey, and José de Alencar and shorter fiction by Lima Barreto, Rachel de Queiroz, Osman Lins, and Moacyr Scliar. He received the Mario Ferreira Award in 1999 and a Prose Translation grant from the National Endowment for the Arts for 2004. His *Literary Translation: A Practical Guide* was published by Multilingual Matters Ltd. in 2001.

Petros Abatzoglou, *What Does Mrs. Freeman Want?*

Pierre Albert-Birot, *Grabinoulor*

Yuz Aleshkovsky, *Kangaroo*

Felipe Alfau, *Chromos* • *Locos*

Ivan Ângelo, *The Celebration* • *The Tower of Glass*

David Antin, *Talking*

Alain Arias-Misson, *Theatre of Incest*

Djuna Barnes, *Ladies Almanack* • *Ryder*

John Barth, *LETTERS* • *Sabbatical*

Donald Barthelme, *The King* • *Paradise*

Svetislav Basara, *Chinese Letter*

Mark Binelli, *Sacco and Vanzetti Must Die!*

Andrei Bitov, *Pushkin House*

Louis Paul Boon, *Chapel Road* • *Summer in Termuren*

Roger Boylan, *Killoyle*

Ignácio de Loyola Brandão, *Teeth under the Sun* • *Zero*

Bonnie Bremser, *Troia: Mexican Memoirs*

Christine Brooke-Rose, *Amalgamemnon*

Brigid Brophy, *In Transit*

Meredith Brosnan, *Mr. Dynamite*

Gerald L. Bruns, *Modern Poetry and the Idea of Language*

Evgeny Bunimovich and J. Kates, eds., *Contemporary Russian Poetry: An Anthology*

Gabrielle Burton, *Heartbreak Hotel*

Michel Butor, *Degrees* • *Mobile* • *Portrait of the Artist as a Young Ape*

G. Cabrera Infante, *Infante's Inferno* • *Three Trapped Tigers*

Julieta Campos, *The Fear of Losing Eurydice*

Anne Carson, *Eros the Bittersweet*

Camilo José Cela, *Christ versus Arizona* • *The Family of Pascual Duarte* • *The Hive*

Louis-Ferdinand Céline, *Castle to Castle* • *Conversations with Professor Y* • *London Bridge* • *North* • *Rigadoon*

Hugo Charteris, *The Tide Is Right*

Jerome Charyn, *The Tar Baby*

Marc Cholodenko, *Mordechai Schamz*

Emily Holmes Coleman, *The Shutter of Snow*

Robert Coover, *A Night at the Movies*

Stanley Crawford, *Some Instructions to My Wife*

Robert Creeley, *Collected Prose*

René Crevel, *Putting My Foot in It*

Ralph Cusack, *Cadenza*

Susan Daitch, *L.C.* • *Storytown*

Nicholas Delbanco, *The Count of Concord*

Nigel Dennis, *Cards of Identity*

Peter Dimock, *A Short Rhetoric for Leaving the Family*

Ariel Dorfman, *Konfidenz*

Coleman Dowell, *The Houses of Children* • *Island People* • *Too Much Flesh and Jabez*

Rikki Ducornet, *The Complete Butcher's Tales* • *The Fountains of Neptune* • *The Jade Cabinet* • *Phosphor in Dreamland* • *The Stain* • *The Word "Desire."*

William Eastlake, *The Bamboo Bed* • *Castle Keep* • *Lyric of the Circle Heart*

Jean Echenoz, *Chopin's Move*

Stanley Elkin, *A Bad Man* • *Boswell: A Modern Comedy* • *Criers and Kibitzers, Kibitzers and Criers* • *The Dick Gibson Show* • *The Franchiser* • *George Mills* • *The Living End* • *The MacGuffin* • *The Magic Kingdom* • *Mrs. Ted Bliss* • *The Rabbi of Lud* • *Van Gogh's Room at Arles*

Annie Ernaux, *Cleaned Out*

Lauren Fairbanks, *Muzzle Thyself* • *Sister Carrie*

Leslie A. Fiedler, *Love and Death in the American Novel*

Gustave Flaubert, *Bouvard and Pécuchet*

Ford Madox Ford, *The March of Literature*

Jon Fosse, *Melancholy*

Max Frisch, *I'm Not Stiller* • *Man in the Holocene*

Carlos Fuentes, *Christopher Unborn* • *Distant Relations* • *Terra Nostra* • *Where the Air Is Clear*

Janice Galloway, *Foreign Parts* • *The Trick Is to Keep Breathing*

William H. Gass, *A Temple of Texts* ▪ *The Tunnel* ▪ *Willie Masters' Lonesome Wife*

Etienne Gilson, *The Arts of the Beautiful* ▪ *Forms and Substances in the Arts*

C. S. Giscombe, *Giscome Road* ▪ *Here*

Douglas Glover, *Bad News of the Heart* ▪ *The Enamoured Knight*

Witold Gombrowicz, *A Kind of Testament*

Karen Elizabeth Gordon, *The Red Shoes*

Georgi Gospodinov, *Natural Novel*

Juan Goytisolo, *Count Julian* ▪ *Makbara* ▪ *Marks of Identity*

Patrick Grainville, *The Cave of Heaven*

Henry Green, *Blindness* ▪ *Concluding* ▪ *Doting* ▪ *Nothing*

Jiří Gruša, *The Questionnaire*

Gabriel Gudding, *Rhode Island Notebook*

John Hawkes, *Whistlejacket*

Aidan Higgins, *A Bestiary* ▪ *Bornholm Night-Ferry* ▪ *Flotsam and Jetsam* ▪ *Langrishe, Go Down* ▪ *Scenes from a Receding Past* ▪ *Windy Arbours*

Aldous Huxley, *Antic Hay* ▪ *Crome Yellow* ▪ *Point Counter Point* ▪ *Those Barren Leaves* ▪ *Time Must Have a Stop*

Mikhail Iossel and Jeff Parker, eds., *Amerika: Contemporary Russians View the United States*

Gert Jonke, *Geometric Regional Novel*

Jacques Jouet, *Mountain R*

Hugh Kenner, *The Counterfeiters* ▪ *Flaubert, Joyce and Beckett: The Stoic Comedians* ▪ *Joyce's Voices*

Danilo Kiš, *Garden, Ashes* ▪ *A Tomb for Boris Davidovich*

Anita Konkka, *A Fool's Paradise*

George Konrád, *The City Builder*

Tadeusz Konwicki, *A Minor Apocalypse* ▪ *The Polish Complex*

Menis Koumandareas, *Koula*

Elaine Kraf, *The Princess of 72nd Street*

Jim Krusoe, *Iceland*

Ewa Kuryluk, *Century 21*

Violette Leduc, *La Bâtarde*

Deborah Levy, *Billy and Girl* ▪ *Pillow Talk in Europe and Other Places*

José Lezama Lima, *Paradiso*

Rosa Liksom, *Dark Paradise*

Osman Lins, *Avalovara* ▪ *The Queen of the Prisons of Greece*

Alf Mac Lochlainn, *The Corpus in the Library* ▪ *Out of Focus*

Ron Loewinsohn, *Magnetic Field(s)*

D. Keith Mano, *Take Five*

Ben Marcus, *The Age of Wire and String*

Wallace Markfield, *Teitlebaum's Window* ▪ *To an Early Grave*

David Markson, *Reader's Block* ▪ *Springer's Progress* ▪ *Wittgenstein's Mistress*

Carole Maso, *AVA*

Ladislav Matejka and Krystyna Pomorska, eds., *Readings in Russian Poetics: Formalist and Structuralist Views*

Harry Mathews, *The Case of the Persevering Maltese: Collected Essays* ▪ *Cigarettes* ▪ *The Conversions* ▪ *The Human Country: New and Collected Stories* ▪ *The Journalist* ▪ *My Life in CIA* ▪ *Singular Pleasures* ▪ *The Sinking of the Odradek Stadium* ▪ *Tlooth* ▪ *20 Lines a Day*

Robert L. McLaughlin, ed., *Innovations: An Anthology of Modern & Contemporary Fiction*

Herman Melville, *The Confidence-Man*

Amanda Michalopoulou, *I'd Like*

Steven Millhauser, *The Barnum Museum* ▪ *In the Penny Arcade*

Ralph J. Mills, Jr., *Essays on Poetry*

Olive Moore, *Spleen*

Nicholas Mosley, *Accident* ▪ *Assassins* ▪ *Catastrophe Practice* ▪ *Children of Darkness and Light* ▪ *Experience and Religion* ▪ *The Hesperides Tree* ▪ *Hopeful Monsters* ▪ *Imago Bird* ▪ *Impossible Object* ▪ *Inventing God* ▪ *Judith* ▪ *Look at the Dark* ▪ *Natalie Natalia* ▪ *Serpent* ▪ *Time at War* ▪ *The Uses of Slime Mould: Essays of Four Decades*

Warren F. Motte, Jr., *Fables of the Novel: French Fiction since 1990* ▪ *Fiction Now: The French Novel in the 21st Century* ▪ *Oulipo: A Primer of Potential Literature*

Yves Navarre, *Our Share of Time* ▪ *Sweet Tooth*

Dorothy Nelson, *In Night's City* ▪ *Tar and Feathers*

Wilfrido D. Nolledo, *But for the Lovers*

Flann O'Brien, *At Swim-Two-Birds* ▪ *At War* ▪
The Best of Myles ▪ *The Dalkey Archive* ▪ *Further
Cuttings* ▪ *The Hard Life* ▪ *The Poor Mouth* ▪
The Third Policeman

Claude Ollier, *The Mise-en-Scène*

Patrik Ouředník, *Europeana*

Fernando del Paso, *Palinuro of Mexico*

Robert Pinget, *The Inquisitory* ▪ *Mahu or
The Material* ▪ *Trio*

Raymond Queneau, *The Last Days* ▪ *Odile* ▪
Pierrot Mon Ami ▪ *Saint Glinglin*

Ann Quin, *Berg* ▪ *Passages* ▪ *Three* ▪ *Tripticks*

Ishmael Reed, *The Free-Lance Pallbearers* ▪
The Last Days of Louisiana Red ▪ *Reckless
Eyeballing* ▪ *The Terrible Threes* ▪ *The Terrible
Twos* ▪ *Yellow Back Radio Broke-Down*

Jean Ricardou, *Place Names*

Julián Ríos, *Larva: A Midsummer Night's Babel* ▪
Poundemonium

Augusto Roa Bastos, *I the Supreme*

Olivier Rolin, *Hotel Crystal*

Jacques Roubaud, *The Great Fire of London* ▪
Hortense in Exile ▪ *Hortense Is Abducted* ▪
The Plurality of Worlds of Lewis ▪ *The Princess
Hoppy* ▪ *The Form of a City Changes Faster,
Alas, Than the Human Heart* ▪ *Some Thing Black*

Leon S. Roudiez, *French Fiction Revisited*

Vedrana Rudan, *Night*

Lydie Salvayre, *The Company of Ghosts* ▪ *Everyday
Life* ▪ *The Lecture* ▪ *The Power of Flies*

Luis Rafael Sánchez, *Macho Camacho's Beat*

Severo Sarduy, *Cobra & Maitreya*

Nathalie Sarraute, *Do You Hear Them?* ▪
Martereau ▪ *The Planetarium*

Arno Schmidt, *Collected Stories* ▪ *Nobodaddy's
Children*

Christine Schutt, *Nightwork*

Gail Scott, *My Paris*

June Akers Seese, *Is This What Other Women
Feel Too?* ▪ *What Waiting Really Means*

Aurelie Sheehan, *Jack Kerouac Is Pregnant*

Viktor Shklovsky, *Knight's Move* ▪ *A Sentimental
Journey: Memoirs 1917–1922* ▪ *Energy of Delusion:
A Book on Plot* ▪ *Literature and Cinematography* ▪

Theory of Prose ▪ *Third Factory* ▪ *Zoo, or
Letters Not about Love*

Claude Simon, *The Invitation*

Josef Škvorecký, *The Engineer of Human Souls*

Gilbert Sorrentino, *Aberration of Starlight* ▪ *Blue
Pastoral* ▪ *Crystal Vision* ▪ *Imaginative Qualities of
Actual Things* ▪ *Mulligan Stew* ▪ *Pack of Lies* ▪ *Red
the Fiend* ▪ *The Sky Changes* ▪ *Something Said* ▪
Splendide-Hôtel ▪ *Steelwork* ▪ *Under the Shadow*

W. M. Spackman, *The Complete Fiction*

Gertrude Stein, *Lucy Church Amiably* ▪ *The Making
of Americans* ▪ *A Novel of Thank You*

Piotr Szewc, *Annihilation*

Stefan Themerson, *Hobson's Island* ▪ *The Mystery
of the Sardine* ▪ *Tom Harris*

Jean-Philippe Toussaint, *Monsieur* ▪ *Television*

Dumitru Tsepeneag, *Vain Art of the Fugue*

Esther Tusquets, *Stranded*

Dubravka Ugresic, *Lend Me Your Character* ▪
Thank You for Not Reading

Mati Unt, *Diary of a Blood Donor* ▪ *Things in
the Night*

Eloy Urroz, *The Obstacles*

Luisa Valenzuela, *He Who Searches*

Paul Verhaeghen, *Omega Minor*

Marja-Liisa Vartio, *The Parson's Widow*

Boris Vian, *Heartsnatcher*

Austryn Wainhouse, *Hedyphagetica*

Paul West, *Words for a Deaf Daughter & Gala*

Curtis White, *America's Magic Mountain* ▪
The Idea of Home ▪ *Memories of My Father
Watching TV* ▪ *Monstrous Possibility:
An Invitation to Literary Politics* ▪ *Requiem*

Diane Williams, *Excitability: Selected Stories* ▪
Romancer Erector

Douglas Woolf, *Wall to Wall* ▪ *Ya! & John-Juan*

Jay Wright, *Polynomials and Pollen* ▪
The Presentable Art of Reading Absence

Philip Wylie, *Generation of Vipers*

Marguerite Young, *Angel in the Forest* ▪
Miss MacIntosh, My Darling

RE Young, *Unbabbling*

Zoran Živković, *Hidden Camera*

Louis Zukofsky, *Collected Fiction*

Scott Zwiren, *God Head*

FOR A FULL LIST OF PUBLICATIONS, VISIT: WWW.DALKEYARCHIVE.COM

WITHDRAWN